The Forest Of Eternals

The Scrolls Of Tralatitious

A Novel

by

Patrick Clermont

Library and Archives Canada Cataloguing in Publication

Clermont, Patrick, 1969-
Artwork by Sharla Clermont & Pebbles Clermont

A Novel (H.C.)

ISBN 978-1-7776504-8-3

This is a work of fiction.

Any resemblance to actual persons, living or dead, events or locals, is entirely coincidental.

To my wife Sharla, thank you for encouraging me every step of the way, and fixing all my grammar and spelling mistakes and for inspiring most of the good stuff in here.

To my daughter Pebbles, thanks for all the artwork I get to look at. It inspires me to write better so this story can one day be as beautiful as your work.

To my daughter Ravah, thanks for telling me what I need to hear, not what I want to hear. Your input has changed the way I write and has made me not only a better writer, but a better storyteller.

Chapter 1 The Window

"Murder! Murder!" yelled Upal. The troublesome minor continued shouting out his window as he pointed toward the western horizon. He turned and tip-toed quietly to his bedroom door and shouted, "Murder!"

The cry startled his old bewitched Keeper who was half asleep. She quickly sat upright, almost knocking over the kitchen table. "Oh no!" she exclaimed as she reached over and grabbed hold of her capsizing glass of Glumvyn.

"Murder!" the sound startled her again. Upal's howls made her heart sink. Her head fell into her hands. She gently yet firmly massaged her temples trying to knead away the sound of his wails. It didn't work...

She quietly whispered to herself. "Precious."

She took a deep breath and repeated the mantra quietly, "*All* children are precious." She struggled with the idea as she hadn't fully convinced herself of it yet (at least where Upal was concerned).

The aged woman had a few misgivings about *some* of her recent life choices. She reached for her glass and lifted it up to the sunlight that was beaming through the north facing window. She looked intently at the remaining muddy colored ounces sloshing around in her glass. She thought she heard a ghostly voice whisper, "No amount of Glumvyn can cover the stains and pains of the past."

"Oh shut up." she said, to her dead husband. The words she heard in her head were the last words spoken by her husband before he died.

She stared out at the shadow on the ground, "It's only noon." she grumbled as she picked up her last bottle of Glumvyn. She stared through the dark green glass to see what remained. The bottle was still half full; she'd be fine for another day. "It's better than being half empty." she said, trying to encourage herself.

Her eyes made their way across the small house and landed on the stairs. A quick movement... she whipped her head to the right and caught a glimpse of a small mouse making its way out through a crack in the door. Oh to be that mouse, no troubles, no worries...

That's right, at this time, in this place, she wished for the life of a mouse. These were hard days for the people of Eternal. Especially those living in the West Gate.

She held her breath and used all her strength to lift her aged and bibulous body from the decrepit old chair. A slow, long *creeeeek,* was released from the chair as she took her weight off of it.

Mrs. Nibbledent was not one to be kept in the dark about the latest gossip or scandal. So, she slowly, painfully made her way to the broken, crumbling (and upon closer inspection... one might add), filthy and rotting clay stairs.

By the time she reached the third step she was exhausted. She had to take a break and rest. She tried to catch her breath before starting her trek up the next few steps. She looked up at the landing and mumbled to herself, "I can't remember the last time I climbed these stairs." Suddenly a piercing pain went through her heart. She couldn't fool herself, she remembered very clearly the last time she climbed this staircase. She looked up the stairwell and a haunting, distant memory flashed through her mind.

A thousand images of a child who lived a lifetime ago. She took hold of a key that hung around her neck and squeezed it tightly in the palm of her right hand. She tried desperately to force the somber memory from her mind. She refocused her energy on climbing. She focused on a crack she spotted on the fourth step. It looked like something, she was sure of it, but her damp, blinking, wine filled eyes had a hard time focusing on it.

She felt a tear rolling down her cheek; she used her index finger to carefully catch it. She looked at it for a moment, then brought the drop to her lips. In it she tasted the pains of past memories, memories she didn't want to think about, but even more than that, they were memories she didn't want to forget.

She bowed her head and breathed out, "I am not young, I have never been young."

She redirected her attention to the next few steps as she tried to distract herself from the previous images. She noticed as if for the first time how years of grating and scratching had taken their toll on the staircase. She realized that time had not been much kinder to her. It was true. The stairs were as old and broken as the Glumvyn drinker making her way up; she could feel it in every crack, snap and pop that came with each step. She paused again and let out a long heavy sigh. Mrs. Nibbledent took in a deep breath as she worked up the courage to continue her journey. As her foot landed on the fourth step, she heard Upal cry out "Murder!" once again.

She shouted up at the teen, "If I come up there and there is no bloody murder," her shrieking voice echoed up the staircase to the boy's room, "there will be!"

She forced her leg up the fifth step, "What kind of a Keeper takes in a demented and bothersome child like this one?" Then she gaspingly shouted up the stairs again. "I must be crazy!"

A handful of steps more and she stopped to take a few breaths. Holding herself up against the wall she shouted up to the bad hat who'd been screaming bloody murder all morning long (or so it seemed). "I tell you this," she struggled to take in a breath. "If I didn't need the money", she paused to take in all the air her aged and smoke damaged lungs could handle, "...if I could find another... less inconvenient discard..." she coughed and hacked, "I would do it in a second. I would make you disappear." She spit out her words between chokes and wheezes, "Then you could never bother anyone again."

Her voice rumbled up the stairs into his room. "Old witch." he muttered.

Mrs. Nibbledent was old, *if* sixty is old? She looked well beyond her years. Her sagging neck complimented her droopy and flaccid eyes which helped to accentuate the face fungus hanging from her feeble chin. Those who crossed her path thought her to be close to a hundred, if not more. Her badly washed out hair did nothing to cover up any of her ripening and aged faults. If that wasn't bad enough she smelled like a decomposing body that had been smothered in smoke and pickled in Glumvyn.

As for being Upal's Keeper? He told anyone who asked, that she was the only one crazy or disinterested enough to tolerate his rebellion. He claimed that she did it solely for the money. After all, those funds kept her glass full. Well, actually, empty (on most days).

His self-proclaimed rebellion wasn't that far off. In his sixteen years (about five of those spent as an orphan), Upal had been discharged by well over twenty Keepers, sometimes spending less than a week with them. His reputation was well documented. No Keeper in their right mind wanted to take him in. Therefore, the C.R.U.C. (Counsel of Refused and Unwanted Children) had no choice but to leave him with anyone they could find who was desperate enough to take him in, no matter how unqualified or incompetent that person might be. And make no mistake about it, Upal believed Mrs. Nibbledent to be both those things.

"Murder! Murder!" Upal shouted again. He was starting to get bored. He took a quick glance back at the stairs. If I'd known it was going to take her so long… he thought to himself.

"Where?" he heard her shriek as she tumbled up the last two steps. "Finally." he muttered as he watched Mrs. Nibbledent's momentum bring her crashing unpleasantly onto the floor of his bedchamber.

He could hardly hold himself back from laughing. He watched as she struggled to get herself onto her hands and knees. It was almost too much for him to bear.

"Who's being murdered, you foolish hob?" she gasped as she pulled herself up with the help of the nearby wall and Upal's sleeve. She stumbled forward toward the window. The boy instinctively reached out and caught her before she made her way out the window. Shaking herself away from his grasp, she braced herself against the ledge and peered out.

She could see nothing strange going on. She leaned in close to Upal. The smell of her breath was nauseating. "What are you looking at, you imbecile?" she screeched in his face. A long gooey brownish strand of ooze left her lips. It landed on Upal's cheek. A small strand of the yukky, acidic smelling sludge found its way into his mouth. He instantly gagged and spit out what he could. He wiped his face with his sleeve and tried hard not to think about what had just happened.

"Right out there your hideousness." He pointed to the distant sky. "A murder of crows!" Upal erupted with laughter at his long and senseless joke.

Her face went red with rage, "Why you little…" she took on the arduous task of bending over. She took hold of her old worn slipper and began to beat the boy with it. He raised his arms to shield himself, but he wasn't fazed by her weak attempt at a thrashing. It only made him explode with laughter. After multiple swats, the aged old hag was exhausted. She reversed her course and walked away, all the while mumbling to herself.

She stopped at the doorway for a moment and glanced at the old wooden chest that made its home at the edge of the bed. She took note that the old rusted lock was still intact. She clasped her pendant, turned back and painfully made her way down the stairs.

Upal watched as Mrs. Nibbledent floundered her way down the stairs, hacking, coughing and scrambling for air the entire way. "Old hag," he whispered, "You'd get to your Glumvyn quicker if I pushed you down."

Upal hated her (as he hated all of his keepers) as much as he did his room or *the dungeon*, as he referred to it most times. It was a dark, damp unforgiving hole that sat on the top floor of the house. It was filled with cobwebs, cockroaches, mice, ticks and other ungodly creatures.

His bed was a burlap bag stuffed with hay that sat on an uneven wood floor. An ancient and tattered wool blanket was used for a covering on cold nights, not that it did much good. Next to the bed leaning up against the wall was a large wooden paddle. It was used to *hit the hay* before bedtime. By doing so (at least in theory), one could dislodge some of the wildlife making their home inside the mattress.

At the edge of the bed was that old wooden chest with a rusted lock. He'd thought about breaking it and opening it a few times. He even thought about stealing the key from Mrs. Nibbledent's neck after she'd passed out at the table. But he thought that not knowing what was inside was more exciting than knowing. After all, what could possibly be in there? The woman had nothing of value. If she did own anything of value she had sold it for Glumvyn long ago.

As for the bed, Upal rarely used it. If he did, it was only when he found the nights outside too cold or too dangerous. He knew that as long as the hag received her monthly stippen, she didn't care if he came home or not. To be honest, she probably preferred the quiet nights his absence created.

Upal turned his attention back to the window and stared out into the distance. He was suddenly stirred by a peculiarly crisp yet mild westward breeze. It took hold of him and sent a chill up his spine. He tried to shake it off. "Death." he whispered. It was believed that any time a chill ran up your spine it meant death was near.

He shook his head and shrugged his shoulders. His gaze returned to the murder of crows. Upal squinted as he strived to get a better view of the distant image he was looking at. Little black dots flying to and fro. "They look to be at the edge of the Rubicon." he muttered to himself.

The Rubicon. With that name spoken, absent of any provocation, he heard the ghost of a voice that might or might not have been his own, whisper... "From where no one ever returns."

Chapter 2 Distracted

Upal's mind was suddenly filled with the legendary tales of Eternal as told by the Old Lady, the caretaker of all Eternal's history. Upal's persistent distractibility turned from the fables to the morning sky. The pinks, blues and crimson colored clouds; they were a sharp contrast to... the winged dots in the distant horizon sidetracked him again. "I wonder..."

An alley cat caught the corner of his eye and his thoughts were redirected to the ground, the crumbling walls and the streets below. He looked up, then down, then up and down again. He stared out at the contrast of the heavenly colored sky and the unholiness of the neighborhood he lived in. The earth and the sky were so far from each other, complete opposites. "If I could only live in the clouds." he muttered.

Alas, Upal's home was not overhead in the soft fluffy cotton filled clouds; it was below in the streets. He looked out and followed a small dust devil filled with debris. He eyed the dirty walls that were stained and soaked with urine. The pee trickled down the walls to the ground where it created small musty-smelling ammonia mud puddles. As if that wasn't enough, the whole scene was topped off with the moderate aroma of *other* bodily excretions too. The scent made its way up to his window. The extreme heat of the day made the smells linger and it burned his nostrils.

He thought it odd that he actually noticed the smells. He was so used to it. Somehow, today it was different. It was as if for the first time his eyes were open to the inescapable sadness of it all. No, it wasn't sadness... it was despair. An endless drought of inescapable despair.

Life as he knew it, was colorless.

He closed his eyes and desperately tried to dream of something more. He let his imagination carry him to what life must have been like thousands of years ago. What it must have been like to live in the fabled world described in the Scrolls of Tralatitious (the good parts anyway). A world where the Rubicon was still the Forest of Eternals. A magical place that fed all the citizens of Eternal. A world where no one ever worried about food, health, loneliness, sadness or whatever it was that he had to deal with on a day-to-day basis.

He fantasized about a place where one didn't have to suffer through the daily onslaught of swatting flies and smacking midges. Yet here he was, slapping, smiting and striking at swarms of mosquitoes on an almost endless basis. It was exhausting. How unfair it was that he should be trapped in this time of history instead of the *good one*.

He clenched his fist and shook it at the sky in belligerence crying out, "Why me? Why have I been forsaken to this wretchedness?"

"Oh, shut up and be happy you have anything!" he heard Mrs. Nibbledent's screech from the ground-floor.

He stuck his head out the window and groaned quietly, "You shut up."

"I have nothing." he grumbled. Everyday life for the citizens of the West Gate was hard and unforgiving. With only a modicum of food and water obtainable, it was a constant struggle to stay alive.

It's true there were some worse off than he was. The truly unfortunate people were those who stayed hungry for days on end. There were many who slept in alleyways, doorways and on rooftops, wrapping their famished bodies in whatever cover they could find. He sighed and lowered his head and shook it slowly.

A full belly, a warm and safe night's sleep were as hard to find as a warm heart in this age of hopelessness.

He whispered to himself "Look at this."

His eyes caught a bunch of unwashed-flyblown children running the streets. He could easily commiserate with them, because just like many of them, he was a parentless and forsaken child, abandoned to a miserable life. He was stuck in the system known as the C.R.U.C., jumping from Keeper to Keeper (at least until he turned eighteen).

Lifting his eyes to the heavens he wondered how such a peaceful and calm looking sky could exist at the same time as the torn and shattered surface, where so little peace existed?

"Oh, yeah!" he exclaimed. His focus returned to the flight of the crows. "What are they doing?"

From what he could make out, there looked to be dozens of them and they seemed to be diving towards the ground and back up again. "Maybe..."

"Oop!" A voice cried out from the street below.

Chapter 3 Meet Preet

Upal looked down to see his best friend Preet standing beneath his window. Preet, who was way too big for his fifteen soon-to-be sixteen years, stood seven feet three inches tall. He was, however, not used to his newly found body. It seemed that he sprouted two feet overnight, and like magic, he became this high-pitched, squeaky sounding man-child. It was a funny thing seeing a giant with a mouse's voice. The only person bold or maybe just boneheaded enough to laugh and make fun of him, was Upal.

For some unknown reason Upal couldn't shake the feeling that today seemed different, maybe even a little strange. For reasons unknown to him, Upal was seeing things in a different light. He stared down at Preet and looked at him, I mean really looked at him, possibly for the first time.

How was it that he never noticed that Preet had the face of an angel? A tiny smirk came across Upal's face. Look at him, he thought to himself. Preet had a beautifully rounded face with bright azure colored titan sized eyes. They popped out against the contrast of his chestnut brown skin. Preet carried a massive mess of an afro that was almost as tall as he was. It was a chaotic coiffure that seemed stuffed with unimaginable debris.

"Hello-oh? Oo-oop?" Preet was waving his arms trying to bring his friend out of his daydream.

"What?" Upal was shaken from his daze.

"Why are you staring at me like that?" He yelled up to the window.

"What are you talking about? I'm not staring at you?"

"Yes you were. You were all like…" Preet looked up with his eyes bulging and his mouth wide open and a little drool dripping out.

Preet was staring up at someone who was his polar opposite. At sixteen Upal had a muscular five foot six inch frame. His wavy shoulder length jet black hair surrounded his face like a frame. He had soft blue eyes with a hint of green. He was a good looking lad with an air of ruggedness.

Upal's physical abilities were unmatched by anyone in the West Gate. He was able to bounce and pounce like a cat and somersault like a trapeze artist.

Preet found that being friends with Upal had more than a few downsides; his big mouth and attitude were just *two* of them. If there was any trouble to be found, Upal could easily find it, if he wasn't already the one creating it.

Ever since Preet's magical mushrooming, Upal's attitude seemed to have gotten a little worse. It wasn't that Upal couldn't take care of himself, he could. He was as proficient with his feet as he was with his fists. He was not afraid of much and rarely if ever avoided a good old fashioned bang-a-rang; the scars strewn across his body could attest to that. But as of late, his troublesome nature had increased. Now that he had constant access to a giant, he took it upon himself to agitate more and more people at once. The problem for Preet was that he was opposed to using his new found size to scare off those Upal would enrage. Nonetheless, Preet's loyalty always stood firm.

"Quit looking at me like that you weirdo." Upal said to him.

"You started it." Preet responded.

Leaning out his window Upal wondered if he would ever leave the house. He shouted down to his friend. "Hey Preet, what do you imagine those crows are doing out there?" He pointed west toward the Rubicon.

Preet turned to look at the splendor of the sky. It took his mind away from his present reality for a brief, almost inconceivable moment. Of course he couldn't see what Upal was talking about.

"Hey genius, I'm tall but not that tall." He paused and turned to look again, "I don't see anything."

He looked up at Upal, "Who cares anyhow? Maybe they're feasting on a dead body." he said sardonically.

"You think it's human?" the curious voice from above asked.

"It will be if you don't get down here. Come on, I don't want to stand here all day in the hot sun waiting for you."

And with that, Upal was finally leaving the house.

Chapter 4 Getting Out

Upal vaulted out the window. He descended the side of the building like a cat. He leapt and seized a frail, weather worn, flagless pole. Even though Preet had seen it done on countless occasions, he still watched in amazement (and a little jealousy) as the boy pirouetted and whirled around with acrobatic beauty.

He went for one final loop around the pole. Upal envisioned himself releasing the pole, flying into a swan-like flip and landing perfectly on his feet (as per usual).

For the last few months this flagpole had taken a regular dose of abuse from the boy. This time was no different. He was a mere half second away from letting go, when a … *creak-crack* was heard. The spinning had finally taken its toll. The rod snapped.

Preet was standing directly below watching the action go down (so to speak). Seeing that Upal had lost all control and not one to stand in anyone's way, he quickly took a step to the side and watched as Upal came smashing down to the ground.

Upal landed awkwardly on his back. Preet looked down at him, his face grimacing with sympathetic pain. He waited a moment to make sure Upal was *alright*, but more importantly that he had his attention. "That must have hurt." He whispered. "I mean, it looks like it hurts. Does it hurt?"

He was used to Upal doing nitwitted things like this. He watched calmly as Upal displayed the typical signs of panic. "Try to breathe." Preet said quietly, a little concerned.

Upal *was* trying. Preet bent over and brought his face close to the boy's and whispered in a slightly mocking tone, "Was it worth it?"

Upal grunted and gave a short painfilled thumbs-up. "Always." he painfully breathe out. He raised his arm slightly and produced his index finger.

"Oh, you think you're number one?" Preet smiled, knowing that wasn't what Upal meant.

"Need... minute..." Upal gasped. The pain subsided a little and he was able to take a few shallow breaths and purred, "Not my best landing."

"You're gonna have to speak up." muttered Preet, "I can hardly hear you through the pain."

Preet stood upright, put his hands on his hips, looked up and shook his head disapprovingly. He looked down at Upal and kicked him gently. "Look, I know you were a little busy falling and all, but did you see my quick reflexes?" Preet gently nudged him again with his foot.

"Man, I was like a cat. It's like..." he waved his hands in the air. "I saw you coming down and *swish*..." He made a side step motion and almost tripped over his feet. "One second slower and I would have been breaking your fall. *Swish*." he repeated the sound and motion. "Like a cat I tell ya."

He paused for a second and rubbed his chin. He waved his index finger at Upal who was still in recovery mode and said, "You know what Lashra would say to you right now if she were here?"

"Ugh." Upal grunted out with disapproval.

Preet ignored his friend's obvious objection. "She'd say," and doing a decent impression of his sister, he continued. "You know Upal, that pole is very much like the average person. This little mishap could go a long way to teaching you a life lesson. What kind of life lesson might you ask?"

"I wouldn't." Upal chirped.

Preet, (I mean), Lashra ignored him. "Well, let me tell you. People, like that post, can only take so much abuse before they break. Stop trying to break things."

Upal was looking up from the ground still reeling in pain. He was not amused in the slightest.

Lashra continued, "Upal, you need to seize the moment. Learn from this, become a better version of you."

"Hey Lashra," Upal muttered, "can you send your slow-witted brother back?" His breath was finally returning to his wounded body.

"Ha, ha, ha!" Cough, cough. Mrs. Nibbledent's head was sticking out the bottom window. She was happy to have partially witnessed the pain that she had so hoped to inflict on the little missfit, just a few minutes earlier. "Your bizarre friend is right, you little…" she didn't finish her sentence, she just shook her head.

"I have to say... I did enjoy witnessing the swiftness of Karma working its magic on you. I haven't felt pleasure like that in years." she said with a rotted laugh. And just as she spoke the words, a loose piece of wreckage fell from the sky and pounded her on the back of the head. Upal and Preet simultaneously broke into an uncontrollable laugh.

The look on her face was so stormy it scared Preet. He reached down and picked his friend up by the arm so fast and hard that Upal was barely able to land on his feet. The two began to run before Mrs. Nibbledent had the chance to reach for her infamous slipper.

Preet could barely keep up to Upal. They took the corner at top speed and Preet tripped over his feet. On his way down, he instinctively reached out to seize onto something that would slow his descent. That something just happened to be Upal's pants.

Preet hit the ground with pants in hand and with Upal's pants now down around his ankles, he unexpectedly greeted the dusty pebbled street with his knees, followed quickly by his elbows and just as swiftly his face. The sounds he uttered were those of pure pain.

Thankfully the humiliation of having his pants around his ankles, got him up instantly and angrily. Pulling his pants up he frantically started looking for the small piece of rope he used to keep his pants up. Somehow it was nowhere to be found.There were only a few bits and pieces strewn here and there.

Upal was furious. He made his way back to Preet who was still trying to get to his feet. "Buggerations Preet! What's wrong with you? Are you trying to kill me?"

Preet sat on the ground looking at his scraped-up knees and elbows. "I was going down." He gestured sorrily. " It was a reflex."

"That was my last piece of rope. I think a rat ran off with it. Now what's going to keep my pants up you half-wit?" he said angrily.

"Calm down Oop. I can see you are clearly angry, and you're saying things that don't make sense. I mean seriously, a tiny person like you calling me a half-wit? If anything, I'm a *full*-wit and you sir, you are the half-wit. I'm the full, you're the half." He chuckled to himself.

"What?" a look of puzzlement crossed Upal's face. "Are you suffering from some kind of brain trauma from that fall?" Upal was in no mood to laugh. "What am I gonna do? Give me your rope, before I lose my patience with you!" He said as he shook the fragment of pants he had bunched up in his hand.

Preet shrugged his shoulders and scratched his head. He slowly made his way to his feet and placed his large hand on Upal's shoulder. "First of all, you don't have enough strength in that little body of yours to carry this much rope and secondly, NO!"

Upal shoved Preet's hand off his shoulder. "Don't talk down to me." he said with a death stare.

"I'm sorry, I'll be more careful next time Oop." he said walking away.

Upal grunted at his friend's attempt at an apology. "You better be, if not, I'll just quit wearing pants, then you won't be reaching out for me."

"You're right Oop, I'd have nothing to hold on to." Preet said as he tried hard not to laugh.

"Ya, ya, real funny." Upal said as he slowed down and tried to clean some of the dust out of his bloody scrapes and scratches. He picked up speed and caught up to Preet. The two walked slowly, trying to shake off the recent tragedy.

"Let's make our way to the Old Lady's house." said Upal, "I'm sure your sister will be there. Maybe she can help me with my pants." he said with a leering smile.

Preet grabbed hold of Upal's shirt and brought him to an abrupt stop. In a rigid and unforgiving tone he stated as fact, "If Lashra even comes close to your pants, I will sit on you, killing you instantly. It's that simple." Preet was very protective of his little sister.

Upal tried to shake himself out of Preet's hold. "Well, maybe you should've thought of that before using my pants as a safety net," he responded. "I just meant that she could probably find me a rope." He cut himself loose and began to walk away. He looked back to Preet and said, "You're sister can do almost anything. After all, Lashra is very pul-chri-tu-di-nous?"

"What?" Preet shook his head and sighed. He could see that it took every brain cell Upal had not only to remember, but to say a big word like… pultudiness??? well, the word he had just said.

"You are a desperate boy, Oop." he patted him on the head. "How long did it take you to memorize that word?"

Upal shoved Preet's hand away, "I told you not to pat me on the head like that."

Preet ignored him, "You do realize that my sister will not be impressed because you memorized a big word. And you know you'll just embarrass yourself by using it wrongly."

Upal unsuccessfully tried to shove his friend away. "I'm not as dumb as I look Preet."

Preet stopped in his tracks. "How could you be?"

"Shut up, you know what I mean."

Preet shook his head. "Let me try and make this clear for you Oop. Lashra doesn't like you. I mean she likes you but she doesn't *like* you, you know, like *that*. And I know you want to kiss her, but ugh… kissing her would be like kissing me. But, if you're that hopeless," he said as he closed his eyes, puckered up and blindly reached out for Upal. "Go ahead, if you want to kiss me I'm right here waiting for you."

"Enough already!" Upal shouted. "You need to have your head checked by the Old Lady. You're babbling. I don't want to kiss your sister and I definitely don't want to kiss you. I just do it to mess with you." He turned around and walked away.

Preet could see that Upal was plainly lying. "You know what would help Oop?"

"What?"

"If you could just shut up once in a while." Preet said quietly.

"I wish it were that easy my friend. I wish it were that easy."

They continued for a while in silence.

Chapter 5 The West Gate

All of Eternal was one large city and the entirety of the city was surrounded by a wall. A wall that was twenty five feet high and ten feet thick. The construction of the wall began after Demorg's departure. It seemed everyone was convinced by the rumors that Demorg was about to seek his revenge on the people at any moment. Many thought that he would seek out all the pieces of the armor by killing its leaders. Then he'd have rule over the whole of Eternal.

Saudj, Preet's friend and a boy Upal considered his nemesis, had been ranting about that very subject a few days earlier.

"Think about it," Saudj had been going on for a while already. "It took them a thousand years to build the wall and all that time they think Demorg is coming to kill them? The guy has been gone for five hundred years and no one thinks... Hey! Maybe he's not coming? Oh wait, maybe he's dead. Maybe, just maybe this story might not be true? I've got an idea. Why don't we stop wasting our time on this wall? No, they just keep building, brick on top of brick, *for another five hundred years. A thousand years to build!* Now it's been thousands of years on top of that... and most people still think he's coming?"

Saudj shook his head in disbelief. "I'm not saying we should tear down the wall, but come on, enough with the nonsense. Why are they still trying to sell these fables to us as if they're real? The way my father tells it, Demorg tried to save Eternal by offering an easier way to feed the people and the other tribes were jealous of him."

Preet put his arm around Saudj's shoulder and pulled him in tight. "You're over thinking the whole thing."

Saudj pulled himself away from the giant boy as he picked up his pace.

"I guess what I'm trying to say," Preet continued, "is, I don't care. Wall or no wall, Demorg or no Demorg, I'm hungry. I want to eat. That's the only thing I believe in right now."

"Fools!" Saudj said as he turned the corner and headed home, "You guys are just a bunch of pushovers for old stories." he shouted back to the boys.

"Ya, well if none of it is true, then why doesn't anyone ever return from the Rubicon?" Upal added. But it was too late, Saudj was already gone.

"That didn't make any sense Oop." Preet shook his head.

"You know what I mean."

*****

"Ugh! I hate West Gate." Upal said, breaking the silence. The West Gate was the poorest of all the gates. Most kids who lived there had one parent. If they were lucky, their parents cared about what they were doing and where they were going. Most kids in the West Gate spent the daylight hours playing, fighting and chasing each other around. The nights consisted of thievery, looting and looking for a safe place to hide and maybe if you were lucky you'd find a few hours of sleep.

Preet was born in the West Gate. Upal started life at the edge of the East Gate bordering the West. It was a working class area of the city. The East Gate had an almost unlimited supply of Dendrocalamus Asper, a long fast growing plant that was both strong and durable. The Dendro as they called it was used to build furniture, houses, utensils, paper… almost anything could be made with it. The work made life a little better there. The Patrolmen were well paid and that meant less violence in the city and most had enough money and resources to buy food and lodging. The East Gate had access to schools, apothecaries and had safer streets.

The Patrolmen in the West Gate tended to bend the rule of law for a stippen. Whereas the Patrol in the East Gate was much more restrained and disciplined and so, the nights were relatively quiet.

When Upal was seven, his family was forced to move to the West Gate, after Upal's father, a drunk who hated having children, found himself a young mistress. He left Upal's sick mother with two children to feed; it wasn't long before things fell apart and she could no longer afford housing. She and her two children were forced to move to the West Gate; she did the best she could under the circumstances.

Moving there was not easy on Upal. He didn't have much experience with fighting or bullying. He found it quite terrifying, but he managed to stay alive. As time went on, he acquired the skills he would need to defend himself and survive.

Upal's brother who was four years older spent most of his days and nights thieving. He eventually snuck back to the East Gate where all his friends were. He rarely came home and when he did, it didn't take long for him to get into trouble. Within a few years he simply stopped coming home. Upal hadn't seen or heard from him in over five years. He simply assumed he was dead.

Soon after his brother left, Upal's mother died. He always believed she died of sadness. Upal found himself alone and before long he was being bumped from house to house, Keeper to Keeper.

He quickly learned to trust no one and found that being alone was the best alternative. That was, until he met Preet and Lashra. Or should I just say, Lashra and Preet?

Chapter 6 Lashra

"Hey Oop." Preet gave Upal a friendly shove.

Upal was lost in his thoughts. His friend's gentle nudge was enough to push him aside and make him momentarily let go of his pants. Startled, Upal caught them before they went too far down. "Hey!" He leaned in the other direction and rammed Preet with his shoulder hitting him hard enough to get a reaction from him.

Preet rubbed his side. "Wake up. You haven't said a word in ten minutes." He was all bug-eyed. "That's pretty spooky." He chuckled.

Preet unexpectedly stopped in the middle of the road, closed his eyes and took in a deep long breath through his nostrils. A peaceful, dreamy expression came over him. "Mmmm, I love the smell of that baking bread."

Yes, it was a good smell, a tasty smell. An aroma so delicious and wonderful that it had the power (if you were close enough to the Old Lady's house and focused your senses), to camouflage the stench of the city.

"I could easily find my way to her house in the dark." he sighed with delight.

Upal smiled as he sniffed the air, "I can actually taste the flavors in that smokey perfume. It smells like magic."

They picked up the pace and quickly found their way to the Old Lady's house. Upal quietly stuck his head in the window. His eyes were immediately drawn to the girl sitting on the floor next to the Old Lady. Her exquisite frame was flanked by dozens of books. His heart raced uncontrollably. Every time he laid eyes on her, it was as if he'd never experienced her beauty before. She was a vision, an overwhelming feast for his eyes. Upal gazed passionately at the pulchritudinous redhead.

She was sitting next to the Old Lady, leaning back against a library of books that had been handed down from generation to generation. The library had been created by the Longevites and consisted of hundreds if not thousands of books and scrolls that depicted the history of Eternal and it also chronicled the fauna and flora that was contained in the Forest of Eternals.

Lashra beamed like the sun. This was her favorite place to be, surrounded by these books and scrolls. She had surely read everyone of them not once but twice and some, maybe more. This is where she liked to spend most of her days. From sunrise to sunset if you were looking for Lashra, odds were you would find her here. She was brainy and known to be wise beyond her years.

No one could have guessed in a thousand years that she was Preet's fraternal twin. People could hardly believe they were related. She stood six feet tall with a thick curly head full of ringlets. Her crimson colored mane was filled with rays of strawberry blonde strewn throughout. When the late day sun hit her head, it lit her up and it gave the impression that her head was on fire.

Her lips were full and cherry red, which contrasted her pale white skin that was lightly mapped with freckles. Her large absinthe colored eyes were stormy and hypnotizing. Every part of her being was a piece of a puzzle that added to her beauty and majesty. Lashra was mystical and Upal believed there wasn't a person alive who could resist her allure.

She was kind, considerate and tenderhearted. She was always ready to listen and truly cared for people. All those things didn't stop her from being strong willed and persistent in everything she chose to do.

Upal loved her. More than that, he wanted only happiness for her and there was nothing he wouldn't give or do to see that through.

Preet caught Upal longingly admiring Lashra. "Can you please stop looking at my sister that way?" he murmured in Upal's ear.

"What way?" said Upal clumsily. "I was just thinking about how your sister is very... uh... how she uh... looks so much like you." he blurted out in desperation. "It's kinda scary." His smile was questionable and his eyes were wide and wary.

Preet, who was easily deluded when it came to compliments, smiled and nodded emphatically. "It is kinda spooky isn't it?"

Upal turned away immediately before his face could give him away. His eyes ran across the room; it was filled with happy children. At this moment in time the Old Lady was part way through a story from the Scrolls of Tralatitious and even though they'd heard it a thousand times before, it still captivated everyone. It seemed the only person smarter than Lashra, was this eight-hundred year old lady.

Chapter 7 The Old Lady

The Old Lady's abode was situated only a short distance away from the outside entrance of the West Gate. Her chimney seemed to billow bread scented smoke day and night. Her homemade bread fed all those who walked through her door and the many who passed by it. If there was any place in this forsaken world that could bring some sense of contentment and a little peace of mind, it was this one.

On her head was a long intertwined weave of colorless horse hair. Her large dark chocolate colored eyes were surrounded by plump rosy cheeks. Her smile was sweeping and her face was cordial and inviting. It had the power to comfort and settle any situation. Even though she was almost a thousand years old, she somehow managed to hold on to her beauty in a most inexplicable way.

As for her size? She was huge. A mountain of a woman, standing over nine feet tall. She was the only one who could embrace Preet and make him feel like the little boy he truly was.

Even with her large size and the fact that she was over eight hundred years old, she moved like someone… half her age? She was still very agile.

"Old Lady"; it was obviously not her given name. No one had ever known her to go by any other name. It had always been *the Old Lady this and the Old Lady that.*

Now understand this fully, there was no disrespect meant whatsoever. She was a well loved and most cherished treasure in everyone's world. Children young and old would sit and listen to her stories day in and day out. She knew more than anyone, after all she was over eight hundred years old.

The Old Lady was the last known living member of the Longevity tribe. She was the only person who could travel from gate to gate and be welcomed by all. Some did find it a little strange that she chose to make the West Gate her home, but, she would always say, "Those who have much should serve and protect those who have little."

The Old Lady was also a Keeper and of all the Keepers in Eternal, she was the most loving, caring, kind, gentle and generous soul that the universe could have provided.

The law of the land stated that all Keepers should love and care for the orphans in their charge like they were their own, and she did.

There were some Keepers who kept children more as slaves or house servants. If you were lucky enough to have a Keeper who was even just kind to you, you learned to keep your mouth shut and be respectful. Otherwise you might be traded in for someone better and then you would simply be shipped out to a more desperate Keeper who was not as kind. Upal knew this situation very well and yet he never kept his mouth shut.

The Old Lady had survived seven husbands. She was never able to have children of her own. For some unknown reason (she kept to herself), she always kept five children at a time, not one more and not one less.

She would never ask or tell a child it was time to leave her care. One person she tended to was *Timmy the Beautiful*. He was twenty one years old and was known to everyone in the West Gate. He would push and pull his cart around and collect debris all day, every day.

Timmy was never difficult. He loved to stop and talk with anyone who would listen. He was always prepared to show you his precious locket. He would open it, so he could show you a faded picture of his mother. He would then give her a kiss and gently return her to his pocket.

Once the locket was safely in place, he would walk away and start singing the song of the people *"We shall live in peace."* When he finished he would shout "Live in peace!" like it was a command, then he would start all over again.

His special needs made him a shining light of hope. The Old Lady used to say, "If we could all love each other the way we love Timmy the Beautiful, Eternal would be a nobler place."

The Old Lady loved to tell and teach her stories. In the last few months she told one particular story more often than others and she seemed to tell it with a sense of urgency.

The story always started the same way. "My great-grandmother told this to my grandmother who told it to my mother who told it to me and now I tell it to you my children."

She was already deep into the story when Upal and Preet arrived at her window. Her smokey, gravelly voice delivered the words in a melodic rhythmic fashion. Every sound she made seemed sacred.

"...the day will come when *The One* will unite the armor..."

"Quit shoving me!" Upal said to Preet.

"Shhhh" muttered Preet as he reached in and easily moved his pal out of the way and took his place by the open window. He stuck his head in the window and quietly mouthed "I love this story".

Upal tried to force his way back under the gargantuan boy's arm. "Come on, let me in."

A choir of "Shhhhh" greeted them from inside the house.

The Old Lady had already stopped her story mid sentence and speaking to all the children in the room said, "My little children, it's time to go and play outside."

"No, please finish the story." they begged.

"Another time, possibly." As the words left her lips, her smile faded for a brief moment and Preet was sure he saw her eyes well up. "I have something to discuss with Lashra's brother and his friends. Go on, outside with you my little nippers." Her smile returned.

Friends? Upal thought to himself.

Chapter 8 Saudj

Upal turned to see who was standing over his shoulder. It was Saudj, Upal's nemesis. He was an inch taller and a year older. They shared the same physique and that's where the similarities ended. Saudj had a head full of curly blonde hair and dark brown eyes. He was an only child.

His father was a maker, seller and drinker of Glumvyn, a poisonous beverage with a high alcohol content. He was a mean drunk and Saudj had felt the back of his hand on many occasions.

Like his father, Saudj had very little patience and at times could be utterly brutal. He enjoyed picking on the weakest people he could find. He reasoned in his mind that he was helping them, by toughening them up and preparing them for the real world.

He had bullied and tortured Upal for the first couple of years after Upal's family had been forced into the West Gate. In time Upal stood his ground and there was a delicate and unspoken truce between them. Deep inside, Upal feared him. He'd witnessed his cruelty often and knew that if pushed hard enough, Saudj was capable of anything.

Saudj, Preet and Lashra had known each other all their lives and yes Preet was bullied by Saudj too, but now that he'd grown so big, Saudj was taking no chances.

"When did *he* become our friend?" he mumbled quietly to Preet.

"Don't be an ass Oop." came Preet's reply.

"It's the only thing he can be. Isn't that why you call him Poop?" Saudj ridiculed.

Upal turned around swiftly, Saudj put up his dukes and Preet put himself between them.

A maternal voice was heard calling from inside the house, "Come now children, we mustn't fight." It was Lashra.

"Come," said the Old Lady as she waved them in.

Excited and eager to sit by Lashra, Upal instinctively dove in through the window or at least that was his intent. He'd forgotten about his lack of a rope. But was quickly reminded when the waist of his pants caught the window sill and stopped him in mid flight.

He abruptly landed halfway through the window. He was bent over the edge and almost fell out of his pants and into the house. There he was dangling, his naked bum in the air. Luckily his quick reflexes got him off the windowsill and outside before anyone was the wiser. Upal pulled his pants up and decided to use the door.

Preet was about to make his entrance when his afro caught the top of the entrance. His head jerked back and he stumbled backwards. "Ah! Darn it! Everytime?" he said bitterly. "Do I have to do that everytime? My neck is killing me." he said as he bent over and made his way into the house all the while rubbing his neck.

"One day buddy, one day." Upal noted.

Saudj was already sitting next to Lashra. Like all the other boys, he was not unaffected by her beauty and charm.

Upal was still a little red in the face and wasn't sure if anyone had seen his misfortune. He assumed since no one was making fun of him, he was probably safe.

Lashra noticed that he was holding his pants up with one hand. She reached into her hallowed hand bag and procured, as if by magic, a piece of rope. She tossed it in his direction, "Catch." she called out. "You wouldn't want to be caught with your pants down again would you?" She winked at him.

"How did you know?" asked Preet.

Upal's face was all shades of red. He quietly tied his pants up, then made his way to the floor facing Lashra.

Preet could only shake his head in disapproval of both boys. He sat in front of the two, to keep an eye on them.

The Old Lady made her way to her old worn and battered up cookstove. She handed each child a cup then grabbed a pot of hot tea. Slowly her celebrated beverage was poured into their cups. Not a word was spoken as she finished her round.

She gently put down her kettle on a short overtaxed wooden stool that stood next to her chair. Gracefully dropping her enormous body down, she sat and stared into her tea for a long thought-out moment. Her face had a somber and serious look to it.

She took a deep breath, exhaled and said, "I have something important to tell you." The children looked at each other in wonderment.

"My time is at hand." she said softly. "And yours has just begun."

Chapter 9 The Prophecy

Seeing the worried look on the woman's face, Lashra's eyes moistened. She didn't know what was going on but she knew enough to know it wasn't going to be good. She began to babble out all kinds of questions.

"I don't understand. What are you trying to say? You said you could live a thousand years. You can't leave us, we need you. Why are you doing this? Why are you talking this way? Why do you look so sad?" She knew what the woman was about to say was going to be poignant and lamentable. Lashra was confused, sad and angry. She couldn't stop herself from going on and on.

"Don't say another word. This is foolishness." She got up, desperate and confused. She threw herself onto the woman, her arms wrapped around her giant neck. Lashra held her tight and began to sob.

Lashra was ready to contest anything and everything the Old Lady was about to say. But deep inside she knew that nothing would change the words about to be spoken. "I love you so much." she whispered sorrowfully in the Old Lady's ear. Her tears had already saturated the old woman's garb. She did not want to deprive herself of the moment, so she held onto her, thinking perhaps, if she just held on long enough, nothing would change.

The Old Lady was patting her hair, "Lashra my darling, my student, my child…" she paused briefly, "my friend." she murmured affectionately. "We must all accept what is to come. We must drink from the cup we are about to receive." As she spoke the words, she guided the young girl back to the floor. Lashra sat quietly at her feet, tears still streaming down her face. The Old Lady rested her hand on the child's shoulder and continued.

"Everyone has a beginning and an end; I am no different. When our light is extinguished all that remains are the lessons we learned and passed on. The love we have accepted and the love we have given. Let all the memories that you leave behind be good ones. Let them be your shining light, the sparkle no one can extinguish." She slowly sipped her tea, giving her a moment to think of her next words.

"It is not the number of years we spend here on Eternal that truly counts. It is the impact that our time here has on others. Therefore, do not mourn for me when I say that my time is at hand. Instead, rejoice in knowing that I have loved you with all my heart, until my last breath." As she spoke the words, she took a deep breath and sighed.

Lashra laid her head on the woman's lap as she continued to speak. "I have outlived…" she started counting on her fingers and muttering names. "…seven husbands." she said with a weak smile.

"I have had a long and prosperous life. I have seen many things. I tell you the truth, my heart has been longing and dreaming and waiting for this day to reveal itself." As she spoke the words her eyes lit up. "When my ancestors wrote The Scrolls of Tralatitious, they did not know the timing of the end of this age. Every one of my descendants had longed to see what I see now. Every generation has dreamed of this day. We dread what comes before and rejoice in what comes after. How wonderful it is for this generation to be the one to witness all that is about to take place. How blessed I am that your identity has been unveiled to me. I am the last pure blood of my tribe, therefore, I had faith that you would arrive in my lifetime."

"When you first came to me I did not recognize you. No, not one of you. However, last night I had a prophetic dream and you were at last revealed to me. I know that today I am experiencing the beginning of the end of this age and you shall bring forth a new age and a new world."

The children sat listening, but were exceedingly confused.

"You have been chosen and are fortunate to be the ones who will fulfill the vision given by the Prophet Of Peace. In *his* own time, he could not find *The One* who could bear the weight of the armor. He knew that one day peace and salvation would return to our world. He prophesied that the armor would be restored."

Saudj stood up and gestured toward the woman. "Quit speaking in riddles, Old Lady. Just come out and tell us what you mean." he said impatiently and brusquely.

Preet asked her, "Why should we be chosen to find The One? We're just a pack of ignorant kids who don't even understand what you are saying."

"You are so wrong my little Preet." she said with a smile. "You are all gifted with skills and talents that will see you through the commission you have been designated for."

Upal got up and paced the room, "Who is this person? The One who should bear the armor? How do we find him? Why can't you go and tell him he's *The One*?" His voice was distressed and anxious.

"It could be a she." muttered Lashra.

"Really?" Saudj jumped to his feet. "That's your big concern here? His use of pronouns? Really?" Saudj said, raising his voice. "The world might be ending…Ugh!" He was visibly shaken and irritated.

The Old Lady slowly got up from her chair and walked to Saudj. She took his face in both of her hands, "My time is nearing its end. Your time is just beginning." She tried to guide him back to the floor, motioning him to sit next to his friends, but he would have none of it.

She returned to her place and sat down before she continued. "During the day of Liberation, Mater the leader of my people said that three must die, that all may live. He sent out Paladin, Protag and Patron with the armor and they disappeared into the Rubicon. Now *I* say, *you* also must enter the Rubicon. This time one must die, that all may live."

Saudj was highly agitated and interrupted her, "I have a question. Do you mean to say that you actually think we believe all those old tales and stories you tell? We're not stupid little children."

Upal glared at Saudj, "Maybe you should shut your mouth and give the Old Lady the respect she deserves."

"And maybe, you should be careful how you speak to me, Upal. This foolish escapade she's sending you on will be much more difficult with only two fools going. Are you willing to be *the one* who dies?" Saudj spoke with a wickedness that took them all off guard.

The Old Lady leaned forward and looked deep into Saudj's eyes. "Do not let your anger betray you." she whispered. "Your time is fast approaching." Her words only confused him more and it only added to his anger and uncertainty.

Saudi was unwilling to listen to any more of her foolishness and so he made his way to the door. He stopped abruptly, looked back and left with these words hanging in the air: "Nothing ever changes. Your great-grand-parents, your grand-parents and your parents, they all talked about *The One* returning in their time. Everyone through history has taught their children to believe it would be within their generation. For thousands of years people have claimed and preached that The One's arrival was imminent. Now, this old lady says she's dying and in her desperation to fulfill some groundless prophecy, she's willing to send you to the Rubicon." Saudj could only shake his head in disbelief.

"She would have you die, or worse, have you tortured and eaten alive by wild beasts. No one ever returns from the Rubicon!" his voice kept rising. "That's the truth we know. Wake up to the reality of her folly. If you choose to listen to this craziness and go, you *will* die! That is the only thing you can be certain of. You know the only true statement of Eternal? The Rubicon Forest, from where no one ever returns. That's it, that's all. That is the only thing we're sure of."

He put his hand on the door latch and threw it open. He took one step out the door and turned around one last time. "Our walls have been standing for thousands of years waiting for the day that Demorg would invade and return to his rightful place. Yet he has not even scratched the surface of our precious walls. The only true invasion is the one these old fools have put into your minds and hearts. Generation after generation of simpletons. They have been controlling our people for thousands of years, poisoning you with lies and deceit. They have trapped and jailed you like mind slaves. They talk of love and peace, but their true objective is slavery. Slavery of the body, slavery of the mind, slavery of the soul. Yes, your soul, your mind, your body. Not mine. They sing you songs of comfort but nourish your minds with fears and phobias."

He took a step backward, fully exiting the Old Lady's domain. "Leave with me now while you still have your lives and some of your sanity. Come with me that you might be free of all this. Come with me and live."

They sat and watched as Saudj became enraged to the point of madness. He raised his fist then pointed to the woman in the chair. Filled with bitterness and enmity he shouted. "You alone are responsible for their deaths, Old Witch!"

The Old Lady looked at the three sitting in front of her. "You are all free to choose your destinies. I will not judge you nor will I love you any less."

Saudj walked out the door, stopped for a moment, turned and put his head through the window. "Lashra, I'll miss you the most." He walked away, then quickly returned.

"Actually, you're the only one I'm going to miss." Then, he left this time for good.

As he walked down the dusty road his anger and resentment toward the Old Lady continued to boil up inside him. "That crazy old hag is sending them to their deaths. Blind, all of them inebriated by her poisonous words. Oh Lashra, you're so smart, why can't you see through her lies?" His mumblings and grumblings continued as he walked, heading nowhere in particular.

The kids were caught staring at the window in a long awkward silence. After a few moments, Upal tried to break the silence. "He's gone mad. It finally happened and not just slightly mad."

"Whatever it is that we must do, we'll do it." Lashra said with confidence.

Upal chimed in. "I know for one that if Saudj would have been involved, he would have been a stumbling block to us all."

"We all have our role to play Upal. Don't be so quick to judge." The Old Lady's mood was somber and she appeared fatigued. "I am tired. Come back tomorrow, then you will know all you need to know."

Lashra was still sitting by the Old Lady's chair. "I'll stay here with you for the night. You shouldn't be alone."

"Go, my child. I must meditate and get some rest. Please come back tomorrow." As she spoke her words, she placed her hands in her lap and closed her eyes.

Chapter 10 Mrs. Nibbledent's

The three teens reluctantly got up and left the Old Lady's home. Preet took hold of his sister's hand and pulled her close. He wrapped his arm around her shoulder and comforted her in silence as they walked along.

Without a word spoken or so much as a look exchanged, they all had the same idea. "We should go looking for Saudj and straighten him out." Upal said while staring at the ground kicking dust up.

"I was thinking the same thing." the other two said in unison.

Their efforts were lackadaisical and they simply spent most of the night walking aimlessly. They found themselves more concerned about the Old Lady and her mysterious message. Little if anything else was said as they traveled throughout the neighborhoods.

Their unintentional wandering somehow led them to Mrs. Nibbledent's. Standing at the entrance of the home they looked to the sky to try and figure out how much of the night was left as the sun had called it a day hours ago. Tonight the moon was in its sixth day of waxing gibbous. It shone as bright as two moons.

Suddenly the night sky was blasted with hundreds, nay, thousands of shooting stars breaking through the moon's light and having the appearance of jetting out from the moon itself. Then as quickly as it started it was over.

The three stood motionless in utter silence with mouths gaping. In the excitement Lashra found herself gripping Upal's hand. She looked over at him. A huge grin covered his face. She awkwardly shook her hand out of his. She took hold of Preet's hand and whispered, "The Tratalitious says…

Tears of fire burned up the sky,
When the prophet went to die.
Shooting from the midnight sun,
Into the forest they did run."

She let go of Preet's hand and grabbed hold of his shirt. "The Old Lady. Something's happened to the Old Lady I'm sure of it."

Upal placed his hand on hers. "She's fine, Lashra... We'll be seeing her in a few hours."

Preet added, "If she thought she was going to die tonight, she wouldn't have told us to come back later. She clearly said she'd fill us in tomorrow. Come on, let's make our way home and get a couple of hours of rest."

"I think we should all stay together tonight, then we can head over to the Old Lady's house at sunrise." she said, still worried.

Preet had stayed at Upal's a few times over the past few months, but never had Lashra ever even considered doing so. Even if she had, Preet would not have allowed it.

"We should go home." Preet repeated. "We'll come get Oop as soon as we see daylight."

Upal was bummed by Preet's insistence that she not stay the night. So, as was often the case he spoke up. "Lashra's right Preet, we should just stay together tonight. The sun will be up in a few hours and I don't think it would be a good idea for me to be alone right now."

He moved closer to Preet and had him bend down so he could whisper in his ear, "Listen, I'm a little freaked out here, you know.. the Old Lady saying she's dying, Saudj going mad and there's the whole fire crying star thing we just witnessed." He tapped his temple, "I'm pretty frenzied up in here. I mean if you leave me alone, in this condition? That's gonna do some extra damage and I think we both know that can't be good for either of us." He smiled curiously hoping his argument was winning Preet over.

"Really?" Preet said, with lighthearted disdain. His eyebrows raised with skepticism. He shook his head disapprovingly but agreed to stay even though he had reservations.

Slowly and with purpose Upal opened the door. They quietly made their way into Mrs. Nibbledent's house. There she was fast asleep at the kitchen table, grasping her glass of Glumvyn.

"Wow, she must have had a hard day." Upal said sarcastically. "I can't ever remember her leaving behind a half empty glass of sauce, let alone one that's half full." He chuckled at his own remarks.

They slowly made their way in. The only light was a small candle on the table next to the empty bottle. It barely had the strength to light her face. As they made their way through the darkness, Lashra bumped into a small stool next to the stairs and knocked over an unlit candlestick. The noise it made partially woke the owner of the house. They all stopped moving and waited. She looked up to see her glass still half full.

"What's this?" she garbled out. They stood in silence, not moving, hoping she hadn't seen them. "What? Is that you my precious?" She lifted her head just high enough to drink the last of her precious juice. Her head fell back onto the table and instantly snoring was heard.

"That's better," said Upal, smiling.

The three friends made their way up to Upal's dungeon. The three were exhausted from all the day's events. Lashra hit the hay and then fell onto the bed. The boys fell to the floor and before any of them could comment on anything that had happened on this whirlwind of a day... they fell asleep.

Chapter 11 Saudj Returns

Saudj spent his night walking and seething. The agony and stress of the situation was crushing him. He thought mostly about Lashra and how he could insulate her from the Old Lady's insane ways.

"I have to save her. She's blind to what's going on. They all are." he said uproariously to no one. "How can I be the only one that sees things clearly? She's been manipulating them all these years. All of Eternal is under her spell."

He was growing more delusional with every step, his brain was swirling with thoughts and images of what would happen if he didn't do something, anything. Saudj abruptly stopped. He was shocked when he unknowingly found himself at the entrance of the Old Lady's home.

He placed his palm on the wooden door. Slowly and gently he ran his hand down. "This is a sign." he whispered ever so quietly.

"Ouch!" He ripped his hand away from the door. He examined his finger and carefully pulled out a small sliver of wood. He squeezed his finger to make sure it was all out. One drop of blood was released. His eyes followed its long journey to the ground. The drip landed in the sand producing an outward explosion. He found himself mesmerized by the small crater it produced.

He put his finger in his mouth and sucked on the tiny yet nagging wound. Carefully, quietly, he stepped to the side and looked through her window. The door to the children's bedroom was closed. His eyes were riveted on the deceitful, lying dragon who slumbered in the chair. She'd fallen asleep holding her beloved scrolls.

He slowly and quietly breathed out, "The Scrolls of Tralatitious. If only they could be destroyed, then the lies would end."

He noticed that the wood stove had been left unattended and only a few red embers were left. The candle by her chair was flickering and darting with its last few breaths of life.

"That candle will be dead in a minute" he said in a hauntingly low drawl.

He glowered at her, his jaw clenched, his teeth grinding. He muttered, "She's going to send them to their deaths. Lashra believes everything this old hag says. She'll be gone forever if I don't do something about it. They'll all be gone."

He heard a dark and sinister voice echo in the back of his mind. "Only you can save Eternal, Saudj. Be the savior they need."

"But how?" he questioned himself. "What can I do?"

"You must rid the world of those scrolls." The despondent voice was becoming less recognizable. "No one should ever be deluded by her fables again. Destroy the scrolls of Tralatitious and you erase the lies. You can bring forth a new world, a new future."

"She'll wake up if I try to take them." he countered the voice. "Then what will I do?"

The articulations of his twisted mind were becoming more desperate. "Stop the lies!" the voice shouted. Saudj's heart was pounding hard and fast. The voice grew more frantic. "The truth belongs to us." His breathing was quick and shallow; the agent crying from within grew more determined. "Do not let this moment pass." He felt faint and confused. The voice was almost unbearable. "Slaughter her, destroy the Dragon."

The dizziness was intoxicating. "I can't kill her?" he said.

"*One* must die, that all may live." The thought echoed through Saudj's mind as he recalled the words spoken by the dragon on the previous afternoon.

"She was begging for you to help her fulfill the prophecy." He pressed his eyes tightly closed and put his palms against his ears in an attempt to block out the voice that demanded the unimaginable.

His attempt to silence the voice failed. "Let her false prophecies be self-fulfilling; she'll die by her own words."

The arguments in his mind were beginning to take a toll on him. Saudj felt himself weakening. The voice was eroding what little will he had left.

"*Your time is fast approaching*; let her revelations be your guide."

At that point, the voice took a comforting and tranquil air. "Help her Saudj. She needs you to help fulfill her dying wish. She knew she was going mad. You are her last hope."

Exhausted and terrified he mouthed, "I will not murder."

Sympathetically the voice replied, "Suffer her to live, but get the scrolls."

Chapter 12 One Dark Night

He scanned his surroundings to see if anyone was in the streets. He was alone. Of course he was alone, it was the dead of night. It felt hot and muggy, his skin was clammy and damp. There was not even the slightest breath of air to refresh him. It was a deathly, eerily still evening.

The moon seemed to shine with the brightness of an afternoon sun. He stood alone and motionless, pressed against the wall by the window of her abode, hopelessly trying to cover himself in darkness. The silence was deafening. He looked around again. Nothing, no one. Not even one stumbling Glumvyn-soaked vagrant could be seen or heard.

Noiselessly he snaked his way over the window sill and secretly he crept in, inch by inch. Slithering and stealing his way down to the hard time-worn floor. Painstakingly rising to his feet he stepped aside so as not to cast a shadow through the hole in the wall.

I don't have much time, the sun will be up in a few hours, I have to hurry. He thought to himself. I can't wake her, I mustn't wake her.

He was eight maybe nine steps away. Suddenly a large cloud passed over the moon and its light disappeared. His head was spinning and his vision was constricted. He tried to focus out of his tunnel vision. She seemed to be a mile away. His vision felt thick, somehow massive and heavy. He found it unsettling.

The distance seemed insurmountable. He counted the steps anxiously. One, he took his first step and *crack*, his knee made a sound that must have been heard throughout all of Eternal. He stopped and held his breath, the woman twitched, the candle's light flickered, then vanished. Saudj went blind. His head was pounding with the hammering rhythm of his blasting heart. The high pitched notes of silence were ear-piercing.

A small sense of relief came when his eyes readjusted to the dark room. He continued, two, he tried to focus on the scrolls in the woman's hands. Three, with each step he tried to embolden and calm himself. Four, I will save Eternal. Five. He softly and deliberately lowered his foot. Si…, his sixth step came into contact with something unusual. He stopped mid-landing, it was merely a cup that was left behind earlier by one of those dim-witted kids, probably Upal. He stepped to the side, avoiding it. Seven, he was distressingly close to the sleeping Longevite. Slowly, carefully, quietly he continued. Eight, even closer. Nine, his trembling hand reached out for one of the scrolls. They were within reach.

The drumming in his chest progressed into an excruciating and uncontrollable pain. He watched her face as his quivering fingers reached out and touched the edge of the scroll, her hands clenched, her eyes opened.

He looked down at his hand and discovered he was holding a large rock. It was heavy, oval and smooth; he could scarcely wrap his hand around it. Startled by its presence and hers and without thought, he swung his arm and it came to a sudden and jarring stop.

The rock's pounding strike made contact with her head violently driving it against the back of her seat. The force fractured the Old Lady's skull. A warm, wet deluge of blood from her injury splattered and sprayed his face; the madness of the situation was quickly unseating any sanity that remained in him.

The moonlight returned and shined in through the window. He saw the woman attempting to lift and straighten her head; he bludgeoned her again. Blood spewed out and covered his face and filled his mouth. He gagged and spit the contents back into her face.

She found the power to turn her head and their eyes made contact. The Old Lady found the strength to reach and grab hold of his garment. She pulled him in close and with her free hand gently touched his face and garbled out of her blood dripping lips, "I forgive you."

Her words propelled him into an uncontrollable and unmanageable silent rage. Over and over he pounded her with the stone. Time slowed to a near halt. Everything moved in slow motion. The room was suddenly bright as day. His vision, crisp and clear. At that very moment he was able to ponder the dull, blunt sounds of the uncontrolled whipping and pounding. It was softer and more hushed than he would have imagined.

Her heavy body tipped to one side and slid awkwardly to the floor. He watched her as she lay on the ground, blood pooling around her head. His blood stained hands reached down and grabbed hold of some scrolls. His feet were drenched in her marrow. In a flash of lucidity he realized he was standing in a quagmire of blood. He stood high above and looked down on her.

"I will not murder." he said to her.

Chapter 13 Run Saudj

His mind was a corkscrew of images, sounds and memories, past, present and future. All of it a crazy, crooked, twisted, tortuous winding spiral of phantasms that could not be controlled. He was running toward the city gate. This portal would lead him to his freedom.

The main gate would soon be open. He knew enough to get out before anyone found out what he'd done. He struggled to unlock and push open the eye of the needle.

This little door seemed to help justify his earlier actions as it persuaded him even more of the peoples' shortsighted, irrelevant, futile, simpleminded ways. "Aahhh!" He let out an involuntary scream of frustration.

The small door had been built for *safety* reasons; the leaders imagined that if Demorg's army ever attacked at night there was no way for his troops to flood the city through the small entrance. The main gate was open from sunrise to sunset, a tradition that went back thousands of years.

The large doors gave everyone access to go in and out of the city during the day. Citizens of the West Gate used this time to trade wares, herbs and trinkets with the Romas (a tribe of gypsies who made the outside wall their domain). At night you could only leave the city through the eye of the needle. It was sometimes used by the Patrol to rid themselves of the *unwanted*. It was better for the Patrol that housebreakers, pinchers and purloiners be cast out for the night, lest they get in the way of the Patrol's evil ways.

He lifted the large bar that kept the door securely locked. He pushed the cumbersome door open. He made his way out and ran a short distance and fell to his knees. He was exhausted.

A thousand questions swirled in his mind. What have I done? I saved my friends. What have I done? I killed The Old Lady? What's going to happen to me? They won't understand. They'll banish me. I don't know what to do. What should I do? They'll banish me. I have to hide. They won't know it's me. Why would they think it's me? It was a painful mind-bending process, a constant reenactment of the night's events.

He prostrated himself. Saudj was stretched out with his face on the ground. He covered his head with his hands trying to stop the unyielding playback of the unimaginable. I have to hide somewhere, but where?

Saudj raised his head from the soil. His eyes met the horizon. The spectacle was transcendent. He gazed in wonderment. Hundreds, nay, thousands of shooting stars showered the Rubicon. The heavens had sent him a sign. The Rubicon; no one will come look for me there.

He scrambled and fought his way to his feet and ran and ran and ran. It was imperative that he make it.

Exhausted, depleted, confused, alone and desperate, he stood at the dreaded entrance. He peered into its tunnel-like structure and closed his eyes.

"There he is! Bring him to me!" The Patrolman shouted. "There's no use fighting it boy. We know you're guilty and you know your punishment."

"You can walk in or we can throw you in. One thing is sure, boy. You will never return. No one ever returns."

Chapter 14 Enter The Rubicon

Saudj opened his eyes and shook himself out of his trance. He was alone. Had he imagined the whole night? He gazed at his blood stained hands and sighed in disbelief.

He looked deep into the Rubicon's entrance. What was he thinking? He tried hard to see through to the other end of the tunnel, but it was too deep and dark.

The first blush of morning light was minutes away from making itself known. The breaking of day brought a warm breeze that worked diligently at drying the long grass that the night had filled with dew. He cast his eyes over the land that separated him from the city. It was going to be a beautiful day, he thought to himself.

He turned back to face the dreaded entrance. "No!" he said to himself. "I can't go in there." Turning away from the exit he proceeded to walk the edge of the forest. The Rubicon's boundaries were partially framed with Euphorbia shrubs. He could smell the perfume of the beautiful pink flowers that bloomed on the poisonous and thorn filled branches. Its barbs were razor sharp and filled with a poisonous acid-venom. It would slowly grow as it ate away at you. Within a few hours there would be nothing left of you. The acid would remove all traces of your existence. A simple scratch was said to be enough to take a life.

The shrubbed flat lands soon turned into a jagged and almost unmanageable sharp rock formation. Slowly and meticulously he made his way up and down and side to side. One misstep and he could find himself pierced through by one of a thousand spear-like rocks.

Saudj was barely a hundred feet into the treacherous terrain when he stopped dead in his tracks. His eyes caught a pile of dried up bones. The human remains had been picked clean of all their flesh. All the stories he'd heard as a child, the same ones he'd repeated to scare the kids he knew, flashed through his mind.

"There are some who try to run from the Patrol when being brought out to the Rubicon. Their escape is short lived. "Run!", the Patrolmen shout as they prepare their javelins and arrows. But they never shoot, they simply watch as the fugitives attempt to make their way past the Euphorbia and through the jagged rocks. It's never long before they slip and are skewered by one or the other. Their destiny and yours if you ever try to escape the Patrol, is to die a slow and torturous death. You could be left out in the sun to be eaten by the venom of the shrubs or die on the rocks and be slowly eaten alive by the condors, vultures and crows. If there was another way to die on the edge of the Rubicon, no one knew. Few people attempted to run. Most chose the uncertainty of the forest.

Lucky for Saudj, he wasn't being chased by the Patrol. He made his way slowly and meticulously. He was tired and thirsty and longed to rest. He continued carefully for a while. He could see flat desert sand just up ahead. With painstaking vigilance, he saw his way through. Saudj reached the edge of the sand and flopped onto the barren no-man's-land, closed his eyes and rested.

He lay still for a few moments. He opened his eyes and could see nothing but an unending desert landscape to one side and the Rubicon on the other. Nowhere to hide. That's all that kept running through his head. Nowhere to hide. It was lingering over him with every breath, every heartbeat, every thought. He felt as if he was sinking in quicksand. It was a sinking, suffocating, strangling, squeezing sensation that was paralyzing and slowly swallowing him up.

He painstakingly made his way to his feet and dragged himself along the Rubicon's boundaries until a few hours before sunset. Saudj spent the day longing and yearning to find a way out of his unspeakable situation.

Saudj had been without sleep, water and food for too long, and the effects were taking their toll on him.

"Bring me the Scrolls." He looked around and could see no one.

He stopped and heard the haunting voice again, a voice that could have been mistaken for the breeze whooshing and murmuring through the trees.

"Saudj." the woods whispered. Yes, it was coming from the woods.

"Deliverance." The sound was almost indistinguishable from the air.

"Solace." The sound became an anesthetic, casually lessening his awareness.

Saudj stood staring at the Rubicon. He was in a dispiriting state of mind. "If I enter I will die."

The wind echoed a comforting, "You will live."

Unknowingly he inched his way forward. "No one ever returns." he whispered to the wind.

"I am Rubicon." the trees rustled.

Unwittingly he budged forward a few more inches. "I will never return."

The woods insisted, "Come to me."

Unknowingly he moved closer. "I need to rest."

In one breath the sky grew dark and the sun vanished. A long booming, roaring, rolling sound of thunder was heard. An ear-splitting crack followed. Saudj looked up to see a tree falling. It smashed down at his feet opening the Rubicon.

A sudden intense gale pushed him closer. The cold wind pierced his ears and he heard, "Come to me my son, I will give you the Rubicon and the whole world."

He climbed onto the slaughtered tree and made his way unintendedly into the forest. At the last moment he realized what he had done and turned to make his escape. It was too late. Thorns had already covered the sprawling tree and the exit.

Overtired and run ragged, Saudj's body gave up and he fell to the forest floor. He tried to open his eyes but couldn't. He suddenly felt comforted by a gentle breeze that caressed his face and hushed gently in his ear, "Everything will be fine, you are home."

And with those final words he passed out.

Chapter 15 Sunrise

It was the beginning of a new day. Upal had slept for about an hour or so. He stared out his window, the black dots were still flying in the distant west. He looked over at his bed and smiled. He was filled with a sense of happiness he hadn't felt since he was a child. In fact it was when he was about eight years old. It was an uncomplicated day that was etched in his mind, a simpler time, an uneventful day spent at the watering hole. His mom had come to watch him play and swim. It wasn't often that she had time to *just* come watch her boys amuse themselves. On that day she brought Upal and his brother some sandwiches and apple cake. That delicious apple cake, with her not-too-sweet icing on top. He closed his eyes and took a deep breath through his nostrils. He could almost smell and taste those wonderful flavors.

"This is going to be a wonderful day." he murmured as he turned to face the not-so-appalling bed of hay. "You sure make that bed look inviting." He whispered as he took in the sight of Lashara sleeping. Yup, a wonderful day he thought to himself.

Preet was lying in a mangled and uncomfortable position. He had three quarters of his torso on the floor and the remainder awkwardly spread out across part of the bed. One of his legs ended up rolling over the chest at the foot of the bed.

His eyes darted back to Lashra. She was still asleep, covered by a thin patchwork that didn't do much to cover her or keep her warm. He observed her quietly and longingly, daydreaming of laying down next to her. He would hold her and keep her toasty and warm. He would gently kiss the back of her neck and stroke her hair all the while trying not to wake her. He would spend his days loving her, caring for her and being loved by her.

"Oh – My – World! Stop looking at my sister like that, you sicko!" Preet's eyes were still closed and to make matters worse he wasn't even facing Upal as he shouted the words. He suddenly cringed when he realized he might have woken Mrs. Nibbledent.

Upal was shaken out of his daydream. Embarrassed and confused he blurted out, "What? What? What are you talking about?" He turned his gaze back to the outside. "I've been staring at those crows by Rubicon for the last hour." He could feel the blood rushing to his face. "We should be going. Wake her up and let's get going."

Yawningly she admitted "I've been up for a while now." Upal's self-conscious face reddened again.

Lashra stretched and spread herself out and playfully kicked the remainder of Preet's body off the bed.

Upal kept staring out the window. He thought he could feel Lashra staring at him. Had she heard his previous murmuring about her? He wondered if he'd even spoken the words out loud. Even though he felt somewhat embarrassed, he took some pleasure in imagining that she might have heard him and was at this very moment smiling at him and the situation. Just to be clear… she wasn't.

"Let's get going." Upal threw the words outside.

"You know he's always staring at you right? Preet said to his sister.

"Shut up Preet." she said.

"Ya Preet, shut up." Upal repeated, "Let's go." He was eager to leave and change the subject.

They quietly made their way down the stairs. When they reached the bottom they could see that Mrs. Nibbledent had not moved one wit. Her hand was still grasping her empty glass. Upal noticed a small puddle of pinkish drool with an almost silk-like thread that led to her lips. He gagged and instantly turned away. They made their way toward the door and Lashra once again knocked the stool over. This time none of them cared about waking her up. Upal slammed the door open and they made a run for it.

The sky had scarcely been lit by the time they hit the streets. Taking a hurried pace they made their way to the Old Lady's house. The thoroughfares and alleyways were quiet. No one could be seen buying or selling. There were no kids outside playing and running a muck. He noticed a couple of roving rats, running from a stray cat and two snoring sots tucked away in a corner seeking shelter from the world and possibly their wives.

This morning's peace and quiet seemed unusual, maybe even out of place, but really he wasn't sure. He rarely if ever got up at this time of day. He was thinking about doing it more often, maybe everytime Lashra spent the night. Why would he bother sleeping when he could be spending time with her?

Their pace must have been extra fast because they were already approaching the Old Lady's home. Lashra noticed the door was wide open. She ran. "There's something wrong!" she shouted back.

Preet started running and just before he reached the door he fell to the ground at the entrance of the house. Upal simply ran on top of him.

Preet looked up from the ground and looked through Lashra and Upal's still legs. Their hearts sank. The Old Lady's giant body was laying in a pool of blood.

Chapter 16 Why?

Lashra, Preet and Upal were frozen in their tracks. For the longest moment the three stood there, confused and unable to register the horror. Their minds tried hard to reject what they were seeing.

A sudden and unyielding sadness filled Lashra, "Why? Why? Why?" she could barely choke out the words. She fell to her knees and wrapped her arms around the Old Lady's shoulders and cried out, "Preet! Upal! Help me turn her over! She's drowning in her blood."

Using all their strength they heaved and rolled her over. Lashra gently lifted her head and placed it on her lap. She reached into the woman's mouth and began scooping out blood and clots in hopes of clearing her air passage. Lashra's tears cascaded down the Old Lady's blood covered face. Lashra used her hair to wipe and clean the woman's blood stained face.

She tried to regain her composure by taking deep breaths and quietly repeating a mantra "Breathe, calm, breathe, calm." she needed to regain her senses in order to think clearly.

Lashra was having a difficult time reclaiming her faculties. Things were moving so fast. The room seemed to be spinning at a dizzying rate. She became queasy and just as she thought she was about to throw up she saw the Old Lady slowly open her eyes. The woman gave a slight groan.

"She's still alive!" the girl screamed as she wiped the Old Lady's face and used her sleeve to wipe slime from her nose.

The aged woman was weary and colorless. She did her best to speak but could only manage a raspy whisper. "You must listen." Her eyes closed and Lashra bent her ear closer. "I don't have much time left, my child."

Lashra pleaded, "No, you'll be fine. I'll clean you up and bandage your wounds. I'll do all the work, I'll take care of the children, the garden, the house; you'll rest, you'll rest, you'll get better, everything will be fine."

The Old Lady continued. "My scrolls, the Armor, Timmy…" she choked then coughed up some blood. "Must gather Armor." She closed her eyes for a moment to rest and gather her strength. "Children, restore peace."

Lashra began frantically quizzing the dying woman. "What do you mean? You should rest. Tell us more later." she begged the Old Lady.

"Three, peace." she mumbled.

"Three what? How do we restore peace? Where is the Armor? Stay with us, you need to tell us more, we don't know anything."

The two boys were paralyzed. The unfolding scene left them helpless, powerless and impotent. They watched as Lashra tried to shake the injured woman awake.

She was weeping and blubbering, her sobs made it impossible for her to speak clearly, but the woman seemed to understand every word. "Please!" Lashra begged, "You need to tell me more. Please don't go, please, please.Tell me who did this to you?"

The Old Lady used the last of her strength and reached her arm up to touch Lashra's face. She gently pulled her down even closer and gurgled her words out through a thick red liquid that was filling her mouth and throat, "My pocket, scrolls, Saudj, Rubicon." She paused. "The Forest of Eternals awaits you." She coughed out more blood. "Three." with that final word she closed her eyes. Her hand fell from Lashra's face and hit the floor with a heavy thud.

Through her tears she cried out to the old woman, shaking and pleading, "No. I don't understand. What are we supposed to do? Why are you doing this? Why?"

Preet was filled with extreme sadness. He took one step toward the woman and his knees gave out. He dropped down next to the lifeless body and leaned into her. He wrapped his arms around her and laid his head on her chest. "Thank you for loving me." he said, weeping.

Upal put his hand on Lashra's shoulder. "What's going on? What are we going to do?" he muttered. He tried to shake himself out of his stupor. He wanted to think. He wanted to be strong. He needed to be strong for Lashra and Preet. "This is all too much to bear. Maybe Saudj was right. Maybe we're all going to die."

The sound of a creaking door made all three turn and look.

Chapter 17 The Children

The creaking sound came from the children's room. Lashra's maternal instincts kicked in. "Upal" she said, grabbing his arm. "Keep the children in their room." She looked down at The Old Lady and back at him. Her lips quivered as she said, "I need to cover her up."

Without hesitation Upal jumped over the body and made his way to the kid's room. He closed the door behind him.

"What's going on?" The eldest asked.

Upal's eyes were wide and jetting side to side. He tried to come up with an answer, but couldn't. He simply stood in front of the door and waited. For what? He didn't know.

Lashra and Preet grabbed the blood splattered blanket from her chair and covered the slain body. Lashra made her way to the kid's bedroom door. She did her best to wipe her tears and snot filled nose. She gently knocked. Upal opened.

"We need to get the kids out of the house." she whispered to him. They opened the door and hurriedly led the kids outside. Preet did his best to shield the children's view on their way past the body.

Once outside, she set Timmy out on his daily stroll and told him to be back for his afternoon snack. She gripped the oldest of the children and pulled her to the side (she was about ten or eleven).

"You need to find a Patrolman and tell him there's been a murder." Lashra was gripping the girl's shoulders and looking her square in the eyes. "You need to tell him that The Old Lady has been murdered..." She paused. "My world." Her eyes grew large. She had a revelation. In an almost catatonic voice she said, "Tell him Saudj has murdered the Old Lady."

The child began crying. "Listen to me." She shook the little girl. Lashra was trying hard to control the quiver in her voice as she told the young girl, "You must also tell him that we have gone to the Rubicon to find him."

Lashra understood the look on the poor child's face. The poor thing was completely lost and confused. Lashra took her in her arms and hugged her tightly for a few seconds. She then placed her hands on her shoulders and held her firmly.

"There is no time to waste. Can you do this for me? Can you?" The child nodded. "Go!" Lashra commanded. "Go!"

Lashra walked over to the other children. Upal had been counting stones with them to keep busy. Lashra gathered them in her arms. "I have a very important task for you." she said bravely. "You must *not* go into the house or let anyone in until the Patrolman arrives." She nodded her head and gave the children a weak smile. "I am trusting you with this giant responsibility, I believe in you." She pulled them back and held them. "Do this for me." she whispered to them. "Remember no one must enter the house." She reached into her bag and gave each child a small candy. She hugged them again and made her way to Upal and Preet.

She grabbed Preet by the hand. "We need to go."

"Where?" he asked.

"The Rubicon." she said in a ghostly manner. "I believe Saudj killed the Old Lady… and he's headed for the Rubicon."

"That's crazy." said Upal.

She let go of Preet's hand and without another word she started running. Naturally the boys instinctively followed her. The three urgently ran out of the city toward the Rubicon.

A short distance away from the city Lashra stopped and turned to face the only home she'd ever known. The feeling of loss was abundant and it came with a heavy heart and a sense of uneasiness.

Upal quickly caught up to Lashra. She stared into the western horizon. "I hear the Rubicon calling me." she spoke with a soft voice.

"If it's calling you it's calling me too." said Upal.

She stared at him with such intensity, that Upal felt as if she was reading his soul. "Is it though?"

Chapter 18 Ray

"Unkindness, conspiracy... that's what they call it buddy." Crawford was bored and desperate for conversation. "Hey Ray, don't you think that's a little mean? Why do you think they call you that?"

The sandy brown haired stripling questioned his black bird. *Caw, caw* his pet responded. "Ah, don't take it personally buddy, I've been called worse."

He sat on the ground petting Ray, who was not only his best friend but his best raven, well, his only raven. Ray was a majestic and ravishing black bird that stood twenty six inches tall and had a wing span just short of four feet. He was a powerful and sinister looking creature. If he was ordered to attack (as he had been in the past), Ray could easily frighten off any would-be aggressor.

Ray was as clever and crafty as he was big, which made sense since ravens are one of the most intelligent animals in the world. This is something Crawford often pointed out to the girls he met, in an effort to keep their attention.

"He prefers to be called handsome." he'd interject when the girls would comment on Ray's beauty.

"He gets that from me, by the way." he would say while attempting a smoldering look (which sometimes worked).

"He knows over a hundred words. He's almost as intelligent as I am." Crawford would say with a smug smile.

If he found a girl pretty enough (and he often did), he'd lean in and secretly whisper, "Why did you know Ray here... he can easily tell the difference between silver, gold, diamonds or rubies; he's a master at finding... *exquisite treasures.*" Then he'd unabashedly chirp, "That's why he made his way to you." It was often enough to make a girl blush. Of course it didn't hurt that he was a tall, good looking lad who came from a wealthy family.

But at the end of the day, it was always Crawford and Ray. Their friendship went way back to a time when Crawford was about seven or eight years old. He was walking home from school on his customary route when he happened to hear something squawking and yelping in an alley. He entered the backstreet to investigate the sound. He spotted a little black bird, limping and protecting his wing.

"Oh, look at you, what are you doing here? What happened?" He carefully picked up the bird, tucked it in his jacket then made his way home.

He snuck the creature up the stairs to his room. He took the bird out of his jacket and said to the bird, "Father won't mind. He's rarely home. But do try to stay quiet in any case."

Crawford was thankful to the housemaid who brought the bird food, water and bandages. Without her help the child would probably have killed the bird with love. After about six weeks of nursing, the raven was looking pretty good. The day had arrived; Ray was ready to return to the sky.

Crawford so badly wanted to keep Ray as his pet, but even at his tender age, he knew something about being locked up and caged. "I wish I could fly out of here with you Ray. I won't hold you back. Fly, be free."

Caw, caw, caw, the sound of his voice echoed against the nearby houses as he flew high into sky. The housemaid held the boy as he sniffled and whimpered. Once the bird was out of sight, she layed Crawford down in his bed, tucked him in and silently patted his head while he cried himself to sleep.

At sunrise the very next day he was awakened by the sound of gurgling and croaking. Ray had returned. Crawford jumped out of bed with wonderment and delight. He ran to his window and grabbed hold of his friend. Ever since then they've been inseparable.

Chapter 19 Nuts

Crawford covered his head with his shirt. He was willingly and happily being pelted and showered with a variety of nuts and berries falling from the sky. He looked up at the hundreds of crows circling above his head. The murder of crows and the conspiracy of ravens stayed busy swooping, gliding and circling, up, down and around the boy.

Crawford gathered up the food and used a couple of rocks to break the hard shells surrounding the delicious fruit. "One for you, two for me." he said as threw out the birds' share a few feet away.

With Ray's encouragement the birds quickly found the human practical, and the human enjoyed the company. It did come as a bit of a surprise to Crawford how easily the birds trusted him and how that trust was rewarded with berries, mushrooms and other treats that seemed to magically appear from the Rubicon.

He remarked to himself more than a few times how they appeared to have no difficulties going in and out of the ghastly forest. "Ray," he said leaning back on a large flat rock, "it seems to me that not *everything* gets trapped in that place."

The notorious saying, *the Rubicon, no one ever returns*, tumbled through his mind and a chill ran down his spine. He reached out to pet the bird and commented, "Apparently that doesn't apply to you or them, does it buddy? Maybe it's because even the Rubicon fears murder, unkindness and conspiracies." A sense of uneasiness came over him after speaking those words out loud. He tried to shake it off by looking the other way and eating more nuts and berries.

The day was heating up and bit by bit the sizzling heat was baking Crawford. He crawled back to his makeshift canopy. It would be a little easier to rest and cool down in the shade provided by the broken branches and shrubs. He got himself as comfortable as possible. He laid there staring longingly in the direction of the city.

Peering through the cracks and crevasses of his makeshift shelter he thought about returning home. It's not all bad, he thought to himself. He stretched out trying to find a more comfortable position. "I may have to rethink my life's goals, buddy." he said quietly to the raven who'd jammed himself next to the chap. "Well, if nothing else," he rolled over onto his stomach and reached out for a handful of nuts, "at least I… I mean, we have food."

Crawford found it hard to get comfortable on the rocky soil. He rolled over onto his back and stared up at the blue sky. I miss my bed. I *miss* the housemaid, he smiled coyly to himself.

"You know Ray," he said in a reflective manner, "being alone isn't all it's cracked up to be."

It was hard for him to imagine that just a few weeks ago he was at home enjoying a peaceful and untroubled life. Well, maybe not *untroubled*. After all, over the past few years Crawford had taught Ray numerous tricks and stunts, many of which got them (but mostly Crawford) into trouble and the years of trouble making had finally come to their natural conclusion.

His home was now a shrub. He was sleeping outside. He was dependent on his raven for food. And as if that wasn't enough, all of it was happening an hour's walk from the Rubicon.

Chapter 20 And We're Walking

They'd been running for almost twenty minutes. Upal was trying hard to keep up to Lashra. Her words... "Is it though?" Kept running through his mind. What did she mean? He wondered. She's confused. Does she think I'm going to abandon her? Does she really believe Saudj killed the Old Lady? The questions looped around in his head.

Lashra hadn't slowed down since she started running. She glanced back and saw Upal about a minute behind her. Where was Preet? She stopped and waited for Upal to catch up. Upal was happy to finally stop and catch his breath.

Grunting and wheezing and hacking, he squeaked out, "You must be the fastest person in all of Eternal. How did I not know you could run like that?"

"You have no idea what I'm capable of." she murmured.

"What? Sorry I couldn't hear you over my grunting and wheezing and hacking."

"Where's Preet?" she demanded.

"He could be hours behind us. Maybe even days." he smiled as he attempted to lighten his situation.

Lashra scolded him with her silence. They waited and waited. Then... Lashra waited and waited while Upal sat and rested on the sand.

"I think I see him." Upal heard the sound of irritability in her voice.

"Seeing a whole new Lashra today." He smiled again.

She was filled with emotion. "Not everything is funny all the time, Upal."

Upal was ashamed of himself. How could he turn so cold so quickly? Lashra was heart broken and all he could do was joke around? "Sorry, it's just how I deal with stuff." he said shamefully.

Preet was still a fair distance away but could see that Lashra and Upal were waiting for him. "Oh, this is so good. They're not shrinking anymore… Oh, this is great. Oh look, they're getting bigger." he wheezed to himself.

He stopped. He couldn't go on anymore. He was tired and breathless. He waved his large arms in the air to show he'd seen them. Then fell flat on the ground. "They can wait a minute or two more."

"I think he fell again." quipped Upal. "He may never recover." he chuckled.

Lashra looked at him.

Upal looked back. "What? That's funny… Come on, that's funny."

Lashra started walking toward Preet. "Let's go and get him."

Upal stayed put and shouted to Lashra. "It's funny 'cause he's always falling down."

Chapter 21 Crawford Must Go

It seemed Crawford had a bad habit, a thing, a quirk, a... *weakness* one might say. He was always bored. The boy found life in South Gate quite dull and so he thought, why should I deny myself a little pleasure? A little joy. A little *adventure?* After all, no one ever got seriously hurt... most of the time.

Every time he got in trouble he'd say the same old thing, "Father, these aged, rusty, senile shopkeepers are behind the times. How can they appreciate my... my resourcefulness? Will they never understand that I'm a man of creativity? I need the freedom to try new things."

Crawford's biggest problem was that his father was an important man. He was a long-standing councilor in the South Gate. Not just any councilor, he was *the* Councilor, that is, the one in charge of advising and instructing the Leader of the South Gate. Second in charge, as it were. He was also a prominent business owner. He spent much of his time traveling, making deals and negotiating terms with various businesses throughout all the gates.

Unfortunately for Crawford, his father didn't see things his way. His long record of stealing trinkets, semi precious loot, vandalism (and one time *maybe* unintentionally and definitely not on purpose), setting the local market on fire, was not helping his father's reputation. All of this and more, had finally caught up with Crawford. He did protest, saying that *officially* he hadn't done any of those things; it was Ray.

However, after years of being defrauded by the young swindler, the vendors had had enough of his little enterprise. Not only was he tormenting shopkeepers in the South Gate, he had taken it upon himself to pluck wares and create havoc in all the gates, omitting only the West Gate. After all, what could they possibly have that was of any value?

The merchants endlessly complained to the councilors of their respected gates. Be that as it may, the prominence and influence of Crawford's father was too much to overcome. Even if the boy was guilty as charged there seemed to be no one around who could enforce the verdict. The shopkeepers felt powerless.

After a long while the merchants devised their own solution. A unionized group confronted Crawford's father and issued an edict; the boy and his notorious crow had to go.

A crowd of vendors gathered at the councilor's house one night. The union's steward ranted and complained to Crawford's father, "You've sat idle for years and have done nothing to remedy this situation."

"He burned down half my shop!" interjected a vendor from the back of the crowd.

The Steward continued, "We've been more than patient with you and the boy. We've petitioned, we've pleaded, we've tried to appeal to your sense of justice and nothing."

"Tell him," a vendor sandwiched in nervously, "he leaves us no choice."

The Steward raised his hand to silence the agitated vendor, "You leave us no choice but to..." he paused for a moment and thought carefully about his next words. "...warn you about the harm your boy is inflicting upon *your reputation*. One might even say jeopardizing it."

The councilor's jaw was clenched in anger, not only toward these men standing before him, but for his son who had been given clemency once too often. "Are you threatening me?" he asked calmly.

The vendor prompted the Steward, "Tell him he leaves us no choice."

The Steward brought his finger to his lips and shushed his companion. "My friend is right. You leave us no choice." He continued nervously but firmly, "We have all agreed that if a solution is not found by the end of the week, all of the shopkeepers, South, North and East will vote unanimously to have you removed from the council and if that fails, we vow that we will discontinue doing business with you. Good luck making a living with only the West Gate to deal with."

"What do you want from me?" came the father's reply. "Would you have me forsake my son?"

"Send him away." they said in harmony.

"Where should I send him?"

"Send him to the Rubicon for all we care." the man said.

One shopkeeper shouted from the back of the room, "Or worse, send him to the West Gate!" and the entire room broke into laughter.

The Councilor fully understood the shopkeepers' position and their frustrations with his son. "I will speak with my son."

The Steward raised his voice. "You need to do more than speak with him." He was growing impatient with the Councilor. "You've been talking for years and nothing has changed." His courage was building. He slammed his fist into his hand. "Action is what is required here."

The group of men turned around and walked away. The steward turned to remind the Councilor one last time. "By week's end."

That night Crawford's father took him aside and layed out his only option. "I can no longer protect you or myself from the merchants. My business, my reputation, my standing in the South Gate and across all of Eternal for that matter, all of it, collateral damage due to your years of mayhem."

Crawford opened his mouth to interject, but was cut off by his father's screams. "It's as if you take pleasure in destroying everything I have worked so hard to create!" He lowered his voice and was almost cathartic when he told him he had been left with no option but to send him away.

Crawford was taken aback by his father's words and the seriousness and finality of his decision. He begged his father, "I'll stop, I'll be good."

Words he had spoken many times before. Sure, he'd be good for a week, maybe two, but then it would start all over again. His father was too familiar with his son's double talk. This time his words were ironclad.

"Your old and worn out promises are no longer good here. You will relocate yourself to the West Gate or live with the Romas outside the city walls. Don't try hiding out in any other Gate."

He warned his son that the merchants had made it clear that the Patrol would be on the lookout for him.

"The merchants suggested I send you to the Rubicon… Go to the West Gate, it's the only place you have left to go. I've had the housemaid prepare your clothes, some food and a few dollars. It will be enough to keep you for a few months, if you don't gamble it away."

Chapter 22 Alone

Crawford was astute and shrewd. Surely someone as clever as he was could come up with a plan that would have him *forgiven* or at the very least excused. With any luck he could come up with a plan that would have his father absolve him of his past sins and allow him to return home.

"We'll be back in business in a few days." he said to Ray.

Despite all his shrewdness, it was two weeks later and he was but a short distance from the bewitched gateway of the Rubicon. In fact, he was no closer to being forgiven than he was the day he left.

As of this very day he still had not figured out a way to safely stay in the city or find a way into his father's heart.

"Well, at least your friends are keeping me from starving." He paused to eat a few berries. "The nights are still manageable. But we have to figure something out before winter hits." he said half jokingly.

His nights were mostly sleepless. He spent a lot of time tossing and turning. The days were long, hot and boring. He was re-thinking his life's decisions and what it would mean to go back home and beg for forgiveness.

"Looks like danger." Ray croaked.

The bird caught Crawford's attention. "It's the Patrol. They've come looking for me."

Crawford layed low and whispered to his friend, "Ray, look over there, is that the Patrol? Why are they looking for me?" He squinted to improve his view. "Maybe they're bringing a criminal out to the Rubicon."

That's how it worked. If you were found guilty of a Rubiconian crime, two to seven patrol men (depending on how dangerous you were) would lead you to the tunnel that led into the unknown world. You would be told to enter it or forced to enter it. Very few made a run for it. Most thought it better to go into the Rubicon with all their senses and limbs intact. It would surely give them a better chance at survival.

Crawford forced his eyes, trying hard to make out the figures more clearly. "This criminal must be marginally dangerous since there are only two patrolmen with him." he said to Ray.

Crawford decided to lay low and stay out of sight. No need to take any unnecessary risks. He would hate for the Patrol to think he had been condemned to the Rubicon, yet somehow managed to avoid entrance. If he was spotted they'd surely recognize him as the son of the Councilor and throw him in without question. He began feeling anxious.

As they got closer he realized none of them were wearing Patrol uniforms. A little closer and he thought they looked like three teenagers not much younger or older than he was. "Hey Ray... is that a girl with them?" he whispered.

"Beautiful girl" croaked Ray.

"Shhhh, not now Ray."

Crawford had taught his raven a few choice words and phrases that he could use to start a dalliance with a Miss Right or at least a Miss Right-now. He found the raven to be a great ice-breaker and a wingman (pun intended).

"They're either in the same situation I'm in or they're crazy. I wonder if I should take a chance and talk to them? It's surely better than being alone."

His raven squeaked out. "Looks like danger."

"Shut up, you're gonna get us killed. "But, maybe you're right my feathered friend, maybe I should avoid contact."

He stayed still and quiet in his little makeshift shelter. The teenagers finally came clearly into sight. The three walked by without even a glance his way. He couldn't make out what the two boys were talking about, but wow! She was beautiful.

"What are they doing this far out of the city?" he breathed.

"Pretty girl" came Ray's response.

Preet stopped dead in his tracks and listened inquisitively. "Did you guys hear that?"

Upal and Lashra stopped and glanced back at Preet. "I didn't hear anything."

"Me neither."

Preet looked around. "It sounded like, pretty girl."

Upal exploded with a loud guffaw. "Dude," he shook his head in a pitiful and hapless manner. "Your obsession with everybody obsessing over Lashra..." He closed his eyes and swayed his head back and forth slowly. "You gotta bring that down a notch. It's getting a little... uh, *eccentric*."

Lashra turned to Upal in surprise, "Wow, Upal, good effort with a new word. But, not the best. I would've used..." She was also growing tired of Preet's overprotection. "...strange, bizarre, idiosyncratic..."

An annoyed Preet responded, "Ya, ya, I get it. You're both really funny, but I know what I heard."

Upal condescendingly added, "You're right Preet, even the bushes and shrubs are trying to charm your sister. Idiot."

Lashra picked up her pace, "Let's go, we need to make up time."

Crawford couldn't quite make out what they were talking about. Then it hit him.

"Of course Ray!" Crawford finally saw the situation clearly. "She's being kidnapped. That giant monster and his miniscule comrade have abducted her. That's the only logical explanation."

He turned over quietly so he could see the three. "I have a plan, Ray. I need you to dive-bomb the giant, and don't stop. While you do that, I'll take care of the dwarf. We'll save that poor girl if it's the last thing we do... But just to be clear... It won't be the last thing we do."

"Go!" He sent the raven off on his task. Suddenly Crawford had a change of mind and decided to stay in position to rethink the second part of his plan.

"Maybe, I'll wait here a little to see how this goes. I don't want to be too hasty." he muttered to himself.

Ray's huge body came down and attacked Preet. "Ahhhh! What's going on?" He tried to duck and dodge the bird. Panic-stricken he shouted, "Help me, that crow is demented. He's trying to kill me."

Without thinking, Lashra picked up a large stick from the side of the trail and started batting at the bird.

Preet continued to scream and wave his arms frantically. "It's the curse of the Rubicon, Demorg's demons are attacking us!"

Upal broke off a branch from a shrub and was coming to help Lashra fend off the bird.

Frenzied and a little delirious, Preet cried out, "Go after Upal, he's bite-sized!"

Upon hearing Preet's comment, Upal dropped the branch and chose to watch instead of coming to his friend's rescue. This gave him time to question why the bird was not attacking him or Lashra.

Lashra on the other hand was busy with her rescue efforts.

Whack, the stick missed the bird and hit the ground. "Get away!" The raven dodged the stick.

Thwack, another miss. "Leave him alone!" Ray weaved.

Swat, "Stop it!" He avoided the large stick again.

Lashra made another attempt. *Whack!* This time she made contact. Her branch hit the raven. "Gotcha!" The raven crashed to the ground. "He's not moving." she cried out.

"Good!" shouted Preet.

Lashra ran to the bird and immediately started caring for it.

"What about me?" cried Preet.

Chapter 23 On A Mission

Crawford jumped out of his nest yelling and waving his arms. "Hey! What's wrong with you? What are you doing? Leave my bird alone!" he growled at Lashra. "Are you crazy? Leave him alone."

Lashra was startled by the sudden appearance of, well, *anyone* out there and she stepped away from the raven. "What the…?"

Crawford was losing it. "What's wrong with you? We're trying to save you from that giant and his sidekick and this is the thanks we get."

"These are my friends, you imbecile!" she said angrily.

Upal looked around as if there must be someone else with them he didn't know about. He elbowed Preet, "Did he just call *me your* sidekick?"

"Hey imbecile," Upal shouted to the stranger.

Crawford turned around, "Are you talking to me?"

"Well you seem to be the only imbecile around, so ya I'm talking to you. Let's be clear about one thing… If anybody is somebody's sidekick it's him." He pointed at Preet.

"What is he talking about?" Crawford mumbled to himself. He turned his attention to Ray and ignored the three. He gently looked Ray over. "You ok buddy? Ya you look ok." he said.

He set Ray on his shoulder and began to question the trio. "What the heck are you doing out here? No one ventures out this far. Unless…" he paused dramatically. "Unless they're criminals."

"Really?" said Upal as he stepped toward him and looked him in the eye. "What kind of criminal are you?"

"The innocent kind of course." He threw an arrogant smile in Lashra's direction.

Lashra ignored his smugness. She stepped in between the two and separated them. "Hold on boys. Let's all calm down and start over."

"Start over what?" Crawford was visibly annoyed. "I tried to save you and for that you tried to kill my best friend."

"Ya, well your best friend tried to kill me, so I think we're even." Preet excitedly added.

"Stop! Everybody, just stop." Lashra just wanted to get back to their prime objective. "Maybe you should go back to your hiding place and let us get back to making our way to the Rubicon."

"On purpose?" Crawford interjected.

"Yes, on purpose." She realized how ridiculous the situation must have looked. "A boy named Saudj murdered The Old Lady this morning and stole some of her Scrolls." She felt herself welling up.

She took a deep controlled breath and continued. "We believe he made his way into the forest. I'm going in after him to retrieve the scrolls and find the Armor of Peace."

"Oh, is that all?" He sarcastically waved his hand toward the Rubicon. "Please don't let me stop you."

"Like you could stop us." Upal said with a strong sense of loathing.

"You said the Old Lady's been murdered?" Crawford had suddenly registered some of her words. He sighed, "I saw her once, when I was about five years old. I remember she came to our house and spoke with my father. She said something that seemed to upset him, then she was gone. Everything else I know about her are the stories that travel through the gates. That's so sad." He paused for a moment and tried to grasp the situation.

"I don't get it." He reluctantly continued. "If her murderer went into the Rubicon, then he's pronounced judgment against himself already. Why go after him? Let him die there. I'm sure you know that no one *ever* returns."

"I just told you." Lashra continued. "We need to retrieve the Scrolls and find The Armor. The Old Lady told us it was our destiny to do so."

"Your destiny? To go into the Rubicon?" he said, obviously questioning her sanity. "You don't actually believe in the Scrolls of Tralatitious? I mean I'm sure they're physically real, but... what I mean is," he wanted to be careful how he finished his thought. After all, he wasn't sure how crazy they were. "What I mean is some people believe the stories about the armor of peace and stuff, but those people are mostly uneducated or they're zealots and scammers."

Upal spoke up, "The Old Lady said that we were the chosen ones. She said we were born to fulfill the prophecy."

Lashra pulled out a scroll from her bag. "The Old Lady had this scroll in her pocket when she died." She waved them in Crawford's face. "It was surely her final message to us."

Crawford grabbed them from her hands and read them out loud.

As I lay down and send you out, to do the things untried,
The forest greets you and protects, 'til deeper you abide.
The one who fell, seeks his revenge, your plans he will curtail.
The armor sought will be revived, but not with friendship frail.

*****

Evil is rising and darkness is growing
The blood he desires is no longer flowing
The sword he is raising to quench his thirst
The one it feeds, let him be cursed.

Enter the forest to change the story

One heart is darkened by their own glory
When it is darkest a light shines through
Peace will return like the morning's dew.

Crawford handed the scrolls back to Lashra. He looked at the three in absolute disbelief. "Hey Ray do you believe this?" he sarcastically questioned the raven sitting on his shoulder. He reached into his shirt and pretended to pull out a scroll of his own. He unrolled it and read it. "We were prophesied to do this story. Enter the forest in all our glory. Have another brew, we're missing a screw."

He backed away, turned and started making his way back to his shelter. He looked back, "That's my prophecy." He laughed uncomfortably.

"Come on Ray, let's go into the Rubicon and DIE! Are you guys kidding me? That scroll is meaningless, you could come up with a thousand renderings for that thing." he said as he continued walking away.

Lashra was filled with all kinds of feelings and emotions. Maybe she was just looking for a reason to explode and release some of her tension. She ran to Crawford, grabbed his shirt and spun him around and let him have it.

"You don't know anything. We've been sent on a mission by the Old Lady, a fact you can't grasp or even begin to understand with your tiny little brain."

He tried to turn away, but she held him in place. "I've known the Old Lady all my life. I spent all my days with her, she taught me everything she knew." Lashra was getting emotional and her anger boiled up.

"She told us the night before she was viciously murdered that our lives were about to change in monumental ways!" She was crying and yelling at Crawford. "I held her in my arms while she died! I heard her final words."

Preet moved in and took her into his arms.

She was sobbing, "I held her while she died. She's dead Preet, she's dead. Gone forever. Why did he do it?"

Preet was overwhelmed too. Tears were streaming down his face. "I don't know. I don't know anything anymore."

Lashra pushed herself away from Preet. She wiped her eyes and took a deep breath. She turned away from Crawford. "We need to get moving. We need to enter the Rubicon before dark."

Crawford was moved by her words and tears, but tried not to show it. "Ok, well, have fun."

Lashra began to walk toward the forest by herself.

"What are you doing out here anyways?" Upal asked the boy.

"Just hanging out." was his response.

"The words of a coward." Upal remarked. "It's more likely that you're hiding out." He turned and walked away.

Preet and Upal picked up their pace and the threesome was restored. Crawford watched for a moment and then decided to follow from a distance. He wanted to see with his own eyes if anyone could actually be so unhinged as to enter the Rubicon willingly.

He walked quietly and whispered, "This is what I'm saying Ray, only crazy people believe the stories in the Scrolls of Tralatitious."

When the three were a few feet away from the entrance, he shouted, "So, you're actually going to go into the Rubicon?"

"Yes we are, coward." said Upal. He pulled on Lashra's sleeve and in a muted tone asked, "Are you actually going in there?"

She didn't respond.

"By the way, it's pronounced Crawford." he shouted. "But I'll let it slide this time, because you don't seem to be too right in the head."

Upal had a slight quiver in his voice, "Whatever Crow-boy." He was feeling anxious about the whole situation. Were they actually going to do this?

Everyone stopped at the entrance. Lashra took a few steps forward, leaving the boys behind. "We've already lost so much time and sunlight. We need to get in before dark." Lashra was trying to sound brave, but inside she was also questioning the validity of her decision.

Crawford was standing only a few feet behind them. "If it's daylight you're worried about, I wouldn't worry too much." he said. "Rumor has it that light does not penetrate the Rubicon. Truth be told, I think you guys are in the dark on just about everything right now."

With small short steps they made their way down the tunnel and closer to the unspeakable point of no return. Upal and Preet stood back and thought that at some point Lashra would come to her senses and turn around.

She slowed her pace and her step became smaller. She noticed that the sound of the birds, the wind, the whole of the outside world started to sound muffled.

She paused but a few inches away from the threshold. All the stories and myths were swirling around in her head.

I can just reach out and touch it, thought Lashra. She slowly reached her hand out. She wondered how close she could get before... Lashra was suddenly in darkness being swatted by some kind of monster... Startled, she fell back. It was Ray. He had flown between her and the Rubicon. Flapping and beating his wings he squawked and cawed his warnings to her.

"Ray, come back here!" The raven ignored the call. He stayed close to the girl, trying to scare her back. Her heart was pounding. She was second guessing her decision to have come this close. "Bird?" she asked. "Are you saying we shouldn't go in?"

The boys stepped forward to join her side. They stood looking and peering into the place from where no one ever returns.

Preet and Upal reached out and took hold of Lashra's hands.

"Am I going in?" she asked.

Preet squeezed her hand, "We should really think about this Lash."

"Preet's right," said Upal. "Eternal has been waiting thousands of years for the prophecy to be fulfilled. What's another day or two going to do?"

All at once the sky grew dark and the sun vanished. The tunnel they'd been standing in went black as night.

Preet nervously squeezed Lashra's hand, "Is that a good sign or a bad sign?"

"I'm not sure." As she spoke the words, a resounding blast of thunder bellowed its admonishment; Lashra leaned heavily forward and pulled herself out of Preet's grip. She felt herself falling and being sucked into the Rubicon. Her final thought was that she'd secretly hoped that Preet could have held her back.

The final sound she heard from the outside world was a roaring voice that seemed to echo from the thunder. A warning. The warning. "No one ever returns!" The words penetrated and cut through her as she pierced the chasm of the known to the unimaginable.

The light returned. She was gone. "Lashra!" Preet and Upal cried out. They looked around. She was nowhere to be found. Without hesitating Preet and Upal ran in after her.

Crawford watched as the strangers vanished before his eyes. He shouted over the sound of the still roaring rumble, "No one ever returns!"

Silence. "Where did they go?" he asked Ray.

"Looks like danger. Pretty girl. Looks like danger." was the raven's response. The bird moved closer to the entrance trying to entice his friend.

Crawford's heart was aching with fear. "I can't." He fell to his knees. "I can't Ray. They're all crazy."

The raven cawed again and went in after them, leaving Crawford behind.

Chapter 24 Into The Rubicon

Lashra kept her eyes closed as she stepped into the Rubicon. An indescribable energy surrounded her as she left everything she knew behind.

She kept her eyes closed and stood silently still. The sounds of singing and chirping filled the air. A distant pecking sound echoed through the woods.

Lashra slowly opened her eyes, but nothing seemed to register except soft low waves of the murmuring wind rustling through the branches and leaves.

She closed her eyes again for a moment and focused on an ambient sound. She was sure she could hear the sound of flowing water all around her. Then other sounds filled her senses, tweet, tweet, peck, peck, caw, caw, shhhh whispered the wind. It was amazing.

She drew in a long slow breath and her senses were filled with the smell of mint and lavender. She opened her eyes once more; this time her sight was filled with lush green foliage topped with an endless array of purple petals.

The sun shone through the trees. A short distance away she could see a path of light. It was filled with every shade of green imaginable. A bird, two birds in the distance. Butterflies and small insects fluttered to and fro. The sun's light was dancing like fire on one long strand of a spee's web that floated on the air high above the ground.

Another flying creature, swooped gracefully down then ascended back up again. Darkness and light, shadows and highlights. The depths and layers, everything was magnificent. She stood frozen. She was hypnotized by the majestic beauty.

She stayed silent and thought about the dreams and stories of what the Rubicon would be. It was not so.

She looked to one side and took in the scent of the damp earth and moss. Her eye caught the bright orange color of a large Pendulous Pudding Mushroom that had nestled into the limb of a tree. It made her smile.

Lashra's attention turned to the mesmerizing song of a Cerulean Crooner that was sitting on a rock a few feet away; a tiny bird covered with every shade of blue imaginable.

Turning in another direction she was instantly absorbed by the freshness of a pine covered path and the enticing smell of life producing trees. It was as if she could smell the aromas of all the colors.

The wind's movement was an orchestra of sound that filled the air. She wondered how all these acoustics had not been audible a few inches outside the forest.

Then it struck her. She turned to see the outside world, it was gone. The Eternal she knew had somehow vanished. It was as if the Rubicon had enveloped her and taken her away from everyone and everything.

Her eyes closed as she paused for a moment to absorb the whirlwind of emotions. It was too much to bear. Tears began to well up and in an instant she was weeping uncontrollably. "I never could have imagined beauty like this. I was expecting death and destruction." she whispered. "I don't understand." she continued. "How could everyone have been so wrong?"

"Lashra!" She heard Preet calling her. He ran to her and said nothing; he reached out and put his arms around her and pulled her in close. In a strange kind of way, she felt at peace, like she belonged here. It was as though her whole life was meant for this moment.

She moved away from Preet and cautiously proceeded deeper into the woods. Upal and Preet followed close behind. Upal was about to suggest trying to leave, when all of a sudden... *Caw! Caw!* The sound of the raven jolted them and made them jump.

They all looked up to see a raven on a branch above their heads.

Preet shook his fist at the raven. "Are you Crowboy's foul bird?" he demanded.

And as if to answer Preet's question, the bird called out "Pretty Girl". He dived down barely missing Preet's big hair. Preet jumped back in fear and tumbled into Upal knocking them both to the ground. Ray smoothly set himself down at Lashra's feet.

"I guess that answers your question, now get off me." said Upal.

Preet was peeved at the bird's attempt at attacking him again. "Lash, shew him away. We don't need him attacking us." He gave the bird a dirty look. "He's been enough trouble already, and if there's one thing we don't need it's more trouble."

They were startled by an unnatural cracking sound coming from behind.

"Noooooooo!" cried Upal.

Chapter 25 Apologize

Crawford poked his head out from behind a large tree. He was astounded at himself and was probably more disappointed than Upal for finding himself here. Why on Eternal had he followed a bunch of crazy strangers *into the Rubicon* of all places?

What if they decided to kill him? He didn't know what to do or say. The momentary lapse of silence felt like hours. He needed to say something, anything... so he blurted out "Yes, of course he's my fowl bird. What other kind of bird could he be?"

Lashra chuckled quietly.

Crawford felt a little soothed by her giggle. Even in the Rubicon, he still had it. He smiled to himself. Preet and Upal on the other hand gave Lashra a disapproving look.

"What?" she questioned their look. "That could be funny."

"Really?" Preet interjected. "Why wasn't it funny when I said it a few seconds ago?"

"Delivery I guess." replied Crawford.

Lashra chuckled again. "Ok, that *was* funny."

Upal let out a disgruntled sigh. "Did you not just hear Preet say we didn't need any more trouble? What are you doing here?" He took a few steps forward, placing himself squarely in Crawford's path.

Crawford gestured to Lashra. "Somebody's got to protect the lady."

Upal shoved him hard enough to make him tumble backwards. "*I'm* here to protect the lady!" he pointed to himself. "I mean Lashra."

"Hello? I'm right here." she said as she waved her arms in the air. "Did I suddenly become invisible?"

She walked up to Crawford, looked him square in the eyes then punched him in the stomach. The force of the surprise blow knocked the wind out of him. "Still think I'm the one who needs protecting?"

Upal watched in dismay. "Why is she flirting with that jerk?" he mumbled under his breath.

She turned to Upal, "What did you say?"

He took a step back, "Nothing." he stammered out in fear.

She placed her hands on her hips and started blasting the three boys. "I am so sick of everyone..." she raised her fingers up making quote signs "... trying to protect me." She shook her fist in the air, "You can all stay right here..." she pointed at the ground full of anger "... and leave me alone. "I don't need any of you to protect me from anything or anyone." Her face had turned as red as her hair. She continued to scold them. "If I need protection from anyone it's from you three."

Preet had never seen her this mad before.

Upal and Crawford took a few steps away from her.

Preet moved closer to his sister. "Don't group me in with those two." he said.

"What? You're worse than Upal!" she yelled at him.

"Ya, worse than me." echoed Upal pointing to himself. "Wait." he pointed at Preet. "How exactly is he worse than me?"

Preet was in shock. "What? Who? How? Oh please tell me how I am worse than Oop?" he exclaimed.

"That's a fair question." Crawford muttered with apprehension.

"Shut up." Upal snarled.

Lashra's fury boiled over onto her brother. "I don't need you to be constantly looking over my shoulder, Preet. I don't need your consent and I don't need your constant protection from every imaginary thing your brain comes up with. I can make my own decisions and protect myself."

"I don't do that?" he said defensively.

"Really? Every time a boy even looks at me, you get upset and start puffing out your chest."

"That's true buddy," said Upal. "She's got you there." he nodded in agreement with her. "Wait… what boys?"

"Shut it Upal you're no better." she growled.

Preet tried to shift some of Lashra's wrath in Upal's direction. "Ya Upal, shut it, you're no better." he repeated.

"Ahhh!" she cried out.

"You're my little sister, it's my job."

"Really Preet, it's your job to protect me from everything?" She took a step toward Crawford who instinctively jumped back a little. She moved in closer and took a hold of his face in her two hands.

Upal silently snickered at Crawford, "Oooh, he's in for it."

Crawford was frozen with fear. He closed his eyes and waited with uncertainty. Suddenly he felt Lashra's lips on his. His knees buckled but somehow he found the strength to stay on his feet.

"There you go Preet, protect me from that."

Crawford opened his eyes. He felt slightly intoxicated and tried not to wobble. Slowly his face was covered with a smile. The awkward smile that covered his face disappeared all of a sudden. He stared at Preet and could almost see smoke coming from his ears.

Crawford began to panic a little, "Uh, I didn't do anything. I was just standing there, I mean here and uh then she uh…then her lips, her soft lips..." The thought lulled Crawford into a joyful daydream and the smile reappeared on his face. That quickly ended when Preet instinctively took a step toward his soon to be victim.

Crawford pleaded with Lashra, "Tell your giant, it's not my fault. I didn't do anything."

Meanwhile lost in the background, Upal gaped at the whole situation. He was confused, stunned, appalled, horrified, shocked, jealous, depressed and it quickly swirled back to confusion. "Why would she kiss the new guy?" he mouthed quietly. "I was right here." he continued to mumble. "Barely five feet away. Why the new guy?"

Lashra made her way to Upal and grabbed hold of him. He was still in a daze. She took hold of his face. Their eyes met and Upal smiled as he closed his eyes. Lashra puckered up and...

"Stop it!" Preet cried out. "I get it, I get it."

Upal opened his eyes. "Nooooo!" A look of shock covered his face. "I mean, no... look at him he doesn't get it."

Lashra let go of Upal and turned to Preet.

Upal reached out and grabbed Lashra's arm. She turned and glared at the hand that had a hold of her. She made reprimanding eye contact with its owner. Upal gently released his squeeze and with an apologetic tone said, "He doesn't get it Lashra." He lifted his shoulders in a pitiful way. "You need to teach him a lesson he won't soon forget." He closed his eyes and puckered up.

"Nice try." she said. She made her way to Preet.

Upal thought he heard Crawford giggle. He looked menacingly at him.

Preet conceded to his sister, "Sorry Lash, I didn't realize I was so possessive."

He looked over at his friend, and quickly recognized that Upal was less than happy with the lip-locking tragedy he had just witnessed.

He walked over and shook his friend. "Oop, tell her you're sorry."

"I'm sorry? *I'm* sorry?" he said, confused.

"See that wasn't hard was it?" Preet chuckled. "There you go Lash, Upal is sorry."

"I'm sorry?" Upal kept repeating as he forgot about everyone else and paced around in a small circle. "I'm sorry?"

Lashra turned to Crawford and raised her eyebrows.

"What?" He locked eyes with her. "You want me to say I'm sorry? Ok. I'm sorry that I'm living in a bush next to the Rubicon. I'm sorry I followed Ray here. I'm sorry I tried to help you earlier. I am sorry I ever made contact with you." He was raising his voice uncontrollably. "And I never thought I'd say this to a beautiful girl who just kissed me." Crawford stepped backward as Preet took a step closer to him. "But I'm sorry you kissed me." He raised his hands and shook his head.

Lashra nodded her head forgivingly. "Apology accepted." she said to Crawford demurely.

"You people are crazy." He reached out his forearm and called his bird. The raven landed on his arm. "Look what you got us into, you stupid bird."

"Looks like trouble." Ray answered.

Lashra composed herself and assumed responsibility for their situation. "Ok, now that we all agree with me, we can set this matter aside. We have more pressing things to do." She looked around. "Which way should we go?"

"This way." Crawford called out. She turned around and she could see he was pointing in the opposite direction.

"Ok, you go that way and we'll go another way." she said. "Preet, Upal, we're going to need some kind of shelter for the night and if we hope to survive for any length of time here we'll need to find water."

She looked around. Where to go? She thought to herself. She searched for clues that might guide her. It didn't take her long to realize she had no idea what to do or where to go.

Upal was still pacing. Preet grabbed him by the arm and led him to Lashra, "Come on buddy everything will be just fine." he said encouragingly.

At this point the boys were still traumatized by Lashra's recent outburst and individually decided not to question anything she said, at least for the rest of the day.

"Crawford? Are you with us?" she asked.

Crawford conceded; he wasn't about to be left alone in the Rubicon.

"Do you think Ray can find us some water? Anything really, a river, a stream, a lake?" she asked him.

"Are you kidding? If I tell him to pick up gold, he doesn't pick up silver." he said proudly.

Upal nudged Preet, "What is this guy talking about?"

Crawford continued, "He's probably the smartest one here. Ray, go find us some water."

The bird left his arm and headed up and over the forest. He began to circle and then started heading in a direction they argued might be North. I hope you're right buddy, thought Crawford.

"Ok, well, let's go." he added, trying to sound confident.

Their pace was quite slow. Every sound or breaking twig made them all nervously stop and listen. Who knew what kind of dark dreadful creatures lurked behind every tree.

Preet felt somewhat vulnerable. He figured his size made him a target for any kind of hell that might be hiding in these haunted woods. His stature did nothing to quench his sense of fear. "Ow." he said when a branch broke the skin on his arm.

Lashra led the pack followed by Crawford then Upal. Preet trailed in the back. He began to feel a little dizzy and then slightly nauseous. A chill went through his whole body, then came the sweats.

Being at the back of the line no one noticed his discomfort. His heart started to race and he felt himself getting increasingly woozy. All of a sudden he could not take in a deep breath and he started panting. He fell over onto a branch and his weight snapped it from the tree.

They all turned to see what had caused the sound. Lashra saw her brother struggling for air. She turned and made her way past Crawford and Upal and went to his side.

"What's wrong Preet?"

He tried but he couldn't make a sound.

Chapter 26 Panic

Preet fell to his knees and leaned up against a tree. He gripped his aching chest with a trembling hand. His heart rate spiked. He thought his heart was about to explode. His mind was getting foggy. He was feeling dissociated. I'm losing my mind, he thought to himself.

Lashra could clearly see he was struggling for air. She grabbed him and held his head against her chest. She gently brushed his face and tried to console him.

"I can't breathe. I feel like I'm choking. My heart's gonna explode. I need to get out of here, I can't stay here…. I'm gonna die… I can't breathe. I'm gonna die."

"It's ok," she said in a soothing voice. "We'll be fine as long as we're together." She held him tightly and tried hard to keep herself calm.

"I don't think I can do this." Tears were rolling down his face. "I don't want to die."

Preet was starting to calm down. She brought her body down to match his and looked into his eyes. "I can't do this without you Preet" she whispered, "Who's going to protect me from Upal?" She gave him a quirky smile. "We can do anything if we're together, you know that."

Crawford stared at the two. He was baffled and disheartened. "We're ten feet into this thing and the giant is having a panic attack? Are you kidding me? What's gonna happen if we come face to face with something worse than trees and fresh air?"

"His name is *Preet, Crawford.*"

He looked to the sky and raised his hands and cried out "Ray! What did you get me into?"

Upal chimed in. "You can leave anytime you want, Crowboy. We don't need you."

"Whatever, I'm better off alone, then with a bunch of wuds." he spewed in Upal's direction. He turned and walked in the opposite direction. "There's got to be a way out of this bewitched timberland."

Lashra paid no means to Crawford. Her only focus was to help bring Preet back down to Eternal. It seemed to be working.

Crawford was only a few feet away from the three and was already regretting his words and his actions. In truth he wasn't sure where he was going. He took several steps off the path and into some soft shrubs and long grass. "The exit is just over here, I'm sure of it." he said loudly, trying to convince himself he wasn't alone.

He turned to look back and was surprised by how quickly the others had disappeared from view. "Did they actually… just leave me behind?" Knowing he was alone made everything seem more frightening. The crackling leaves and broken branches beneath his feet resonated throughout his body. All of his senses were suddenly on high alert.

He looked around for something familiar. Strangely enough the outside world had been swallowed up by trees and shrubs. In some mystical way he had traveled much deeper into the forest than the few minutes he had actually walked.

"What's going on, what kind of trickery is this?" he questioned out loud.

The ground cover was becoming impenetrable. "I should probably turn around and find those stupid wuds." He called out hoping to get some kind of response back from one of the three. Sweat poured down his brow. He turned and couldn't figure out where he'd just come from. "Did I already turn?" he questioned himself. "It's got to be this way." He thought about calling for help but his stubbornness prevented it. But he did make a great and loud effort to conquer the vegitation as he worked his way through. He continued clawing and climbing his way through and over brushwood and thicket. Within a few minutes he found himself toiling and plodding a dense almost unimaginable growth. "Are you kidding me?" he cried out and tried another direction. "It's as if this stuff is just growing around me." he nervously mumbled.

He thought he scanned a bit of light from the outside world. It was a spark of hope. He stepped towards it and from out of nowhere a root jumped up to trip him. He fell face first onto the ground hitting the base of a tree.

He tried to shake off the fall and work his way up, however his feet were tangled in vines that covered the forest floor as far as his eyes could see. He noticed how they weaved themselves around the trunk of the trees. He pulled and pushed with legs working one free. He quickly devoted his time to freeing the other leg. He was able to move it partially out of the vine's grip. He gripped a vine a few feet in front of him. He pulled with all his might. He felt something on his hand. He looked up from the ground and came face to face with a horrifying sight.

The terror threw him back. He urgently pulled, pushed and shook his leg. Regardless of his efforts he stayed stuck and his eyes remained glued to the nightmare before him.

He put his useless pride aside and called for help, but nothing came out. He continued his fight with the woods, only to become more entangled in the wiry brush. It was as if it had a mind of its own. It was working on holding him down. The harder he tried to free himself the more difficult it became. He knew this thing he was glaring at was in control. The tree had a face in it. It had eyes and they were locked onto his. He had no doubt they were alive.

This face was frozen in time, yet its eyes were alive. It was crying out for help. It was a visage filled with suffering and torment. "It's me. That's *my* face!" he cried out.

He was horror-struck as he discovered his hands were bound. The vine's grip was getting tighter. Crawford was scared to death. He attempted another call for help.

"Somebody help me! Help! I'm sorry, don't leave me! Help me!"

Could anyone even hear him? Had they already made their way without him? He was quickly losing strength and energy. His heart was pounding a thousand beats a second. He tried to take in a deep breath but his chest could no longer expand. The vines had wrapped themselves around his chest. He could no longer gather enough air or strength to yell for help.

Even the trees were moving closer and leaning down toward him. The forest floor was gripping him tightly. They were about to overtake him at any moment. How could this be real? It can't be. He must be in his bed having a nightmare. Then again what if it was, what if this was to be his fate?

Crawford could see nothing but a trapped soul, locked in the tree in front of him. He was in a near state of madness. He felt himself being sucked into the ground. He could hear the voice of the underbrush crinkling, whispering in his ear. "No one ever returns."

There was no way out. A feeling of hopelessness engulfed his whole being. He tried one last time to yell for help, but not a sound could he make.

Exasperated, he closed his eyes so as not to witness the final calamity that would soon overtake him. Visions of his father flashed through his mind's eye.

He was completely depleted. Without choice Crawford surrendered himself to the woods. One final thought passed through his mind. No one ever returns.

Chapter 27 All For One

"He's over here!" Crawford opened his eyes to see Preet standing above him. His large hand was wrapped in Crawford's shirt. He grunted as he heaved Crawford's haggard body from out of the brush. He hoisted him in the air and planted him on his feet. Preet looked into his eyes, reached around and wrapped his giant arm around Crawford's shoulder and pulled him tightly into a monstrously affectionate hug and in a calm and gentle way he comforted him.

"It's ok. I'm right here with you." he whispered.

Crawford bowed his head in shame and relief. "Thanks for saving me and I'm sorry for what I said earlier."

"Are we done here girls?" Upal shook his head in disbelief. "You know we're going to regret this decision at some point don't you?" he said to Preet.

The four gathered together and collected themselves. Lashra insisted that if they were going to weather further storms and the calamities that were sure to arise, they had to work together as a team. She emphasized that if any of them should have a moment of weakness, the others needed to rise up to the occasion and be strong.

She looked each one in the eye and in a motherly tone said, "We're all going to falter at some point. We're going to have days when we're weak. We need to be here for each other. Whether we like it or not, we need each other. The Old Lady used to say, "The bonds of friendship can be broken by the pointing of one finger."

Upal shook his head. "Look, I'm not pointing any fingers," he said as he nodded towards Crawford, "but you know who doesn't belong here with us. Sorry to be the one to tell you, Crowboy, but you shouldn't have followed us here."

Crawford's heart sank and he felt disheartened.

"This is what I'm talking about Upal." she said disappointedly. He's here and we need to make the best of it. After all, how do we know he's not meant to be here?"

"How do we know?" Upal responded. "Uh... I don't know... He makes fun of Preet for having a panic attack, then he calls us a bunch of wuds, then he takes off only to have to be rescued by Preet." He raised his hands exasperated. "I can go on if you want Lashra."

She reached out and placed her hand on Upal's shoulder. "Like I said, we're all gonna make mistakes. I pray that in my time of weakness," she placed her hand on her heart, "that you will do for me, what I am prepared to do for you."

She reached her arms out and forced them into a tight ring, arms around one another. "I need you. We all need you. We all need each other." she said quietly.

Upal bowed his head. He knew in his heart that Lashra was right and there was no way he was going to let her down. He swallowed his pride and spoke at a volume that was almost inaudible, "We need each other whether we like it or not."

She added, "Our alliance needs to be real and it must be strong and most importantly unbreakable."

"Unbreakable." they repeated.

Lashra once again took the lead. "Ok, so we all agree with me again." she said with a coy smile. "We need to stick together and start moving." She noticed a small path and made her way to it. Unbeknownst to them it was leading them west.

Crawford followed a few feet behind Lashra while Upal and Preet walked the back of the line together.

Preet, speaking loud enough to make sure Crawford heard his words, quipped, "Hey Oop, I hope I didn't look as foolish as Crowboy did when I was having my panic attack?"

Crawford turned to look at Preet who had a big smile on his face. "It could have happened to any of us, big guy." he returned Preet's smile and turned around. The smile left his face immediately. What did I get myself into? he thought to himself.

"Anyone but me." Upal noted.

They continued on their walk, occasionally looking up to see if Ray was still guiding them. He would disappear and return about every fifteen minutes or so.

"There he is." Crawford stated, "We must be getting close."

"What makes you say that?" asked Lashra.

"He hasn't left; he's just circling us now."

"Of course. I should have noticed that." Lashra quietly noted to herself.

"I wonder how much farther we have to go?" she queried.

Crawford stopped in his tracks and pointed to the sky. "You see the way he's circling? He makes ten circles then flies straight, then he returns and does another ten. Every circle represents 10 minutes of time. So he's saying we've got about 100 minutes before we reach our destination." He seemed so proud of himself "It's a fact that ravens, much like crows fly instinctively towards water." He nodded in agreement with himself.

"Wow!" Preet remarked, "You can tell all that just by watching him fly? That's pretty cool."

"Wait a second..." interjected Lashra, "Crows instinctively fly for land not water. You just made all that up didn't you?"

Crawford shrugged his shoulders, "Maybe." he chuckled.

Lashra wasn't sure if she was amused or annoyed by him. "Ha, ha. So, as I was saying, I wonder where he's taking us."

Sunlight was fading fast and they all felt a sense of urgency. They had to find a safe place to stop for the night.

They spent long moments walking in silence, each praying and hoping that Ray wasn't leading them down the wrong path. But what choice did they really have?

"It's starting to get pretty dark." Preet remarked.

The day was coming to an end and none of them wanted to spend the night in the middle of this thickly wooded forest.

Preet was starting to feel uneasy again. "Hey guys, I really don't want to spend the night here surrounded by who knows what and not being able to see, *who knows what*. Not that I want to *see*, who knows what." his voice was getting higher. "So… Can we please move faster so we can get somewhere else?"

"Calm down buddy," Upal patted him on the back. "We're all in this together. You're not alone… Yet."

"You're not helping, Upal." Lashra shouted back at him. Then she suddenly realized she was hungry and was wondering why no one had complained yet.

"I wonder if there's anything to eat here?" cried Preet from the back field.

She smiled to herself, "What took you so long Preet?" Just as she spoke, she spotted a cluster of mushrooms. "Hey guys, look at this."

Preet ran up and looked at where she was pointing, "This is awesome! They look just like Spems."

"What are Spems?" Crawford asked.

Preet gave him a strange look. "Where have you been your whole life? Spems are a delicious treat." he said, shoving Crawford aside. "The Old Lady handed these out all the time." He was so excited at the prospect of food. "I love these things."

Lashra bent down to pick one up; she took a closer look. "Yup, they sure are." she said enthusiastically. "She grew these particular S.P.E.M.s in her garden all year round." She picked one and took a bite. "Mmmm." she smiled, "Oh my, they never tasted this good."

Preet reached down and started picking, eating and harvesting. Crawford stood by and watched.

Lashra reached out to Crawford and held one for him to take. "You seriously have never eaten a Spem? Try it."

He took it... looked at it... and carefully placed it in his mouth. His grimace soon turned to joy. "These things are delicious," he smiled.

They used their shirts as baskets and filled them. There seemed to be an endless supply. Preet was about to put it in his mouth when... "Hey Lash, take a look at this one it has a small Spee on it. Oh, it looks like it's pooping into the spem. Oh well, that one's no good." He threw it over his shoulder and grabbed another one.

Lashra broke into an uncontrollable giggle. "Have you never been in The Old Lady's garden before? Those are Spee-shrooms. That's what they do. They find these Burnt-Umber mushrooms," she picked one and held it up close to his face for him to see, "then they poop in them. When the mushroom is full, the universe appears on it." (They said this because tiny yellow dots would appear on the S.P.E.M.s and with the burnt-umber color as a background they looked like little stars.) "That's how you know they're ripe and ready to eat."

Preet was starting to worry that she might be telling the truth. "You're making that up. How do you know that?"

"Preet, they're called S.P.E.M.s. It stands for Spee Poop Edible Mushrooms. What did you think it stood for?"

"I don't know? Special People Eat Mushrooms?"

"Ya, you're special all right." quipped Upal. "Are you sure about this?" he questioned Lashra.

"What do you think I did every day at that house? I read all the books, helped her in the garden, and learned everything I could. All you, Preet and Saudj ever did was play and eat. So, yes Preet" she said to her brother. "That creamy filling you love so much?" she continued with a massive grin on her face.

"No way?!" Preet started to gag. "I'm gonna puke."

Upal reached into Preet's stash. "Hey, if you're not going to eat them I will."

"Keep your hands to yourself, these are mine." He turned away to protect his supply.

"It's Spee poop." Upal said disgustedly.

"If it tastes good, I'll just eat it and won't ask anymore questions about anything." Preet replied with a sour look. "Hey Lash, they are safe to eat right?

"Of course they are." she said as she put one in her mouth.

"Ok then, let's eat up." Upal attempted to grab a few more from Preet's supply and was shoved away. "You don't want to eat Spee poop do you Preet?"

"I'm hungry." he said disappointedly. "I'll eat just about anything right now."

They carried what they could and continued to walk. Suddenly Crawford realized Ray had disappeared. Crawford looked around and tried to listen for his call.

"Quiet for a second! Ray's gone." He craned his neck forward, "Listen. I can hear something."

Chapter 28 Good Night

"It sounds like water! He did it!" shouted Lashra. They followed Ray's cawing.

"There he is!" Crawford shouted.

It didn't take long for them to join the raven. They all fell to the ground and started drinking from the stream with him.

"Good boy Ray." Preet said in between gulps.

"Ya! Good boy Ray!" the rest shouted as they continued to guzzle and slurp as much of the miracle liquid as they could take in.

"I didn't realize how thirsty I was until I started drinking." Upal said as he dunked his head under water.

"This is so good, we couldn't have done this without you Crawford." Lashra noted.

Upal was instantly annoyed by Lashra's apparent gushing over the stranger. "The bird did all the work you know. You should just stick to thanking the bird."

"You're so right, Upal." she said sarcastically. She walked over to the bird, who happened to be standing next to Crawford. She bowed down next to him and petted the bird. "Good boy Ray. He's such a good boy isn't he, Crawford?"

"Yes he is." Crawford agreed with a sly smile.

"That's not what I meant." mumbled Upal.

No longer thirsty and having rested a few minutes, Lashra got up and started collecting branches, shrubs and any dry kindling she could find. "We should try and start a fire to keep warm and have light overnight. We'll need some twine and a bendable piece of wood to create a bow drill."

"What *don't* you know about?" Upal flattered her, trying to shift some of her attention to him.

Preet sighed heavily and shook his head disapprovingly.

Lashra gathered all the pieces together and after thirty minutes of hard work, she exclaimed, "Fire!"

They all praised her skills and helped her build the fire by adding branches and twigs, little by little so they wouldn't put it out, as they were so gratefully told multiple times by the fire starter.

The day was gone and night had crept its way into the forest. They all laid around the fire exhausted by the day's events.

"Looks like it should be a full moon in the next day or two." she said casually.

For a moment Lashra almost felt like she was camping. Just a few friends sleeping out in the Old Lady's backyard, relaxing under the stars. Somehow, the Rubicon didn't seem that dangerous. Of course she wasn't about to take any liberties. As they climbed deeper into the night Lashra suggested taking turns keeping guard.

"We should change every two hours, that way we all get some sleep." She collected a few twigs and held them up. They drew straws to see who would go first, Upal drew the short straw.

"I'll wake you up in about two hours." he said to Preet.

"Better get some shut eye, it'll come quick." Lashra said to her brother.

"What are we going to do tomorrow?" Upal questioned out loud.

"Where do we start looking?" Lashra asked.

"Do you even know what you're looking for?" asked Crawford.

"Of course we know what we're looking for." Upal said defensively.

"Are we only going to be eating Spems from now on?" Preet was hungry again.

"Ray's pretty good at finding nuts and berries." Crawford answered him.

"I have no idea what we're looking for." Lashra said.

"I wonder if Saudj actually did come in here by himself." asked Upal.

Crawford observed his surroundings and thought about the Scrolls of Tralatitious. Could they be real? I mean, he knew they were real, but were they true? The fact that he found himself in the Rubicon made him hope the stories were true. Otherwise what was the point of all this? And... What about this crazy threesome? Were they willing to lose their lives *in case* the scrolls were true? It didn't make sense.

The more he thought about the scrolls and their stories the more he had to admit that he really didn't know much if anything about them. He got to thinking about his school lessons on the subject.

"I probably should have listened a little more." he muttered.

"Did you say something?" asked Preet.

"Oh, no... Well, I was just thinking about the scrolls and how I should've listened more attentively when I was being taught about them." Crawford continued to stare at the night sky. "You guys were lucky to know and learn things from the Old Lady. I know almost nothing about the Scrolls of Tralatitious." he said disappointedly.

Lashra didn't take her eyes off the stars as she pointed out a simple truth. "You're not the only one. Those two dum-dums never listened either. Most people think they're just fables. Sure there are a lot of symbolistic tales in the scrolls, but I don't think it's all allegory. The problem is that everyone seemed to have their own translation. Look at Saudj and his family for example. They seemed to believe that the scrolls were used to enslave the people."

Crawford was lying a few feet away from Preet and gave him a nudge with his foot. "Hey Preet, what do you know about the scrolls?"

"Uh? Plenty..." He rolled over and away from Crawford. "But uh... ask Lashra, she knows everything." he whispered. "Just know that once she starts she doesn't stop." He rolled over pretending to fall into a deep sleep.

Crawford asked Lashra to tell him what she knew. And, she did. She went on and on and on.

"Let me know if I'm going too fast." she said, not wanting to stop.

"So far so good." Crawford remarked. Just then he thought he heard Preet chuckling.

"Anyhow..." Lashra threw a small rock at Preet's head and threw him a nasty look. She turned her attention back to her audience of one.

"The Prophet of Peace divided the magical armor between Bravo, Beria, Purdah and Demorg and granted Mater and his tribe the gift of a thousand year lifespan. That's the Old Lady's tribe, the Longevites. That night he left and entered the Forest of Eternals where he died."

"For a period of time everything went well and the people lived in peace. They all worked for the betterment of the other. Then, one day Demorg was spotted in the west returning from the forest with a large number of his tribe's people.

There was an electrifying and somewhat disconcerted buzz felt with the sound of his return. He led his people home, arms filled with large objects. Their cheering grew louder and became more aggressive as they approached the city. Eternals from every corner of the city gathered to see what all the commotion was about. As Demorg came into plain view, they clearly saw the item he held above his head.

The people were shocked and dismayed. He had returned with dead animals to feed them. The other leaders who were there to share in the harvest were appalled.

"What is this thing you are doing?" they asked Demorg.

"I have found a way to use the sword to bring more food!" he exclaimed boldly, so that all the city could hear him.

114

"We can work less and have more to eat."

"Flesh does not eat flesh." said Purdah.

"The Patriot of Peace said that we would surely die if we ate flesh." added Bravo.

"Look at me you fools." Demorg raised his arm up and turned around, smiling and nodding in agreement with himself. He made sure everyone gathered could see him. "Not one of us has died from eating this animal."

"The Patriot said it's wrong!" shouted someone in the crowd.

Filled with rage, Demorg furiously spat out, "The Patriot lied to us when he told us we would die the day we ate flesh. I am here to show you that this is not so."

He shoved his way through the crowd, pushing and thrusting people side to side. He stopped abruptly and yelled, so that all might hear, "Are these ghosts that surround me? Did I pass through them or did I have to make my way through with force? As you can see we are all alive and well!"

He grabbed his belly and laughed. "Full and satiated bellies, that's what we'll die of." He spoke with a mirth that made him sound mad and his words were full of disdain. His tribe joined in the laughter and began to clap and cheer in unison.

The other leaders did not approve." Lashra was excited and spirited. She couldn't help herself, she stood up and started acting the part. "Flesh does not eat flesh." repeated Bravo.

The tribes quickly discussed the issue among themselves and came to a unanimous decision.

"Demorg, we can not in good conscience accept or tolerate this action. You must cease this madness." Beria continued. "We live in peace and are well fed by the Forest of Eternals. Let us remain at peace. If we begin breaking our traditions, where will it end?"

Demorg was incensed. "Do you dismiss me so easily?" He shouted at them, "We must develop and change our old and rotting traditions! All of you can see with your own eyes that we are alive. The lies of death did not come upon any of *my* people and they will not fall upon you either."

He raised his arms and wrapped them around two of his men standing next to him. "The opposite is true, eating flesh has opened our eyes and made us stronger and wiser."

He made his way through the crowd halting in front of the leaders. "Beria, Bravo, Purdah…" He paused for a moment. "Are you all fools?" he snapped at them.

He turned to face the crowd. More and more people gathered. "Do you wish to remain entrapped and blinded by your old and dying ways?!" he cried out to the crowd.

He paused for a long moment. He could hear the people murmuring in dissatisfaction. Growing frustrated, he pointed at the leaders and howled, "If you make this declaration against me and my people, I swear with my life and the lives of those who follow me," he raised his weapon, "my sword will not stand idly by and watch this world decay because of your fear!"

"Flesh shall not eat flesh!" cried out Beria.

"Flesh shall not eat flesh!" Purdah shouted. She could see the crowd was becoming feverish and agitated.

As the multitude pressed closer to Demorg, he could sense that he was beginning to command the situation and that his dominion was fast approaching. He declared his hostilities toward the leaders. "Flesh can eat flesh!" he repeated his claim to the frenzied throng.

"We did not die! You will not die! The time for change has come. Let the old traditions die with these muggins. Do not tolerate their lies any longer. Join me and my clan if you want to live forever. With me as your ruler, you shall be free. You shall be released from all *their* useless laws and rules! Come with me, or stay and live in shackles and bondage!"

Many in the crowd started to chant his name…
"De-morg, De-morg!" Soon thousands upon thousands were chanting in unity.

"Leave with me, embrace freedom; together we will make a new city where abundance will reign. All will taste the nectar of independence. Let us build a place where lies, deceit and plans made under the cover of darkness have no place." Demorg's voice rang out like thunder. "My sword will be used as a tool to feed you and as protection against those who would see you starve and keep you blind." Many people from all tribes were persuaded and embraced a union with Demorg and his clan.

Word of Demorg's promises traveled quickly. Talk of building a new nation and of newfound freedoms and liberties traveled throughout the land. Over the following weeks the procession out of the city was over a million strong.

There were but only a few handfuls of people from the Sword Tribe who chose to secede (Demorg's wife being one of them). Some of his clan chose to be absorbed by other tribes while others chose to remain leaderless in the west end, the rest chose to live as gypsies.

Demorg gave the signal and led his new found kingdom into the Forest of Eternals. They were never seen from again.

Soon after Demorg and his people had vanished deep into the forest, people began to notice that the Forest of Eternals was losing its ability to feed the masses. Food became scarce. Eventually there was so little to harvest that people stopped entering the forest. Then it was discovered that those who did enter it in search of food, were never seen from again.

It was then that the Council of leaders decided that Purdah should proclaim that Demorg had brought death and destruction with his choices. They gathered the citizens and Purdah spoke.

"The Forest of Eternals is no longer a safe place for us. I decree from this day forth that the forest will be known as the

Rubicon Forest, because Demorg and his people have cursed the land. A line has been drawn and it is forbidden by all to enter it. Those who cross it will be damned and salvation from its curse will be unattainable."

As time went on, the stories surrounding Demorg's departure grew. Some said that he and his people found their way through the forest. On arrival, he enslaved all those who were not from the Sword Tribe and made them build a tower, his tower. When it was done Demorg had all the slaves killed. He and his clan feasted on their bodies for seven years." Lashra had been getting louder and very animated during her long drawn out retelling of the story. Crawford on the other hand was slowly fading away.

"Then what happened?" he yawned and closed his eyes. Boy, Preet wasn't kidding, he thought to himself.

Lashra was getting tired, but she was so excited that she'd found someone who was interested in knowing the tales that she simply continued. "He then began to wipe out his own clan. Slowly and meticulously killing everyone and absorbing their life force. It was whispered by the people of Eternal that the tower was surrounded by a moat filled with the blood of his victims and that it fed all kinds of wild grotesque animals and insects."

Lashra stopped for a moment and yawned, "Crawford, are you still listening?"

He was almost asleep and wasn't really listening. "Insects." he mumbled.

Her eyes were getting heavy, but always one to maximize an opportunity to share her knowledge, she continued. "So, from that day forward, anyone who broke the law and was found guilty of an unforgivable crime was banished to the Rubicon Forest."

Tired, she lay on the ground, rolled over and made herself more comfortable. "If you were unlucky enough to be relegated to the Rubicon," she yawned and closed her eyes, "it

118

was believed that its magic would lead you to Demorg's tower, where he would without a doubt devour you, absorb your life force and add your blood to the deep wide trench that surrounded the walls of his dreaded black tower." She forced her eyes open for a second and stopped talking.

"He's sleeping." said Upal. "He's been out for a while."

"Oh? Well..." She was nodding off. "...I was talking... to all of you. Maybe *you* learned something tonight?" she said as she fell asleep.

"I learned something all right." He looked up from his resting place and could see that all three were now sound alseep.

Chapter 29 Exhausted

Saudj flew back, his body slammed against the wall. His face was burning and pounding.

"Husband!" Saudj's mother cried out. "The boy's only five years old." His mother came to his rescue.

"The boy needs to learn." He was drunk. "And I'll be the one to teach him good."

Saudj had dropped a small bottle of Glumvyn on his way up from the storage room and his father's discontentment was swift and clear. "That's four weeks of hard work in that bottle!" he yelled at his wife.

"He fell on the stairs. He's got such little legs and he works hard for you." she defended her son.

"Fine!" he cried out. "*You'll* get the rest of his beating." She bowed her head submissively. Saudj watched as his mother took two hard slaps to the face. His punishment.

"I should give you another for making me raise a coward!" his father shouted as he staggered out of the room.

Saudj jumped awake from his nightmare. It was still dark. How long had he been sleeping? He picked himself up off the ground. He was cold and shivering. He moved in and tucked himself into the cavity of a tree. He clutched his knees and made himself as small as possible in hopes this would help him stay warm.

His mind drifted back to the nightmare. Saudj's father was a mean, unforgiving man who was angry at the world and all the unfairness he spewed at him on a daily basis.

Husband, as his wife called him, was a proud member of the Sword Tribe. His family's heritage could be traced back for generations. He believed himself to be a true successor of

Demorg. He was not ashamed of it and he made sure everyone knew it.

He was feared by his neighbors and trusted by no one. His small fortune came from making and selling his Glumvyn to the poorest and loneliest. From the moment Saudj could walk he was responsible for being the runner. That is, running up and down from the storage room with bottles of the toxic liquid. Saudj was also charged with delivering to those too weak to make the trek to his father's house.

For some reason Saudj's dream led him to the memory of a lonely, homeless man who showed up to the house four or five times a week. He was one of the many people who made their way around the city collecting apple cores and peelings to sell to his father.

"What do you have today, old man?" his father grabbed the bag of scraps from the man.

He looked inside and dropped the lot on the scale… "Looks like it's just under two pounds." He'd always grunt the numbers disapprovingly.

The pitiful old man looked up, "Well, that's ten pounds for the week master, I'll take my bottle."

"Saudj, go fetch me a small bottle. Consider yourself blessed." he grumbled. "I should be giving you half a bottle for what you bring me."

"You're too kind, master." the old man said as he bowed his head to avoid eye contact with the pinchfist.

Saudj ran down the stairs and grabbed a small bottle of Glumvyn. He held it tightly and was careful not to slip and fall on the damp stairs. He handed it to his father who gave it to the old man. That one little bottle would make the old man's day.

Glumvyn was a sour apple wine. It was easy to make, it was cheap and it had an alcohol content that was high enough to start a fire. The potent formula had put many homeless men to sleep for the night. It was also used for cooking, cleaning and as a cure for many ails.

"Boy!" the sound of his father screaming echoed through the forest; Saudj jumped awake once more. He sat alone staring into the darkness and waited for the sun to rise.

Saudj started walking at first light. Where was he going? What had he done? He didn't have an answer to either question. So he walked and walked and as the sun faded he found himself another small hole in a tree where he tucked himself in and away for another night.

Chapter 30 Return To The House

The young girl found a patrolman. He was a well known figure around the neighborhood. He himself had been placed in the care of the Old Lady as a child. This honest, caring man was now on his way to the Old Lady's house.

"The Old Lady's been murdered?" said the Patrolman. He didn't believe it. He couldn't believe it. "How is that possible? Why would any living soul want to harm the woman who loved everyone as if they were her own? She survived over eight hundred years, and this is her end? Impossible." This was all just one giant mistake. The child must be delusional. As they approached the home, he realized there was no smell of fresh baked bread in the air.

The Patrolman grew frantic. "Who is this Saudj? His punishment will be so severe that it will be remembered for as long as *she* was alive." He spoke with a passion that was uncommon to see in a patrolman.

He looked down at the child who was pulling his arm to speed him up. The man was surprised by the calmness shown by the child. She was delivering horrific news with hardly an emotion to show for it.

Of course... he explained to himself, the child was in a deep state of shock. "What will we do without her?" He spoke the words under his breath.

The Old Lady's abode was surrounded by dozens and dozens of people. The children of the house did their best to keep people from getting too close.

As they got even closer, the Patrolman realized something was sure amiss. A large swarm was moving toward the Old Lady's home. When they arrived he gasped. She hadn't been discovered for an hour yet and it seemed the entirety of the West Gate was making its way to her house. Rumors were already circulating that councilors from the other gates were well aware of the situation and were on their way to confirm the unimaginable.

Although they all wanted to, no one had dared to enter her house. Citizens circled and surrounded the area. It was a dense assortment of every kind of person. There was a humm of whisperings with sudden waves of people wailing and crying out. The Patrolman had never witnessed such a scene. His heart was heavy; he could not recall a time he'd been more saddened or shaken.

The young girl and the Patrolman fought their way through the crowd. He stood at the entrance door trying to prepare himself for what he was about to see. "Stay here." he told the children. He opened the door and entered the home. "What the…" He could not find the words to finish his dreaded thought.

He fearfully approached the large mass that lay on the floor. His hands began to tremble uncontrollably as he reached down. He turned his head so as not to see what was laying underneath. He reluctantly lifted the blood soaked blanket. He gathered all his courage… He looked down. The pain was too much to bear. He fell to his knees and started sobbing uncontrollably.

Chapter 31 Sweety-Pie

Crawford had accidentally dozed off a couple of times during his watch. His eyes were getting heavy again and his blinks were getting longer. He was almost asleep again when he fell off the log he was sitting on. Startled by the sudden fall he jumped to his feet and looked around to make sure no one had seen the crash. "I'm done..." he said to himself. "It's got to be her turn by now." he yawned.

He walked over to where Lashra was sleeping and kneeled down to wake her up. He stopped short of shaking her awake. He watched for a moment as the firelight illuminated her face. She looked so peaceful. She had a huge tuft of hair tucked between her head and her arm and her handbag was perched comfortably between her knees. He watched her sleep for a minute or two. This was the first time he actually got to look at her. The last thing he wanted was for Preet or Upal to catch him staring at her, he had enough troubles with them already.

Crawford had seen and met many beautiful girls, but Lashra was different. She was more than beautiful, more than just a girl. She was...

Lashra opened her eyes. "Can I help you?" she asked quietly.

Crawford was taken off guard and fell back onto his but. "I uh, I was just about to wake you up." His heart was racing. It wasn't often that someone could make him anxious or embarrassed. He was sure his face was red and hoped that being slightly back light by the fire made it hard for her to notice. "Umm, it's your turn to keep watch." he mumbled out.

Lashra kicked her handbag aside and stretched out. "Ok, I'll get up in a second. Get some sleep."

She stretched a few seconds more then got up and paced around the fire a few minutes to help wake herself up. Having the last watch allowed her to have a long and unbroken sleep during the night. A few hours later she was wide awake and glad to see the first hint of morning. The forest's understory started filling with long shadows and color was slowly returning to the enchanted woods.

Lashra casually rose from her wooden seat. She made her way around the perimeter of the camp as she had been doing for the last few hours. She collected a few more bits of fuel for the fire. She knelt down close to the small and smoldering flames and warmed her hands. As she watched the boys sleep she wondered what this day would bring.

She got up and walked around nudging the boys with her foot. "Wake up, wake up, wake up you lazy boys." she sang.

Upal rolled over onto his back and placed his arm over his eyes to block the light from the morning sun. "Mm not ready." he tried unsuccessfully to garble out of his still sleeping lips. His arm blocked out just enough light to let him fall back asleep.

Preet slowly opened his eyes. For one brief moment he'd forgotten all about the events of the last couple of days. "What? What's going on?" he asked himself drowsily. "Uhhh, we're actually here?" he squeaked out of a yawn. "It's not just a bad dream?"

He stretched his arms out and after a few minutes he sluggishly made his way to his feet. He embarked on a voyage that took him around and around the fire pit. "Yaaawn." Still half asleep he stretched his arms out and purposefully thwacked the back of his sister's head while making his rounds.

"Hey!" she squealed as she shoved him.

"Oh, I'm sorry. I didn't see you there." He giggled to himself. As he walked he shook and jiggled his king-sized trunks, "Come on legs, wake up. I feel like I'm walking on pins and needles."

Crawford had not heard a thing. His second wake up call came in the form of a raven pecking at his head.

"Stop it." He tried to wave the bird away.

Peck.

"Stop it." Another wave.

Ray simply jumped up to avoid Crawford's arm.

Peck.

"Stop it." he uttered, as he failed a third consecutive time to halt the bird's jabbings.

Peck.

"S-T-O-P I-T! *I said!*" This only encouraged another peck.

"Ray." He paused for dramatic effect. "One more time and I'll convert to the sword tribe and have you for breakfast."

His comment made Lashra smile. "So you were listening." She gave the bird an appreciative thumbs up.

"Good boy Ray." she giggled.

"I'll help you eat that black bird for breakfast." Preet voiced half jokingly.

Ray turned and cawed angrily at Preet. He took flight and charged the juggernaut. He came down toward Preet's head just missing him. He flailed his arms in all directions and screamed out, "Are you crazy?"

The ebony devil made a second raid at the terrified boy. Preet recoiled and leaped out of the way. He tripped over the rocks that surrounded the fire pit and fell into the last smoldering remains of the fire. He leaped out and alarmingly launched himself into a dance of snuffing out embers from his smoking clothes. He turned his back to Lashra, "Am I still on fire?" he said as he continued to sweep himself.

She brushed off a few pieces of hot dust with her hand and assured him he was no longer on fire.

"I swear Ray," he said under his breath. "Come at me one more time and I *will* eat you!" he bleated discreetly and somewhat cautiously as he finished dusting off his pants. "Foul bird."

"Looks like danger." Ray gurgled out from a branch above Preet's head. He spread out his wings and came down for another close landing. This time it was a peaceful descent next to Lashra. "Pretty Girl." he whistled.

"You are so cute." she replied as she bent down to pet him.

Preet reprimanded his sister. "He's trying to kill me, Lash. Why are you rewarding him?"

Lashra smiled. Thanks to the bird's buffoonery, at least Preet was fully awake, she snickered to herself.

Preet made his way to Upal and sat on a log next to his *trustworthy* friend. He stared at him in amazement.

"There is no way he slept through all that noise." he stated.

"Oop?" he fired out. "Yup, still sleeping."

He moved in closer. "I know what will get him up." He leaned down slowly and with his best Lashra impression, whispered into his friend's ear. "Wake up sweetie pie, it's morning time."

Upal's face instinctively smiled as his semi-dreamland fantasies played out in his mind. He could see Lashra next to him, speaking softly and lovingly. He slowly opened his eyes only to come face to face with Preet. His whole body jerked, he shoved Preet away and jumped to his feet.

"What's wrong with you?" exclaimed Upal.

Preet was laughing uncontrollably.

Upal was flustered. "What's wrong with you?" he exclaimed. "Are you having some kind of mental breakdown?" Preet's wake up call had whipped him into a small frenzy. "You should never mess with a man when he's sleeping."

Preet was in stitches, "I was just helping Lash out. She begged me to wake you up since she couldn't." He was still cracking up.

Upal was fully agitated, and growled, "You could have been *severely* hurt pulling a stunt like that." He was trying his best to regain some sense of composure.

Crawford snickered, "Oh yeah, killer instincts there sweetie pie." he said as he poked the fire, trying to revive it.

Preet added, "I had no choice. She's been trying to wake you for hours."

Upal looked up at the sky, "Hours? The sun is barely up."

He turned his attention to Lashra and Crawford, "What happened to one for all and all for one? We need to be able to trust each other."

Upal was thrashing his arms around and feeling defensive. "No more stupid pranks or else I'll have my revenge when you guys fall asleep." In a sinister voice he uttered, "Oh, it'll be just as funny. Oh yes, *just as* funny."

Lashra attempted to ease his mind. "Upal, take a deep breath. The boys have only been up a few minutes and for what it's worth, I think it's kind of sweet that you believe I'd actually call you sweetie pie."

"Whatever." he said in a lackadaisical fashion. "You could do worse." he continued as he gave a passing glance at Crawford.

She playfully smiled at him, "You really think so? *Sweetie Pie.*"

"Ok, ha-ha-ha, we've all had our fun. You do realize however that I am now seriously traumatized by this whole thing. Who knows if I'll ever sleep or trust any of you ever again." he said with a dispelling groan.

"I'm sure you'll get over it, Upal." She winked at him, "After all you're a big boy."

"Not really though." Crawford muttered under his breath.

"Did you say something?" Upal turned around and stared at Crawford.

"No, just clearing my throat." he said.

Preet and Crawford spent some time drying their dew-filled shirts while Preet went on about the boredom of the previous night's watch.

Lashra debated with herself about what course of action should be taken. Upal continued pouting in silence. Meanwhile Crawford seemed to be lost deep in thought.

"Well?" Lashra questioned them. "What should we do?"

"What should we do about what?" Upal sulked.

Befuddled, she exclaimed, "About what? About anything. About everything, about this… this… this whole situation we find ourselves in." Her voice rose in volume. "What other about could I possibly be talking about Upal?" She massaged her temples in frustration.

Preet looked over at Upal, who was still moping and chose to ignore him. He turned his attention to Crawford who was daydreaming. "Hey Crowboy?" he gently elbowed him, "Are you pouting too? 'Cause I think Upal's already got that one locked in."

Upal paid no attention to him.

Crawford was still lost. Preet reached over again. This time he gave him a little shove, "Wake up!"

"What? Sorry..." he said and immediately returned to his daydream.

Lashra walked up to him and put her hand on his shoulder asking sympathetically. "Are you ok Crawford?"

He sighed heavily. "I don't know."

"Do you want to talk about it?" she asked supportively.

"I was just remembering an uncanny dream I had last night. I forgot it until just a minute ago." His face was pale and his eyes distant as he uttered in a disquieting tone, "Now I can't seem to be able to think of anything else."

Chapter 32 Crawford's Dream

Lashra was instantly made curious by Crawford's air of mysteriousness. "Please tell us all about it." Her eyes grew at the idea of hearing a strange and veiled nightmare. "Well, let's have it." She pressed him. "I'm sure we could all use a little more weirdness to start our day." She half giggled and winked at Upal.

"I remember so little of it. It's more of a feeling, something like a thick fog."

"Try." She waved her hands trying to encourage his memories forward.

Crawford closed his eyes and concentrated. "I was walking through the forest…" he mumbled quietly. "I was collecting firewood and…"

"Hey, speak up!" Preet interrupted. "You're mumbling and we can't hear a word of it over here."

"You can't hear a word," Upal said to Preet. "I'm fine with not hearing *anything* you say."

Crawford cleared his voice. "I remember hearing birds chirping. No. They were singing. No that's not it either. Maybe they were plucking?"

Upal was getting annoyed, "Making sounds. We get it." He waved his hand trying to shoo him away. "Please, move on before we lose all interest."

"You're right, tiny boy." Crawford mockingly nodded at him then continued. "So where was I… oh yes they were making sounds, but it was a familiar sound." Crawford turned his eyes to the sky and searched deep within his mind to remember. "I remember, it sounded like a lyre harp and the birds were singing a song…" They could see he was trying hard to remember the details from his dream. "I can almost hear it." He moved his head around trying to find where the sound was coming from. He quietly hummed the tune. "That's it, yes, they were singing the Roma's ancestral song of hope." He sang a few lines. "I've heard them sing it often in the marketplace of the Crossroads."

"Crossroads? Music? Harps?" Upal grimaced. "Where are you from?"

Preet was also curious, "Doesn't sound like *our* part of the West Gate. Where did you say you were from?"

"Uh, I live on the edge of the West Gate near the doors of the Crossroads." He was getting nervous. "My older brother took me a few times when I was young. He was always stealing trinkets from the vendors and he used me as a distraction." Crawford hoped his story was believable.

"I don't know," quipped Upal. "It sounds like you're making everything up." He shook his head disapprovingly. "I trust you even less than I did five minutes ago. Why are you here with us?"

"Yes, that's right, Upal," Lashra said sarcastically. "I remember now... Last night he was talking in his sleep and he mentioned being a rich Westender who has nothing better to do than to die in the forbidden forest with three dystopian kids from the bad part of the West Gate."

Preet burst out laughing. "He did not." he got serious for a second, "Did he?"

Crawford grimaced and laughed uncomfortably as he tried to mask his anxiety. He quickly continued his story to avoid the subject of his home. "Anyhow... All of a sudden it sounded like they were calling my name. It was mesmerizing and I couldn't stop myself from walking toward the music. I kept moving forward, collecting branches and twigs as if I was in a trance. I just kept moving along." He stopped speaking for an instant, the expression on his face showed everyone that he'd just remembered something important. "That's right." he said to himself. He stood up, "All of a sudden I was in a clear patch and there was this old witch sitting on a throne; it was made of stone. Behind her was an endlessly long golden path. It flowed all the way into the horizon."

Lashra's eyes widened as she waited for more details.

Crawford closed his eyes trying hard to remember. "She sat in her chair kneading dough. She looked up and saw me staring at her. I was frozen in place by her gaze. She pointed to an old wood stove with a tea kettle on it.

"Come, sit with me, my child." she said. She pointed to her stove and spoke to me in rhyme.

> *"My children left to gather wood,*
> *but now I fear they've gone for good.*
> *My fire now is sure to die,*
> *unless on you I can rely."*

Crawford continued, "She went on talking in rhymes and then asked me if she could purchase the pile of wood I'd collected. She then tells me that she has no money, even though I can clearly see that there's an endless stream of gold behind her. So I asked her, and this is where it gets weird,"

Preet nudged Upal and whispered, "So none of this was weird before this point in the story?"

"I started talking in rhymes."

"Wholly smokes, it did get weirder." Preet exclaimed.

Crawford ignored his remark and continued.

> *"If not a purchase with gold I pleasure,*
> *You'll pay me how, if not with treasure?"*

Then Crawford raised his hands and shook his head nonchalantly. "Blah blah blah, she tells me that she has a much more precious gift that she's willing to exchange for the wood. I ask what it is, she tells me it's a poem, I say, "A poem?" She says not just any poem, this one is a map to an ancient treasure. Blah blah blah, I gave her the firewood and then I woke up."

"Wait a minute" Upal chimed in. "You're going to take a poem instead of insisting on the gold? What's wrong with you? It's no wonder you had to steal stuff."

"It was a dream and I... anyways, I said yes... BECAUSE I like helping little old ladies in distress. Is that ok with you, Oop?"

Upal's face dropped. He stared Crawford in the eyes and in a deadpan voice he said, "Don't you ever call me Oop. Understand me?"

Crawford tried his best to not show any emotion, but couldn't help but swallow hard.

Lashra walked over and tapped Upal gently on the face. "Do you always have to be so melodramatic?"

She picked up a stick and stirred the embers. "That was truly gracious of you Crawford." Lashra said as she patted Upal on the head with the warm tip in an effort to break the tension.. "Don't you think that's gracious of him Sweetie Pie?"

Upal grunted his displeasure.

"That's it. I'm done" said Crawford.

"No, no, go on, we're sorry. We won't interrupt you anymore." she asserted.

"No, I mean, that's it. That's the whole dream."

"She never told you the poem?" interjected Preet.

Crawford stood there for a moment looking around, up and down, side to side, searching his mind, trying to remember. "Oh ya... she did tell me." His eyes widened. "She asked me to put the wood inside the stove. When I was done, I closed the door and she gently patted me on the head with her staff. She sang the poem to me and the next thing I know Ray is pecking at my head."

"Do you remember the poem?" asked Lashra.

"Hmm." He thought for a moment. "I think I do?" He recited the words.

"Lore and visions are guides for your duty.
Anguish will grip you with sunlight's beauty.
Safely guided through the golden path,
Hunting widows, you'll escape their wrath.
Retrieve from the rock what is incomplete,
Altruism bestows you death's defeat."

"What does altruism mean?" asked Preet.

Lashra and Crawford responded in unison. "It means putting others before yourself."

Upal rolled his eyes upon hearing their chorus. Great, he thought, now they're finishing each other's sentences.

Lashra added. "Or being selfless." She paused and thought for a moment. "Hmmm… There is something familiar about that poem. I just can't put my finger on it."

Upal stared at her in disbelief and a smattering of incredulity as he haphazardly blasted out "You're kidding right?"

She was surprised by his outburst and confused by his demeanor. "About what?"

Upal returned her glance with a suspicious and disbelieving glare. "Really? Something familiar? Like you didn't notice that the first letter of every sentence spells your name?"

Chapter 33 A Long Walk

Upal turned his attention to Crawford. "When did you find time to sleep?"

Crawford was confused, "What?"

"I can only imagine that it took you all night to come up with that *load* of gewgaw." He stood up and faced Lashra. He tried to mimic Crawford's mannerisms and sang out,

> "Please oh please listen to my dream.
> Reality, reality is not what it seems.
> Everybody, everybody come and see.
> Exemplar, exemplar this is me.
> Toast me, toast me for my apogee."

After finishing he curtsied and bowed to Lashra. "Seriously…" he shook his head.

"You must think we're a bunch of dim-wits, if you think we're going to believe you had some kind of vision." He waved Crawford away.

Crawford had an odd smile on his face. "Hey Preet? Does that little poem remind *you* of anything?" His smile grew wider.

Preet shrugged, "Not really."

"That's funny…" Crawford let out a little chuckle. "Because the first letter of every line spells your name." He couldn't hold it in any longer, he broke out into all out laughter.

"No it didn't!" Upal retorted.

"Please oh please listen to my dream." Preet started. "Something, something, something… what's the rest Oop?"

Upal was feeling flustered, "I don't know, I just made it up."

Preet looked over at Lashra. "Well?" he said to his sister. "I know you have it locked up in that brain of yours... how does the rest of it go?"

A grin slowly appeared on Lashra's face, "Sorry to break it to you Upal, but Crawford is right." She giggled as she recited the poem back to Upal.

> "Please oh please listen to my dream.
> Reality, reality is not what it seems.
> Everybody, everybody come and see.
> Exemplar, exemplar this is me.
> Toast me, toast me for my apogee."

Upal wasn't very happy with Lashra's memory of his unrehearsed poem. He immediately turned his attention back to Crawford and in a very displeasing tone he continued to air his grievances. "I don't think you really appreciate what's going on here, Crowboy." He moved closer to Lashra and placed his hand on her shoulder. "We don't have time for your ridiculous gewgaw."

Lashra gently removed Upals' hand from her shoulder. "Ok..." she took a side step.

"Buggeration!" Crawford exclaimed. "You're right. It does spell Lashra but I didn't do it on purpose I swear."

Preet placed his giant arm around Upal's shoulder and stared at Crawford with him, "So you didn't make all that stuff up?"

"No, I'm telling you the truth, I dreamed about it." Crawford said, a little exasperated.

"I don't believe him." Upal stated.

Crawford pointed at Upal, "So then, you meant to write a poem about Preet?"

"That's completely different, I was being you... so really..." he paused a little confused at where this sentence was leading, "Well, I guess really you wrote a poem about Preet."

Preet squeezed him a little, "You know how nutty you sound right now right?"

A look of excitement suddenly covered his face. Preet hysterically pointed at Crawford. "Oh, oh, oh... oh buddy... It's a message from The Old Lady." He walked over and grabbed Crawford by the shoulders and shook him briskly. "The Old Lady is the witch in your dream. She's trying to help by sending us a...a..."

"A delusion?" Upal chimed in.

"No, the other thing." Preet said.

He looked over at Lashra for help. She stood there in silent astonishment. Within a few seconds all three boys were staring at her and waiting... and waiting.

Her mind was moving at light speed. Was it possible that Crawford had actually received a vision from the great beyond? It wasn't impossible, or was it? Why Crawford? He wasn't part of their inner circle. He hadn't even met The Old Lady. He'd only seen her once as a toddler. What connection could he possibly have to her?

Be that as it may, what if The Old Lady really was sending them messages? If so, what were they supposed to do with it? How could they decipher the communication? What did all this mean? If The Old Lady was trying to correspond with the kids, wouldn't she have given them clues to solving this riddle? What did all this mean?

Preet waved his hand back and forth in front of Lashra's face. "Hello-oh, are you there?"

She pulled his hand away, "Stop it."

She looked at Crawford, "Do you remember anything else about the dream?"

He shook his head. "No I don't think so." He thought for a second. "That's everything."

She thought out loud as she paced the area. "There's got to be more to it. You're forgetting something. If this dream of yours is a message…"

Preet interjected, "What do you mean if?" He raised his hands and looked at her in disbelief, "The witch literally spelled out your name."

"*Lore and visions are guides to your duty?*" Lashra had memorized this poem too, having only heard it one time.

"Well, Crawford's dream must be the vision." she continued, talking out loud to no one and everyone. "What's the duty?" she murmured, meandering around the camp. "Find the armor and find The One." She continued to answer her own questions. "Retrieving from rock what is incomplete."

Upal begrudgingly spoke up. "I'm not saying that I'm buying into this dream thing… but, that could be referring to the armor. After all, it has multiple pieces and therefore it's incomplete." He couldn't admit it outright, but his gut was telling him that the dream was probably real. "Maybe it's buried under a rock somewhere?"

Preet slapped Upal on the back, "Thanks for joining the team buddy."

Upal continued, "What else are we here to retrieve besides the armor? Unfortunately, the whole *rock* thing has me confused. Hmmm. I hate to admit it, but this dream might actually be a real thing."

"I think you might be right about the armor Upal." Lashra said.

Upal bounced his shoulder off Preet. "I think this place might be making me smarter. Is that possible?"

"Sorry Oop, no magic's that powerful." Preet said as he slapped his short friend on the back.

"Can you please stop slapping me on the back? You're killing me."

"Hey guys, I think we're forgetting the most important verse." Crawford seemed a little uneasy. "*Altruism bestows you, death's defeat*? What the heck does that mean? According to this we have to figure out a way to defeat DEATH? Maybe we should focus on that part of the riddle..."

Upal interrupted Crawford before he could finish his thought. "I really think we need to focus on getting a move on. We're not gonna find anything standing around here." he said.

"To where?" asked Preet.

Lashra gave the area the once-over. "If this secret message is truly from The Old Lady, I'm sure she'd expect us to continue with our mission." Lashra kicked sand into the fire pit. "I never thought I'd say this, but Upal may be right, perhaps we should just start moving. Judging by the sun, I'd say this way is west." She was right. "I think we move west until something changes our minds or our direction."

"What were the first couple of lines again?" Upal asked.

Crawford thought for a second. "*Lore and vision are guides to your duty. Anguish will grip you with sunlight's beauty.*"

"I think we figured out that our duty is to find the armor, but what does "*Anguish will grip you with sunlight's beauty* mean?" asked Upal.

"I don't know." Preet uttered. "But it doesn't sound good."

Lashra put her hand on Crawford's back and moved him to the front of the pack. "I think you should take the lead. After all, it was your vision and I think you may have forgotten some of it. Maybe you'll see something, anything that looks remotely familiar. I'm hoping that something will trigger your memory."

Crawford looked around at his environment. Nothing came across as being familiar. No, not one thing. He decided to go with his gut. "In my dream I was in the forest carrying firewood. I think we should go this way." He pointed into the thickly wooded forest. He sent his bird to go look for food as they pushed and fought their way through the greenery.

"I sure hope he gets a poem dream about me," said Preet. "I mean yours was ok Oop but his just seemed nicer."

"You know I can hear you right?" shouted Crawford from the front.

They laughed. Except for Upal. Upal didn't laugh.

The grass was long and filled with condensation, the warmth of the sun's beams had limited access to the floor due to the full and lush canopy overhead. Within just a few minutes of walking their shoes were sodden, their pants dank and their shirts clammy and smothering. The ever rising temperature was only made worse by the humidity. It didn't take long for them to start complaining about the mugginess and crying out for the sun's rays to take it all away.

"My kingdom for dryness!" cried out Crawford.

"His kingdom." Upal muttered to himself, "Who does this guy think he is?"

Then, as if by magic the late morning sun appeared through a few thinning spots in the canopy. In a short time they found themselves wandering through a giant open field, where the bright sun vanquished any and all traces of moisture. Therefore they had nothing to complain about, except for the excruciating dry heat.

The last few spems disappeared as quickly as the moisture. Preet's complaints of hunger returned just as swiftly.

Crawford kept an eye on the sky, hoping by some miracle that Ray would bring them some kind of food or lead them to a patch of edible goods.

Every once in a while Lashra would stop to study flowers and shrubs to see if they were edible. Sometimes she'd stop just to satisfy her curiosity. The drawings in the botany books she'd read during her time with The Old Lady had nothing on the real thing. She'd seen and read about many of these plants but never thought she'd experience touching and smelling so many of them. Once in a while she fell behind as stopped to make notes in her diary about the smells and textures of the plants.

They walked quietly for a while. A few more hours passed and they found themselves back in the thick bushes of the forest. They silently continued slowly plodding through.

Crawford was desperate to break the long silence. "Lashra, tell me more about the scrolls. Last thing I remember you saying was that Demorg eats everyone who comes in here."

"Well that's what people thought happened. Since no one ever returns, no one really knows." Lashra was happy to talk to anyone about the stories. So, she went on, and on.

"With Demorg gone, struggles and conflicts between the remaining three armored tribes began. Beria, the leader of the Shield Tribe, went mad trying to gain power and Kingship. He believed that he was *The One, The Shepherd*, that could protect the people from the coming onslaught that would surely be ushered in by Demorg. Beria's words and actions began to worry and strain relationships with the other tribes. His demands to be the sole possessor of the remaining pieces of armor were worrying. One night on the way home from a briefing, he was assassinated."

"Bravo of the Casques, believed it was his sole duty to resolve and administer judgment against Beria and the precarious situation he was creating. When the Shield tribe discovered Bravo's involvement in the murder of their leader, an insurrection ensued.

Those who supported Beria and his leadership, planned to assassinate Bravo as an act of retribution. This was referred to as *The Rebellion of Sagacity*. Their success created a series of vendettas."

"As these battles were occuring between the Casques and the Shields, there were also struggles for leadership within each of those tribes. Multiple splinter groups began to form. For three and a half years there were battles both within and between them. A time known as *The Cabal*."

Lashra tapped Crawford on the shoulder. "You are paying attention right?"

"Ya Crowboy, there will be a test." Preet chimed in.

"Sagacity. Cabal. Got it." Crawford nodded.

Lashra was happy to continue. "The Cabal was a period of murders, suicides, assassinations and massacres. As quickly as a faction was formed it would fall. Discord and distrust were rampant amongst all."

"For all their fighting and disagreements, the leaderless Casques and Shields were united on one matter; the belief that Purdah of the Breast Plate Tribe could not be trusted. Her constant contact with both sides began to be worrisome.

Although she spent all her time trying to build bridges, the paranoia and conspiracies were too great. It was understood by both the Shields and the Casques that it would be prudent to remove Purdah from her position permanently, lest she join forces with one side and give them the advantage." She stopped for a moment. "I'm not going too fast am I?"

"I'm not as dumb as I look. Go on." Crawford said.

"Hearsay and rumors were widespread throughout the two rudderless tribes. Confabulation took hold of the masses. Every type of paranoia and hysteria was put on display, and it became natural for everyone to behave in this manner."

"*She's preparing to take control of us!*" they cried out from the windows.

"In the gin mill they would whisper, *she's plotting to hold all the pieces of the armor. She will be invincible if she's not stopped.*"

"On city streets they cried, *Purdah will kill us all!*"

"An agreement was reached by the two distrustful groups during a covert merger. They agreed that on the morning of her 75th Jubilee, she would be purged."

143

"Quiet." Crawford interrupted her. "It looks like another open field just ahead." He felt a sense of uneasiness come over him. He thought he saw something moving through the gap in the distance.

"Thank goodness," cried Preet.

Lashra gave him a stern look.

"Oh come on Lash, It's not that I'm not happy that you have to stop talking for a minute or two... Wait... I am happy." He chuckled. "Also I have more branches and leaves sticking out of my hair than most of these trees. Can you please help me?"

"I don't see why I should." she said.

Preet was picking through his hair trying to remove some of the debris. He looked at his sister with a pitiful look on his face.

"Come here you big baby." she said. "Kneel down and let me help you."

Crawford picked up his pace and left the others a fair distance behind. He stopped in his tracks when he arrived at the entrance of the field. His eyes bulged out at the sight. His jaw dropped as he took in the scene. His heart started pounding harder and harder as the feeling of panic rose within him.

"This can't be good." he said to himself.

Chapter 34 The Orchard Of Souls

"What's going on up there?" shouted Preet. "Did you find food? Are you eating right now?"

"Keep still." Lashra said as she tried picking through his hair.

Upal slipped by Lashra and Preet and quickly caught up to Crawford who was motionless. He stood silently behind Crawford and tried to get a look at what he was staring at.

What Crawford was looking at was an ominous orchard-like setting. Only this one was not filled with trees containing fruit.

"I've seen this before." Crawford said, thinking he was speaking to Lashra.

"In your dream?" questioned Upal.

He was surprised to see Upal behind him. "Yes and no. Remember yesterday when I tried to leave the Rubicon? I saw something very similar."

"*Anguish will grip you with sunlight's beauty.*" he quoted his dream, almost unaware he was even speaking.

"What are you talking about? Move out of the way, I want to see inside." Upal squeezed his way past Crawford. As he did he tripped and tumbled almost landing into the troubling plantation. He slowly looked up and his curious facial expression soon turned grave. His eyes and brain struggled to assimilate what he was seeing. "This is wrong… so very wrong."

Lashra reached the two, and when she peered into the open field she was instantly taken back to The Old Lady's house. She could hear her voice as clear as a bell.

"There is a place they call, *The Orchard of Souls.*" Lashra remembered how The Old Lady's description of this place affected her. It had the power to freeze her blood and cause her hair to stand on end. A chill went up her spine, as she heard the woman's gravelly voice narrate what her eyes were now seeing.

"The Orchard of Souls holds thousands of trees each one containing someone's soul. Each tree's roots are weaved in such a fashion as to create a chain that winds itself around the giant stone that sits next to it. A stone that is used to hold its victim in place. Pray that your eyes never fall upon this orchard."

Lashra could now clearly see with her own eyes these nightmarish individuals wrapped in thorn bushes. She never imagined anything like this. She stared at the long slender branches laced with prickles and barbs. It seemed as though they were frozen in mid-fight. It looked like they were fighting off the prickles and barbs and lost the battle.

All four were mesmerized by the creaturesque beings. Their heads were covered with light greenish-brown moss-filled dreadlocks that swayed in the breeze. Each one was uniquely ornamented with a sublimely radiant arrangement of large colorful blossoms. Some with yellow golden flowers that twisted and curled. Others were filled with explosive spurs and outlined with a sharp blood red contour. Still others had round glowing moon-like colored flora that wrapped around their necks like a choker. There was also an endless multitude of petals and polychromatic blossoms that encircled the sorrowful prisoners. The calm cool breeze that made its way through the grave, gave them the appearance of being adorned with long flowing garments.

Lashra stood gazing at the sardonic tableau. A beautiful orchard filled with tortured souls. The visible screams of agony were surely caused by the giant thorn spike piercing their thorax and exiting out of their backs.

146

Every life, every being, every soul, bent over backwards, arms reaching out to the sky, crying out for mercy to the heavens above. There was nothing they could do to escape. They stood there tormented and cursed forever.

She was fixated on the scene. She wondered if these trees were really living people at one time? Was that even possible? She knew one thing; simply looking at them filled her with an intense feeling of fear and anxiety. She was sure that their entrance into the orchard would bring death.

"Do you think this is the *sunlight's beauty* we're looking for?" Upal whispered to Crowboy.

"I hope not." Lashra responded.

Preet was slowly making his way to the entrance. He scanned the ground and nearby bushes hoping to find something to eat. His eyes happened to skim the entrance of the orchard and he spotted something moving inside. The snake-like object slithered on Upal's foot. "Oop! Your leg. Get out of there!"

Preet's warning came too late, the snake had him.

Chapter 35 Trapped

Upal had inadvertently stepped into the Orchard of Souls. The vines that covered its floor were making their way around his foot. Hearing Preet's cry, he instinctively tried to lift his leg. It was too late. A blood curdling feeling filled him.

The orchard felt Upal's foot rise. The vines spontaneously clutched onto him and climbed his calf in an effort to stop him from fleeing. Upal pulled harder but the orchard had its hold on him. The vines tightened their grip on his leg. A look of terror covered his face. He fell forward trying to get out. Crawford instinctively reached out and caught him. He grabbed hold of his arms and tried not to let go.

"Pull!" Upal's plea was filled with spine-chilling fear.

Crawford tried to pull but he quickly found himself slipping and sliding toward the orchard. "I'm sliding in!" he cried out.

"Don't let me go." pleaded Upal as he tightened his grip.

Lashra jumped in and wrapped her arms around Crawford's waist in an attempt to stop his sliding. She leaned back and tried hard to put an end to his slow drift.

"I won't." Crawford grunted. He managed to brace one of his feet against a large root.

Upal's hands were slowly slipping away. Crawford couldn't hold on much longer. He let go of one hand and hurriedly wiped the sweat off and regripped himself onto one of Upal's arms. He cried out in desperation, "Preet! Help me!"

Preet had totally spaced out. Crawford's cry shook him from his trance. Preet lunged in and the two teens did their best to pull Upal out. The harder they pulled, the more the vines worked at imprisoning him.

Lashra dropped to the ground, picked up a rock and launched herself into a pecking frenzy. She attacked the flourishing creeping plant with power and precision. She banged and smashed at the vines trying to cut them or at least make them loosen their grip.

Terror-stricken and on the verge of becoming fully hysterical, Upal cried out. "Pull harder! Harder!"

Preet and Crawford heaved with all their might.

"My arms, my arms," Upal yelped. The tugging was causing him great pain. "You're going to rip them out of their sockets."

"I can always let go." Crawford exclaimed.

"No, no, no I'll be fine, don't let go." said Upal.

From out of nowhere Ray joined Lashra in a continuous attack on the stalks. Lashra had chipped away a fair portion of the vine and after a frenzied battle the twine snapped and the three boys flew backward onto the ground piling up on top of each other. Upal was free.

They broke into awkward laughter as they released their joy and relief of escape.

"That was insane." Upal said as he rolled over and sat up against a tree. "Thanks for not giving up on me. I really thought I was going to become one of those things."

Upal kept his eyes on the orchard and in a hushed trembling tone said, "I vote we get as far away from this place as we can."

"You think so?" the rest said unanimously.

They sat for a while in silence taking a long hard look at the orchard. It was immense. They deliberated on the subject for over an hour, concluding in the end that it could take days to walk around the orchard, if they could even manage the task at all.

They moved back a few more feet to sit in the shade of the trees and to be farther away from the bedeviled gateway.

"Anguish will grip you, with sunlight's beauty." Crawford broke the silence.

"Ya so?" Upal retorted.

A light went on in Lashra's mind. She looked over at Crawford who gave her a knowing nod.

"Anguish will grip you with daylight's beauty." she repeated Crawford's words. "Well, if those trees don't look anguished, I don't know what does and they're being gripped by those beautiful thorny vines that almost got you Upal." She stopped for a moment, trying to take in her own words. "I think if we try to cross at night, we may be ok. I'm hoping that the grip is only in the daytime." She didn't seem very convinced about what she was saying.

"That's what I was thinking too," said Crawford.

A green-eyed Upal mumbled under his breath, "That's what I was thinking too."

With a trembling voice Preet questioned the decision, "Oh, great, not only are we going to walk into a nightmare, we're going to do it at night? Why do we even have to go this way? Let's go south or north or we could just go back from whence we came."

"That's exactly what I was thinking." said Upal.

"No," whispered Crawford. "We need to move west." He paused for a moment, "This is the way to the witch, I know it."

"Ugh," Upal grunted. "I guess we're bound to die here at some point. We might as well get it over with today."

No one responded to his remark. Deep inside they knew he was probably right.

They spent the rest of the day sitting around waiting until nightfall. Not much was said most of the day. Preet might have mentioned his hunger once or twice and wondered where Ray and his hopeful bounty of food could be. He'd left them soon after they'd freed Upal. He'd been gone for hours.

Other than that, they rested in the coolness of the shade and were caressed by the breeze making its way across the open field.

At one point or another they'd all fallen asleep for an hour or so.

"It won't be long before it's dark." Lashra commented.

Crawford nudged Lashra. "Hey, were they successful?"

The expression on her face was that of confusion.

Crawford smiled at her and explained. "At purging Purdah? You said the leaders were in agreement, *she will be purged.*"

That was enough encouragement for her to continue the story and so she went on and on as she tended to do.

"True to their words, Purdah was ambushed on the way to her jubilee. All of her entourage was killed. Her body was found slashed in two. The tribes were so deep in their misgivings they believed (falsely of course), that by slicing her body in half, her followers would believe that Demorg was somehow responsible for her death. Of course Purdah's tribe did not even consider this."

"All three tribes were now without leaders. Panic was followed by hysteria, which soon led to lawlessness. Leaders rose and fell by the week and sometimes the hour. Eventually this led to chaos, disorder and finally anarchy."

"All three armored tribes were at war. Any efforts to build truces between one another, to try and gain an advantage in their power and position, fell apart before the ink could dry."

"The feuds brought with them famine and an immeasurable amount of gore. Blood flowing from the city at its most wicked period of combat was said to be waste high. The blood contaminated the water supply and made it undrinkable. Within a few months the food supply was almost non-existent and most went days without eating. It became so bad that people were eating clay to stop the pain of hunger."

"The smell of death that came with the decomposing bodies was atrocious. The dead bodies were mounting and the streets were overflowing with carcasses. Left with no choice, the living dumped cadavers and the bodies of those who were effectively dead, over the city walls. Many of the carcasses were bloated from the long warm days and when the bodies were moved they often forced out gasses and human waste. Some had laid in the streets so long that their bodies were split and they were filled with pests who ate them and sometimes took refuge inside."

"There were so many bodies that it seemed there were more slain than alive. In the dark of night when the fighting slowed, you could hear the moaning and whimpering of those not fully deceased. It seemed to many that the sound of battle during the day was easier to bear than the sound of the mournful anguish cries of the night. After three and a half months of combat, and extinguishing thirty percent of the population, an armistice created by the Longevity tribe was subscribed to by all. They knew that if they continued to fight much longer there would be no survivors."

"During this fragile peace time, a pestilence soon followed as a result of the internment. Four more years of slow, painful and feverish death followed. Another forty percent of the population was lost. The survivors had no other option but to help each other out. It wasn't enough not to be at war. If they didn't ban together soon, not one soul would be left alive."

"During the war, the Longevity tribe was a neutral party. However, neutrality was not an option during the time of the plague. They were hit the hardest. When the blight finally ended, only twelve Longevites could be accounted for."

"The night of the last death from the plague, all twelve members of the Longevity tribe received the same prophetic dream."

"I hate to interrupt all your talking Lash… but I think it may be time to go?" (Preet didn't really hate interrupting her.)

"Real funny Preet." she said, "I was done for the night anyways." Lashra stood up and took a deep breath. "Well, at least we'll have the moon to light our way." As she spoke a thick patch of clouds rolled in to darken an already dark night.

"Great." they said in one accord.

"I'll go in first." Upal said, trying his best to garner up the courage to actually follow through with his offer. I really have to think before I speak, he thought to himself.

Lashra spoke up quickly. "No. We should all go together."

Upal made his way to the entrance. "We can't *all* go in together, not this time anyhow. The Old Lady needs us to finish this and we can't do that if we're all frozen in time. If I walk straight ahead it should only take me a few minutes to cross the field. I'll yell for you to come when I'm safely on the other side."

"What if you don't make it?" Preet accidentally uttered.

They all turned to face him and if he could've seen their faces in the dark, he would surely have died that instant.

"*Well*," Upal groaned. "I guess you guys will have to figure another way around."

"Lashra," Upal took her hand, "If I don't make it, I want you to find someone else." He was trying to let her know his feelings, but even at a time like this he was too afraid to let his guard down and chose instead to make a joke. He did it mostly to stave off the fear of what he was about to do.

She gave him a quirky half smile and quietly told him, "I don't think it will be that difficult." Then her tone became serious. She put her hand on his shoulder, "Are you sure you want to do this alone?"

Upal was having a hard time breathing. "No." he said as he turned and placed his foot into the Orchard of Souls.

Chapter 36 The Other Side

His foot touched the ground and he waited a few seconds. He slowly raised it off the ground. He was successful. "So far so good." he whispered back.

Upal's pace was slow and careful at first. Everytime he was able to raise his foot freely and take another step his heart lightened.

Preet shouted lightly, "Are you ok?"

"I'm good." he responded.

The night was dark, still and silent. As he moved deeper into the Orchard of Souls he thought he could hear hushed long-drawn-out sounds. The low inarticulations were sounding more and more like a distant whimpering. The volume of the cries seemed to be climbing.

Upal was trying to stay calm but he could feel the panic rising within him. "What was I thinking?" he mumbled to himself. Suddenly his mind flashed back to a childhood nursery rhyme that appeared to be describing this very situation.

Full moon, full moon, makes you groan.
You're trapped in the orchard and you're not alone.
You fight and you scream in the full moon night;
The Rubicon has you and it's holding tight.

Full moon, full moon, your wide awake,
Living a nightmare with no chance of escape.
No one can save you from the full moon night;
The Rubicon has you and it's holding tight.

The childhood poem gave him the willies. He shook his head vigorously. No, it can't be about this place, the thought sent shivers up and down his spine. He tried hard not to listen to the vibrations in the air but it was impossible for him not to hear the sounds of tortured souls and internal suffering. Somehow he knew that it was the trees that were moaning and the notion of it made his skin vibrate.

Upal picked up his pace. He did everything he could to not get too close to any of the tortured trees. He was only a few minutes in and he was already second guessing his choice to go first.

"Are you still ok Oop?" he heard Preet call out.

Upal stopped, looked back and could no longer see his friends.

"Oop?" he heard his friend cry out again.

"Yes, I'm fine. Can someone please shut him up?" Upal didn't mean what he said. He was actually grateful to be hearing something other than moans and groans.

Without warning something touched his leg. He pulled up quickly. He was still free. "Stupid clouds," he muttered, "I could use a little moonlight right now."

He'd had just about enough, he wasn't taking any more chances. He wanted… No, he needed to get to the other side as quickly as possible. He picked up his pace and started running, hoping beyond hope that he didn't run into a tree or get snagged by something ghastly. Upal did his best to keep his feet off the ground, as much as humanly possible.

After *much less* time than he first anticipated, he found his way through the darkness and safely to the other side, no thanks to the moonlight. He was fully charged. He couldn't believe how fast his heart was pounding. It was racing faster and pounding harder than the first time he met Lashra (and that was saying something).

Taking no chances, he walked a little farther into the woods away from the orchard. He looked back and started laughing and jumping with joy. He fist-pumped the air and gave himself a few high fives.

"Way to go Upal, you did it!" he shouted. "You did it!"
He cried out a loud and harsh "Yawp!"

The threesome across the valley responded with a thunderous and encouraging "Yawp!" of their own.

Upal was hoping to see some form of moonlight. He was worried that without it they might not make it through the orchard. After all he was quick and nimble, Preet on the other hand… As luck would have it, the cloud coverage was getting thicker and pressing down lower and lower. He reached out his hand. He could feel the moisture in the air.

He waited anxiously for their arrival. Out of the blue he heard loud shrieks and the crackling of vines.

"Are you all right?" He moved in a little closer to the orchard. He could hear grunts and loud whispering sounds. They weren't far away.

"Go on without me." he thought he heard Preet whimper.

Chapter 37 Luciferins

Upal couldn't stand it any longer. He decided to run back in and help. *Thud! Bang!* He was knocked to the ground.

"Ahh!" Lashra moaned.

"It's me, it's me!" Upal shouted.

"Where are you going?" she exclaimed.

"I was coming to help."

"We're fine, Preet just tripped and fell a few times. You can only imagine how that played out." she said sarcastically.

Before long they had all gathered safely on the other side. Then as if to mock them, the clouds thinned out and the moon returned to light the night sky. They shook their heads in disbelief.

As they moved away from the plagued orchard and deeper into the forest, the woods started to flicker. Tiny dancing sparkles were appearing here and there. The farther they traveled into the woods, the closer they got to the twinkling star-like objects. The lights were getting bigger, burning brighter and increasing in numbers.

Lashra was leading the way. "Look at all those blinking lights." she whispered. "I need to get closer."

"Uh, no Lash, you don't *need* to get closer." Preet said as he grabbed her sleeve to slow her down.

She pulled away and dashed toward the light leaving the others behind. She stopped suddenly. "Oh my." she mouthed silently.

She gazed at a long line of bright fluorescent yellow and purple flowers that were lighting up the area as bright as day. As she moved in closer she realized it wasn't the flowers that were glowing, it was the insects inside them.

"What is wrong with you?!" shouted Preet.

Lashra shushed her brother. "Be quiet and follow my lead." she said to them.

She carefully guided the troop down an open path. As they made their way closer to them, the insects would glow with an intense brilliance, then as they passed the lights would die down to a faint haze.

She stopped and looked into the center of a large glowing flower. "Luciferin Apoidea" she whispered to Preet. "These insects only pollinate at night." Lashra's face lit up almost as bright as a Luciferin as she continued educating her brother and anyone else who would listen. "When they sense any kind of danger, they light up. That's how they warn the others."

Preet was feeling quite nervous. "I've got an idea." he whispered as quietly as possible. "How about we get out of here, then you can share everything you know about these things with us later?"

She looked at her brother disapprovingly. "Quit being such a craven, we'll be fine. We're perfectly safe as long as we leave them alone and don't give them reason to attack us."

"Attack us?" Crawford yelled from the back.

The Luciferin's glow became almost unbearably bright. Preet shielded himself behind his sister.

"Stay calm." she muttered softly. "Don't do anything foolish. You'll probably survive one sting, but never two. The first sting is a warning that comes with a mild venom. It's the second sting you really need to worry about. That one comes with a toxic poison."

She looked over at Upal and Preet and repeated the particulars.

"Ya, ya, one bite good, two bites bad, we get it Lashra, you're smart and you'll outlive us all." Upal quipped almost soundlessly as he waved his hand in a disconcerting manner. Upal was just as nervous as Preet was about the massive species.

Lashra was hypnotized by the beauty of it all. She tried her hardest to stay calm and did her best to absorb the marvel she was witnessing. "This bright light shines from such a cute and delicate, yet dangerous insect. I just want to take one in my arms and squeeze it." she whispered. "They look so harmless."

The Luciferin was about the size of Lashra's hand. It had beautiful translucent oversized wings. Their fluffy, furry bodies were constantly changing from crimson to gold to a fluorescent green. Four black hairy legs were outlined with bright green razor sharp lines. They had two large black eyes on each side of their head and four tiny eyes at the top. This one's legs were filled with pollen to take back to its hive.

They carefully continued their journey away from the notorious orchard, their path being constantly lit up by the Luciferins. Even though they were surrounded by a swarm of large hazardous insects they didn't really feel like they were in any kind of danger.

They were going to need a place to camp for the night and Lashra felt it would be best to camp in an area *sans* deadly giant light-up bugs. So, they kept walking.

Crawford had been uneasy ever since Ray had left his side earlier in the day. He rarely slept a night without him. He worried the bird might have been captured or killed by some wild animal. "I hope Ray's ok out there on his own." he said in an apprehensive and fatherly tone.

Preet reassured him that Ray would be fine, all the while looking around almost expecting the raven to attack him at any moment. "I wouldn't worry about him."

They stopped in an open patch that was well lit by the moon high above their heads.

"I think we should stop here for the night." Lashra said.

Still unnerved by the day's and night's events they sat back to back in a small circle. The sun would be making its appearance shortly and it couldn't happen soon enough for the troop.

Crawford was still worrying about Ray's situation. "I'll stay awake for the first watch. I can't sleep right now."

"I think this place is trying to starve me to death." Preet said in the middle of a yawn.

"Tomorrow is the third day." Lashra said pensively.

They silently nodded to themselves. Lashra's reference to the third day meant it would be the final day of mourning in the city. The day of The Old Lady's funeral. No one said another word.

Soon everyone but Crawford was sleeping. A half hour into his duty his alertness failed him. He was fast asleep. The crack of dawn brought with it a soft glowing orange light and the patter of crackling twigs.

Floating on the morning breeze was the constant echo of croaks, gurgles and shrills. The sounds were fast approaching the sleeping clan. But it seemed nothing was going to wake them from their lifeless coma.

Chapter 38 The Third Day

It was daybreak on the third day. The gentle morning light calmly bathed the sea of people standing quietly, shoulder to shoulder.

The Old Lady's requiem was about to begin. It was common knowledge that anyone who could attend her funeral would. For the first time in more than a thousand years, Eternal held its farewell outside the city walls of the West Gate. The crowd was so large that it seemed to flow into the Rubicon.

The Leader of the South Gate stood on top of the West Gate's wall, next to its entrance. As he looked over the scene, he struggled to grasp the number of mourners. Did Eternal truly have this many citizens? he questioned himself. He began to speak; his voice echoed down the valley and over the crowd.

"Is there anyone alive who was not in one way or another impacted by The Old Lady?" He bowed his head in silence as the words lingered in the air.

"You could have been two hundred years old, and to her…" he took a deep breath and looked to the sky, trying unsuccessfully to compose himself.

His voice trembled as he choked out his words "... and to her, you were but an infant." His lips quivered and he paused again. He found it difficult to keep his composure.

"There is not a soul dead or alive, not one, who in the last eight hundred years did not want *and need to* know her." The eulogist was speaking from the heart and the crowd held on to his every word.

"Everyone… As parents, we made a commitment to our children before they were even born that in their lifetime they should be blessed by the presence of this woman. Not only our children, but their children's children." He went on to exalt and honor her life for over an hour.

A second Leader took the stage and continued the dirge.

"She was charming, mysterious, and mythical. She was more than just her years, more than her stories, more than her patience, more than anything we could ever fathom. She was a combination of all the love and goodness that, in our deepest hearts, we desire to be. She was all that we dreamed her to be. She was a healer, a teacher, a peacemaker; she was... *our* Keeper."

Another Leader rose to the stage. "She's been gone for only three days and in that time, a thousand years has passed us by. Our world has lost a shining star, but let me assure all of you who stand here with me today, that her light will shimmer and sparkle for an eternity. We will tell her story to our children and they will tell it to their children. Yes, it will be an everlasting, imperishable story for all the ages. She will live forever and the brightness that was her life will shine; it will never be diminished."

The lamenting crowd broke into applause and cheers.

The Leader of the West Gate was the last to speak. "As we leave here today, may we go in peace. If you can, live as she would have lived, love as she would have loved."

Each of the Gates' Leaders had given their parting words and tributes in remembrance of The Old Lady. A decision was reached the previous night by all the Gates' Leaders and Councilors, that the day of her departure would be considered an annual holiday.

Every year, on the *Day of The Old Lady*, all the doors to all the gates would remain open from sunrise to sunset. This included the doors to the Crossroads. Travel throughout all the gates would be encouraged. It would be a day of kind words, sharing of drinks and food. It would be a celebration of her life, the sharing of stories, a day of love, laughter and cheer. On that day no one would be a stranger.

The Leader dismissed the crowd with these words. "We will be a symbol of her light, she will shine through us. We will honor her memory with the same compassion she showed the world."

Chapter 39 Timmy

As the people made their way back to their respective Gates, some chose to travel outside the city walls, while others *risked* passage through the West Gate. No one living there could ever recall seeing so many people in their part of the city.

Meanwhile... Timmy and the four children had spent the previous days alone at the Old Lady's house. A few of the West Gate Councilors debated what to do with them. They took care not to dishonor the Old Lady's memory.

An agreement was reached by the Council. They realized the children had been through unimaginable grief and enough heartache to last a lifetime. They consented to keeping the five together, if it was at all possible.

They charged the Patrolman (who had once been in the care of the Old Lady) with the duty of stopping by the house frequently to monitor the children.

Timmy had spent the last two days asking everyone he met if they had seen Lashra. He'd grown attached to her over the years. She was as much a staple in his life as the Old Lady.

One of the young girls told him over and over, "Lashra went to the Rubicon with Preet and Upal to find Saudj."

"Timmy should go to find Lashra" he would answer.

"No, Timmy can't find Lashra." she said sadly. "Lashra is gone forever, like the Old Lady."

"Timmy will find Lashra." he said with a smile.

On the day of the funeral the crowds filled the streets. Timmy was unfazed by the amount of people. He did as he always did. He left the house with his cart and made his way around the West Gate and continued to question everyone he came into contact with.

The kids spent the day doing their daily tasks out of habit. They still were not able to fully grasp the recent events. Every time they looked at the Old Lady's empty chair, they simply imagined her working in the garden or out doing one of her daily chores.

The world they lived in was a hard one and they weren't new to the concept of death. If it were not for the fact that the Old Lady was an everlasting fixture in their world, maybe then they could have registered their loss, but their minds simply rejected the notion of a world without her. And so they went about their daily lives doing what was expected of them.

"Where's Timmy?" asked the ten year old.

"I don't see his cart. He must be out questioning everyone about the whereabouts of Lashra." one of the four said casually.

"He'll be back for his noontime snack, he never forgets that." said a third.

At high-noon Timmy hadn't returned. By two o'clock the kids began to worry. The eldest of the children began to ponder Timmy's obsession about finding Lashra.

"Timmy's not back for his snack? That never happens." she stated as a fact.

"He's been yammering about Lashra nonstop over the last two days. NO!" she yelled out.

"He wouldn't have?" Panic filled her voice. "Oh my! Do you think Timmy's heading to the Rubicon to find her?"

Chapter 40 Lashra Gone

The young girl threw the door open and headed toward the main gate with three bodies trying to catch up to her. As they made their way through the crowded streets they asked anyone and everyone if they had seen Timmy. No one had.

When they arrived at the gate, the ten year old told the youngest to go and find the Patrolman who'd been charged with their guardianship. "Tell him that Timmy has headed to the Rubicon and that I've gone after him."

The ten year old watched as the young girl ran to find the Patrolman. "Go back home and wait for me there." she said to the other two.

She turned and started running toward the Rubicon. They followed her. A few seconds later she stopped. She repeated her orders to the two children. They shook their heads no. She didn't have time to argue and so she ran and the two followed as closely as they could. The three ran toward the forest as fast as their feet could take them. The adrenaline coursing through their bodies made it almost impossible to control their feet. They reached the dreaded forest in record time.

The ten year old cried out, "Look, it's Timmy's cart!" It was at the edge of the path leading to the entrance.

With great caution the kids slowly made their way into the long corridor. The three were filled with unspeakable fear. They held hands as they guardedly walked down the long path.

"There he is." the eldest quietly said as she pointed into the deep.

Timmy was standing at the very edge; his feet were only inches away from the entrance. He was yelling into the woods.

The children stopped a fair ways away. They didn't want to unwittingly startle him into the Rubicon.

The ten year old whispered, "I think he's calling out for Lashra."

Carefully they continued their approach. The ten year old was right. She could just make out what he was saying.

"Lashra! Lashra! Timmy will come find you."

Even with his slowness of mind, Timmy somewhat understood the dangers of the Rubicon.

The children gently pushed forward, inching their way in closer and closer to the young man.

The ten year old gently called out his name. "Timmy? Timmy?"

He turned his head to see them. "Timmy will find Lashra." he said.

"Lashra is gone, Timmy." The child took on a motherly tone. "Timmy should bring his cart home and have snacks."

"Timmy needs to find Lashra." he said.

He reached into his pocket, took out his locket and kissed it. He safely put it back into his pocket. He looked back once again. The children carefully moved in closer.

He smiled at the children, "Timmy will find Lashra." As he spoke the words and without taking his eyes off the children he took one small step forward and vanished forever into the unknown world from where no one ever returns.

"Noooooooooooooo! Timmy! Timmy!" they called out as they ran to the spot he had just recently occupied. They stopped, their noses bordering the edge of the forbidden zone.

The Old Lady's warning permeated their minds. "No, not even your little finger should enter the Rubicon, lest you be pulled in and disappear forever."

"How can he be gone already? He just stepped in." the kids asked themselves as they observed the woods with amazement and fear.

"I have to go find him." said the ten year old. "When the Patrolman arrives you must tell him that I've gone in to bring Timmy home."

The two children were crying. "You can't leave us."

She took the children in her arms and held them for a moment. "I must and you must be brave for me." She let go and moved ever so close to the woods.

She raised her hand anxiously moving it forward, guiding it in a most delicate fashion. All of her attention was focused on the tips of her fingers as they approached the unsearchable, the unexplained, the undiscovered. How long would it be before she was pulled into the hidden universe that would take her far away from her world? A scream of terror ran through her mind as she was brutally propelled away.

"Are you crazy?" a voice yelled at her. "What are you doing, you foolish child?"

In an attempt to save her life, the Patrolman had grabbed her shirt and flung her backwards a great distance. He quickly realized that she was as frightened by the situation as he was.

He ran to her, knelt down and held her. He spoke softly, "You know the danger. No one ever returns."

"Timmy went in." she sobbed.

"Nothing can be done now, my child. You know that, don't you?"

He looked back with sadness and wondered what kind of monstrosities resided within the woods. He picked up the child, dusted her off and gathered the others.

"Come on, I'll take you all home."

The ten year old uttered, "We no longer have a home."

The Patrolman camouflaged his sadness with a frail smile. He did his best to sound reassuring and comforting, "Yes you do. I've found someone who is willing to take the five of you." He paused briefly realizing what he'd just said. "You'll have to help me break the news to your new Keeper."

The Patrolman had no children of his own, and with all the calamities that had befallen the West Gate in the last few days, he wasn't sure he'd be able to ever manage the responsibilities of safeguarding the lives and emotions of such tender creatures. There is so much tragedy for these deprived children, he thought to himself.

The youngest of the children pulled on his jacket sleeve and asked, "Who is this Keeper that we are going to stay with?"

"This old lady told me that her last child had sadly departed her dwelling and that nothing would please her more than taking the lot of you into her home."

The little girl pulled on his sleeve once more and smiled at him, "Who is this Keeper?"

He smiled at the little girl and gently said, "Her name? It's Mrs. Nibbledent."

The little girl smiled. She grabbed hold of his hand and said. "That sounds like such a friendly name. She must be so lovely."

Chapter 41 The Witch

Preet sleepily shooed away something that was trying to land on his cheek, then his nose and back to his cheek. He forced his eyes open. He thought he felt something bounce off his hair. "What is that?" he grumbled.

He darted his eyes back and forth but saw nothing suspicious. He closed his tired eyes and this time was sure he felt something land on him. He opened his eyes and saw something bounce off his nose. He was startled by the size of the object and jumped to his feet. "Buzz off!" he shouted as he waved his arms around frantically.

He was suddenly being pelted by all kinds of debris. Then it stopped as quickly as it started. He looked up but the brightness of the sky blinded him. Then from out of nowhere something small like a pebble hit him, then another, then another; all of a sudden everyone was being pelted by rocks falling from the sky.

Preet's vision adjusted to the light and he looked up again. The sky was filled with crows. He looked to the ground and realized that in fact they weren't being pelted with rocks, it was nuts and berries falling from the sky.

Crawford heard the familiar caws of his friend echoing in his dreams. Preet was still looking up when he backed up and tripped over Crawford. He fell to the ground and landed next to Upal whom he accidentally elbowed in the gut as he landed. Upal jumped up from his resting place thinking he was being attacked and Crawford woke up with the sight of Ray looping the sky above.

"Ray you're back!" he shouted excitedly.

The bird had returned with hundreds of crows and ravens. All of them were carrying a variety of nuts and other fruitlets. The deluge was overwhelming. After a few minutes the birds were all gone. Ray circled the sky and cawed, thanking the flock with whom he had roosted the night before. He came down once again and was greeted by a cheerful crowd and a very relieved Crawford.

It wasn't long before the kids were all going around the camp gathering food. With shirts full they sat around, rocks in hand and smashed open their breakfast from the sky. They gorged themselves until they were full and satisfied.

After breakfast they did their best to gather every leftover morsel. With full bellies and the successful crossing of the Orchard of Souls, their spirits were lifted. They resumed their walk and wondered what was awaiting them around the next tree.

Crawford once again led the group. Lashra stayed close to Crawford continually asking him if anything seemed familiar.

"How about now?" she'd say.

"No" he'd respond.

"How about now?" and so on and so on.

Getting tired of the same question, Crawford raised his hand in an effort to stop her from asking it again and interjected, "I'll tell you when I see something familiar. In the meantime, why don't you tell me about the Longevites' prophetic dream?" He figured that would keep her occupied for a while, and, truthfully, he was enjoying the stories.

Preet and Upal took that as their cue to fall back and talk about anything else. They'd heard the stories plenty of times before. They knew Lashra could tell a good story, but nothing compared to hearing it from The Old Lady.

Lashra smiled as she continued from where she'd left off. "Oh yes, the dream. Well… the next morning the twelve gathered together and summoned the newly elected leaders of the three tribes. They instructed them to unite all the people and bade them to gather in West Gate on the first day of the week. It was mandated that all who were able, must attend."

Lashra was having difficulty narrating and keeping up with Crawford's pace. She raised her voice, "On the first day of the week the populace had gathered to hear from the Longevites. They stood motionless and soundless. An unprecedented calm filled the air like a sea of tranquility."

"Does it actually say *like a sea of tranquility* in the scrolls?" Crawford needled.

"Do you want to hear the story or not?" she responded, slightly out of breath.

Crawford stopped to let her catch up. "It just sounds like you're making some of this up as you go." he said.

She stared at him in dismay, "If you knew anything about the Scrolls of Tralatitious you'd be amazed at my ability to be so meticulous in detail."

Crawford couldn't help but smile at her. He watched as she reached for a clump of hair and tied it up and away from her face. How can someone be this beautiful? he thought to himself. The sound of Preet and Upal's voices getting louder shook him out of his trance. "We should keep moving." he mumbled as he turned and continued walking.

"Where was I?" she said, completely unaware of Crawford's gawking. "Oh yes, the twelve stood great distances apart from each other on top of the walls of the western part of the city. They spoke as one and the people were amazed."

"*I was standing in the darkness. It was a lightless and dreaded night.*"

"The people were astounded at the thundering sounds of their proclamations."

"*The smell of bursted bowels and decay was in the air. The sounds of lamenting surrounded us. As the sun slowly started rising, I could see that I was standing in a circle with the others, facing three beautiful and hearty trees. A chestnut, an olive and a plum tree. Outside of our circle I could see thousands upon thousands of our dead and withering brothers and sisters. The cries of torment lingered and my soul was filled with anguish. Why have you betrayed us? They groaned. Is death and destruction our reward? The dead and decayed rose from their graves and pointed to the trees in our circle."*

"Oooooh… scary stuff." Preet crooned from behind.

"Go easy on him, Lashra. You're going to give him nightmares." Upal chipped in.

Preet and Upal could be heard giggling in the background like two little boys.

She ignored their childish comments and continued. *"I turned to see that the trees were infested with palmerworm. I watched as the trees were being eaten. What might we do, that you may rest in peace? we trumpeted."*

"The Longevites' voices were filled with misery and remorse. The crowd was silent. No one understood the meaning of the vision. The Longevites continued."

"The dead laid hands on three of us. Unearth the trees, they whispered. We did as we were told. Each of us was commanded to carry our tree away to the Rubicon forest. We were told to hold the tree and to not bury its roots in the ground. They obliged us three to sit with our tree and mourn its passing for the remainder of our lives." The twelve paused, bowed their heads and wept."

"Many people were moved to tears. *What does this mean? they murmured to one another."*

"The meaning of our dream will not be hidden from you! they shouted. *This is the meaning…."*

"Hey Crowboy!" Crawford's attention turned from Lashra's history lesson to the voice calling him.

"Can you send Ray out for more food?" shouted Preet.

"I was talking, Preet." Lashra reprimanded him.

"Surprise, surprise." retorted Preet. "How about it, Crowboy?"

"Well, first of all, my name is Crawford not Crowboy." he finally let them know. "And how is it possible that you've eaten your stash already?" He turned and continued walking.

"Don't be mad Crawford, Crowboy is just a smooth appellation they gave you." said Lashra.

"It's not a smooth anything." Upal wholeheartedly disagreed with Lashra.

"Kids." Crawford mumbled. "Ask him yourself Preet." he responded.

He looked up at the bird that was sitting on his shoulder. "Ray, go sit on the giant." The bird took off and headed toward Preet who immediately panicked. He yelled and waved his arms around. "This isn't funny Crowboy!"

"Just calm down and let him land on your arm or shoulder." said Crawford.

Preet took a deep breath and stopped flailing. The raven landed on his large shoulder. It didn't take long before Ray was pecking at the boy's immense hairdo.

Nervously Preet asked, "Hey Oop, what's he doing?"

"I think he's eating."

"Hmm... that actually feels kinda good." Preet's eyes closed a little. "A little to the left, Ray. Ya, that's it."

"Hey Crowboy, what do I say to him if I want him to find food?"

"Go find food?" he responded.

"That makes sense," said Preet. "Go find some food Ray." The bird took off and landed a few feet behind Preet. Ray began foraging under a large leaf of a nearby tree and brought him back a cluster of tiny, dark purple berries.

"Hey!" Preet shouted to everyone, "Those trees have berries."

He walked over to where Ray had gotten the berries. He lifted the large leaf and found hundreds of clusters of the beautiful (and as it turned out) delicious berries. Almost every leaf he turned had a cluster hidden under it.

How did I not see that? thought Lashra.

"Hey Lash?" Preet cried out. "How did you not see that?"

Her face turned red and she threw her arms up in the air. "I was giving a history lesson. Sorry. And it may surprise you to know that this is my first time here too, big brother." She turned away frustrated more at herself than her brother."

Why is she so hard on herself? thought Crawford.

Preet on the other hand, did not hear a word she said after "I was". His head was already under the leaves in search of more berries.

The rest of the troop joined him. They'd been walking a few hours already and felt they deserved a short break. They feasted on berries until they could eat no more. Their hands and faces were covered in the purple dye of the sweet pulp.

"That's some ugly tattoos you got going on your face Oop." he said pointing.

He looked over at his sister and Crawford who had not fared much better. He wondered what he looked like.

Preet took advantage of the copious amounts of berries and loaded his pockets. He stuffed berries in until they were falling out.

"What are you doing?" questioned Upal.

"Duh? Loading up for later on." he replied.

Upal shook his head as he watched his friend filling his pockets with the juicy berries.

"What?" Preet asked him as he continued to stuff his pockets.

"Nothing."

Crawford was once again leading the way. They continued trekking, working and fighting their way through sometimes almost impenetrable brush. Within a short period of time Preet understood Upal's dismay and his pocket filling blunder. The berries in Preet's pockets had turned to juice and it trickled down his legs and left him quite sticky.

Not letting all this sweetness go unnoticed, were the gnats surrounding his legs. All of his complaining fell on deaf ears.

"Why didn't anybody stop me? Ray, why didn't you say something? I thought we had something."

They walked, climbed and fought their way through all kinds of wild mazes throughout the day, only resting here and there so as not to get completely exhausted from the day's heat.

To pass the time, Crawford questioned them about what life was like with The Old Lady.

Lashra and Preet told him that they didn't know life without her. Their earliest memories all involved her. "I've been reading books from her library since I can remember." Lashra mentioned.

Upal, on the other hand, had only known her for a few years. Ever since he became friends with the twins. But he'd collected a few choice stories in his short time with her.

As the day progressed they realized they'd have to start looking for a suitable site to rest for the night.

After a short moment of silence, Lashra returned to *educating* Crawford on the history of Eternal.

"What was the last thing I told you, Crawford?"

"About what?" he joked.

"The Scrolls."

"I'm kidding." he said. "Let's see… people, tears. What does this mean? And the meaning of the dream is..." he finished.

"Oh?" She was pleasantly surprised. "You were listening."

"I heard everything."

She continued. "Yes, well." She cleared her throat. *"The meaning of our dream will not be hidden from you.* They shouted. *This is the meaning… the vision tells us that our shame has been exposed. Not one of us is worthy of the armor. Therefore it must be taken and concealed in the Rubicon. But know this. Like a tree that was once thought dead, a branch will grow from its root and from this branch a giant tree shall rise from the forest and cast its shadow over all the people of Eternal. On that day we shall be refreshed by its shade and comforted from the burning sun."*

"Yet, there will come a time when your children will be delivered to the forest and many calamities will come to fall upon them. After a time they shall conquer and suppress the beast that tortures them. On that day the Armor of Peace will be once again reunited and peace shall be restored."

"The crowd was silent. Their thoughts turned to themselves and they began to whisper, *Who will go? Who will bear this tragedy that befalls the whole of Eternal? Who will give up another brother or sister?"*

"The Longevites knew their hearts and spoke up. *We understand your fears. We will not ask any of you to sacrifice a life. Three of us were anointed in our dream. These three will die, so that you may live."*

"Three remained silent, as their names were pronounced. *Paladin, Patron and Protag will make their way tonight."*

"That evening everyone bade them farewell. Hands were laid on the chosen as they made their way out of the city gate. Not a word was spoken. Only the somber sound of tears and mourning could be heard as they made their way toward the Rubicon Forest. When they entered, each went in their predetermined direction. North, South and West.

Paladin with the Shield, Patron carried the Helmet and Protag the Breastplate. They were never to be seen again. After they had vanished into the Rubi…"

Crawford raised his hand and hushed Lashra with an almost inaudible volume. "Shhh. I see something moving."

"Did you just shh me?" She felt slightly disrespected. "When did you stop listening?"

"Shhhhhhhhh!" he forcefully repeated.

"That's funny." Upal shook his head in a drolly disagreeable fashion as he watched the event unfold.

"What did you say?" Lashra turned and asked Upal.

Upal hadn't realized he'd spoken out loud. "I said, uhm... that's not funny."

He turned his attention to Crowboy. "Why would you disrespect Lashra like that Crowboy?"

"Shhhh." Crawford begged.

"I'm hungry." cried Preet from the back.

In frustration Crawford yelled out. "Can everyone, please, just shhhhhhh!" He emphasized it with all his might.

"Look, out there." he whispered. "I thought I saw something move."

He'd gotten their attention. "Where?" Lashra spoke quietly.

Crawford's eyes locked with another's, just past the bushes. A chill ran through his spine.

"She saw me." he stated despondently.

"Who?" whispered Lashra.

"The witch."

Chapter 42 Angry Widows

They all peered quietly through the foliage trying to see. Suddenly the witch jumped out and they all saw her at once.

Lashra's eyes bulged out, "Is she the one from your dreams?" she whispered to Crawford.

They silently stared at an old decrepit hunchback on a giant throne. Her body leaned forward and her large hands braced each side of the majestic chair in a way that she appeared to be raising up from it. She had a large face with a wide nose and an oversized mouth. The corners of her mouth were turned upwards, revealing her few remaining rotting teeth. The witch had two colossal aquamarine emerald stones for eyes and her bug-eyed gaze surely had the power to see through any soul that might dare come this close.

All four were frozen in time. The witch hadn't moved. Had she even seen them? Crawford was suddenly freed from her hypnotizing gaze and broke into an ill-timed laugh.

"It's a rock." he said light-heartedly. "It's just a rock formation."

He's right, Lashra thought as she snapped out of her trance. She quickly moved in for a closer look. She instinctively reached into her bag for her book and started sketching. She was astounded by every crack and crevice and how it created this beautiful and mysterious illusion.

She took note of the tremendous dark purple bell shaped flowers on the top of her head. She stepped back a little to admire how the flowers sat slightly above her head in a way that it looked like a crown. At the base of each flower's petals was a wide gold colored band. It looked like the sun setting in the horizon, with streaks of silver shining upwards back through the purple petals. On either side of her crown grew two large burgundy orchids. Lashra was stunned when she saw two tiny rainbow colored hummingbirds come to occupy the orchids.

Her eyes traveled to the woman's cape, which upon closer inspection looked more like enormous wings. The first layer was made up of small faint, wispy feathery petals the color of lavender. She could make out dozens of layers, each one larger than the next and their color grew more transparent by the layer. She leaned in and her senses were filled with a delicate floral scent.

Lashra carefully moved closer to better see the golden river of petals that lay behind the throne. There was a river of a thousand golden leaves floating a few feet above the ground. Over each one of those leaves there dangled from the branches of the trees above a flaring purple flower. The flowers had a blue stigma in the shape of a tear-drop.

She moved back away from the object so that she could see it all at one time. She was amazed by the beauty and details of what could only be a natural formation, or was it? Either way, she marveled at the majesty of it all.

Lashra smiled to herself. "She's not a witch." she said. "She's a queen."

Crawford approached the witch and placed his hand on hers. "Safely guided through the golden path," he said.

"I remember something. After she finished her poem, she turned and pointed to the path of gold. *Follow the path of gold to your reward.* she said to me."

"This is the path we need to follow to find the armor. Come on, let's go!" he shouted excitedly.

"Wait." Lashra said.

There was something about those flowers that she knew wasn't right. She'd been searching her mind.

"Just a minute… The flowers above the path, they look familiar. I've seen those flowers before. I just need to think."

She scratched her head, closed her eyes and combed through the books in the Old Lady's library. "I've got it." she said excitedly. "They're called Veuve-en-Colère."

Upal did his best to repeat what he heard. "vuvencollar?"

Lashra corrected him. "Veuve-en-Colère. Loosely translated it means "angry widow. From what I remember," she paused, "these *Angry Widows* are poisonous."

She picked a branch up off the floor and pointed to the purple flower. "You see this little drop of liquid?"

The boys moved in a little closer to get a better look.

"It's going to fall on the golden leaves here…" The drop fell right on cue. "It falls onto this leaf and the leaf absorbs the liquid before it has time to roll off of it."

They were truly unimpressed.

"So what?" Upal commented, casually.

Crawford and Preet seemed bewildered.

Lashra stood up and made her way to them. "So what?" She held her chin and shook her head disappointedly. "These are highly acidic drops." She waited for a reaction, but didn't get any. "Hello? Acid… Ugh!" She was so frustrated that she couldn't help but let out a deep sigh and rolled her eyes at them. "IF! they get on your clothes they'll eat through them and if they get on your skin," she paused for a moment to make sure Preet and Upal were paying attention.

"Go on, we're listening." Preet was a little annoyed with her.

Lashra tilted her head and hesitated.

"I was listening. You said that we can eat our way through them."

She shook her head in disbelief.

"I'm kidding Lash." This time he rolled his eyes and said, "Acid bad, acid bad, I get it." in a sarcastic tone.

Annoyed with her brother's lack of seriousness, her voice took on a stricter tone. "*If*… a drop lands on your skin, you'll get a burning rash that spreads rapidly. It's so severe and angry that it will drive you insane before you have the time to die from its effect." She hoped to scare the boys straight.

Preet tapped Upal and smiled. "So you're saying we shouldn't make any rash moves." He giggled at his own senseless wisecrack.

Upal looked up at him in dismay. "You'll have to do much better than that."

Lashra took a step forward and kicked Preet hard right in the shin.

"Ow!" he screamed.

"You think that hurts?" Frustrated, Lashra laid out the hard facts. "This rash works its way through your entire body. As it eats you it grows and it continues eating you from the outside in, and by the time it's done you're just a pile of edible liquid. Then, the ground will absorb your mindless, unlistening, irresponsible dead bodies."

Upal patted Crawford on the back. "I'm sure you're going to want to take the lead again, *right*?" he said, smiling and nodding.

Lashra was at her wits' end, pacing back and forth, she tried hard not to pull all her hair out as she muttered to herself. She tried hard to figure out a solution to her problem. "This is serious, we could easily die crawling under this path."

Crawford and Upal were too busy with each other to hear anything Lashra had just said. "Come on Crowboy, take a run at it?" He pushed Crawford toward the poisonous path.

Crawford stumbled over a root and fell to the ground sliding almost a full body length underneath the golden flowers.

Just as he was about to get up Lashra shouted, "Crawford Stop! Don't move!"

A drop of acid was forming on a flower right above his head. They all stood still, hearts racing. The drop fell onto the golden petal and rolled slowly toward the end. It seemed as if it was just about to drop onto Crawford.

Lashra held her breath as she watched Preet jump forward and grab Crawford by the legs and drag him out at light speed.

Crawford was furious. He jumped to his feet and started toward Upal.

Lashra stepped in between the two boys. "Stop these antics now!" She was irate. "We don't have time for this. Upal you need to watch what you're doing. You could've killed him."

"Sorry Crowboy." he said. "I just nudged you. I didn't realize you were so delicate."

Crawford clenched his jaw. He wasn't convinced that Upal was actually apologizing.

Preet tried to deescalate the situation by putting his arm on Crawford's shoulders. "Yes!" he said to Crowboy, sensing his dismay. "That's as sincere of an apology as you'll get out of him."

Lashra grabbed Upal's arm and walked him over to the golden path. She knelt down and looked as far as her eyes could see. "Someone has to try and make it through. I think Crawford's right. This is the way to the armor." she said in a solemn tone. "I'll go first."

"Slow down a little bit." Crawford was standing behind them. "We're not going to just let you crawl through there."

She pointed to the sky, "We still have some light, I should go now." she persisted.

Crawford walked away from her and sat down in the middle of the opening a few feet away from the witch. "We should camp here tonight and think about what lies ahead of us. We can't even see beyond the path. I for one would like to make plans for tomorrow, one that keeps us all alive. You're not going." he stated firmly. "We're all staying right here." Crawford cleared a spot on the ground and stretched out.

Unwillingly and with great regret Upal spoke up, "I hate to say it Lashra, I mean I really do hate to say it. But I agree with Crowboy."

"Me too," said Preet.

The vote was three to one; the decision was made to rest for the remainder of what little daylight was left. It was decided that it would be best to think things through with a clear and rested mind. They could make their move at the first sign of light if need be.

Chapter 43 The Spee-Eyeder

They built a fire and settled in for the night. They sat silently staring at the dancing flames. After a short while the fire began to flicker. Lashra started to get up but Crawford motioned for her to stay seated. "I'll get up and pick a few branches and shrubs to keep the fire going for the rest of the night," he said softly. "I need to stretch my legs a little."

Lashra sat back down on her small stool sized rock that happened to be under an umbrella shaped tree. It was just high enough not to be set on fire and low enough to keep some of the heat down and around her. She looked up and studied the bluish moss-like plants hanging from some of the branches. She climbed onto her seat and grabbed a handful.

Preet watched as she placed a small amount on her tongue. She immediately scrunched up her mouth and nose and started spitting out the bitter moss.

"Are you regretting that decision?" asked her brother.

"I'm pretty sure this blue moss is edible." she said as she used her fingers to get the remaining bluish stuff off her tongue. "There's something about it…" She hesitated before going on. "Oh, I think you have to cook it slightly first before you eat it."

She reached over and grabbed the stick she'd been using to stoke the fire. She put a little moss on it, she placed it over the fire, just high enough to dry the moss out. After a few seconds she removed it from the fire. She stretched out and placed the tip of the stick in Preet's face. "Want to try some?" she giggled.

"I'm good." he said as he pushed the stick away.

"How about you Upal?" she asked.

He shook his head, "It didn't look tasty the first time you tried it." he smiled, "It's all yours."

Lashra brought the stick back to her mouth and took a bite of the moss. Preet and Upal waited in anticipation for her reaction.

"Mmmm... it tastes like candy." she said smiling.

"I don't think so," said Preet.

Lashra took the rest of the moss off the stick, put it in her mouth and ate it with a smile. She climbed back onto her stool, grabbed more of the bluish candy to be and started roasting it over the fire. After a few minutes she was eating more of it.

That was enough for Preet and Upal. They both jumped to their feet and ran to the tree. "There's hardly any!" they complained.

"It grows all around the tree." She shook her head and laughed.

The boys made their way around the tree and collected the candy. They headed back to the fire with an arm full of blue moss and a stick.

Lashra entertained herself simply by watching Upal and Preet trying to figure out how long to cook the moss. They put some on a branch just long enough to dry it out, but the excitement was a little too much for them. Every time they tried to pull the sticks off the fire they dropped the candy moss into the flames.

Lashra used her motherly inflection to caution the boys. "Take your time or you'll never eat."

"Success! Oh yeah, this is the perfect amount of time. Oh, that's good." Upal said with a smile. "Who knew moss could taste so good?"

"Let me try that." said Preet, as he reached over and snatched Upal's branch and ate the rest of what he had on it. "You're right, that was the perfect amount of cooking time. Make me some more."

"Hey! Come on. Cook your own candy."

While the boys were busy arguing, Lashra spent some time looking up at the shapes, sizes and colors of the leaves. She loved watching the flickering shadows created by the fire. The leaves looked like they were dancing.

She spotted a little Spee making its way down a silken fiber it was slowly weaving. "You're such a tiny little one, but I see you coming."

"Wait... I know you..." Before she could finish her sentence the spee fell from its lattice and landed in her eye.

"Ahh!" she exclaimed, "A spee fell in my eye."

"Just blink it out." commented Preet, who was more focused on Upal's moss than his sister's problem.

"I can't," she said in an eerily calm yet spooked voice.

"I've seen this spee in the book of spees." she said panting and trying unsuccessfully to stay calm.

"This is a Spee-Eyeder. One small bite and I will be paralyzed."

She had their attention. "Paralyzed?!" cried Preet. "Upal do something."

Upal's eyes widened and he looked around trying to make sense of the situation. "Uh?, how paralyzed are we talking about here?"

Preet shoved him off his log, "What kind of question is that?"

Lashra was trying hard not to lash out, "The paralysis makes its way to the heart and..." she took a few shallow breaths and continued as she held her eye open with her fingers in an effort to avoid blinking. "within two hours I'll be dead. Is that paralyzed enough for you?"

She looked up toward the bright light of the full moon. "I'm afraid. I don't know what to do. Preet don't let me die."

Chapter 44 The Rescue

Upal scratched his head. "Let me think," he said nervously. "What if we wash it out with water or something?"

"I'm afraid guys... I don't want to die like this." Lashra sounded unnerved.

Preet had never seen his sister panic and it horrified him. "What about the water idea?" he repeated nervously.

She shouted, "We don't have water!" She was trying hard not to cry. "I know that if they feel threatened they'll bite."

"It's kind of ironic eh Preet?" It was staggering how quickly Upal could be distracted. "I mean it's a Spee-Eyeder and it's in her eye." he quipped.

"You idiot!" Lashra lashed out again. "It's called a Spee-Eyeder because it looks for eyes to lay its eggs in. The first bite is to paralyze, then it lays its larva into the eye."

She continued berating him. "The larva takes less than an hour to eat your eye, *while you're still alive*." She was beginning to hyperventilate and gulp for air. "Are you happy you know everything about them? Think of something before I die."

"What is she going on about now?" Crawford mumbled to himself. He was plodding his way back with a large armful of fuel. As he walked in from behind Upal and Preet he could see Lashra with her head back and her finger holding her eyelid open. He said nothing as he dropped the pile of wood next to Lashra. He stood above her for a second. He leaned in and could see the tiny spee making its way across her eyeball.

He raised his eyebrows, shook his head and looked over at Preet and Upal who were just staring at him. He couldn't believe what he was seeing. "What is all the commotion about?" He leaned in closer to take a look and without question or hesitation he blew a puff of air in her eye.

Lashra was caught by surprise and fell back onto the ground and let out a short shriek.

Upal and Preet jumped up and shouted at the same time. "Are you crazy?! She's got a Spee-Eyeder in her eye!"

Lashra was laughing hysterically. "It's out, it's out. I'm ok, I'm going to live."

She jumped to her feet and wrapped her arms around Crawford and covered his face with kisses.

"Thank you, thank you, thank you." She laughed merrily as she danced circles around the fire. She made her way to Preet and gave him a big kiss on the forehead. "I'm going to live!" she yelled out.

She reached Upal and held her hand up excitedly waiting for him to clap it. He didn't. So she simply grabbed his hand and helped him.

She made her way back to Crawford. "I'm going to live. Thank you." She grabbed his face and covered it with kisses once more.

Upal grumbled under his breath, "More kisses?" He looked at Preet. "Are you going to do something about all that kissing?"

"Those days are over my friend. She can kiss whoever she wants. Except you of course." Preet said with a smile.

Upal decided to direct his green envy toward that witless Crowboy. "You know you could have killed her?" He was standing and flailing his arms wildly. "That was a Spee-eyeder in her eye you fool!"

Crawford was still confused by all the excitement and the kisses. (Not that he was about to start questioning the kisses.) "A what?"

An animated Upal continued, "A Spee-Eyeder, you know? Everybody knows." He was wild and angry. "You could have killed her with your dim-witted eye blowing stunt Crowboy."

Crawford still had no idea what was going on. He decided to bluff his way through the moment until *he could* figure it out. Calmly he said to Upal. "Well, from where I stand, it looks more like I saved her life."

He smiled a proud smile for doing whatever it was he had just done. "You, on the other hand, seemed to be doing a great job at being dazed and confused."

Upal took a step closer to Crawford, who dug in his heels.

Crawford crossed his arms and in a passive aggressive tone he said, "I think what you meant to say to me was, *thank you*." He took a gracious bow and waved his hand in Upal's direction.

"He's right Upal." Lashra said as she placed a hand on Crawford's shoulder. "The dazed and confused part and the saving my life part too."

"They do make a good point," said Preet trying hard not to laugh at the obvious jealousy Upal was displaying.

Upal gave Preet a death stare.

"What? He's right Oop. You just sat there and she is alive after all. You'd think you'd be happy about that?" he giggled out as he made his way over to the pile of wood and tossed a fresh piece onto the fire.

Upal was fuming. He couldn't do anything but walk away.

"Where are you going?" asked Preet.

"None of your business. If that's alright with you?" he said bitterly.

"I'm happy that she's alive. Even if she is my sister. You big baby." Preet called him out on his sour mood.

Upal walked away ignoring Preet's comments and grumbled his way into the bush. "Buggeration... that dull-witted-half-wit. I can't believe she kissed him again." he said kicking debris around.

"He saved her by accident. At least when I save her I do it on purpose." he kicked up more leaves and shouted *"On purpose!"*

Upal was referencing the first time he met up with them... It happened a few years earlier, before Preet's growth spurt. Upal had put himself in harm's way to protect Preet and Lashra. He stood up to a group of about twenty teenage boys and a few female zealots, who were walking the streets at night looking for trouble. Once they set their sites on Lashra, things quickly escalated.

Preet had no choice but to try to protect her. Upal had watched the situation develop and could plainly see that these two strangers were outnumbered. Wanting to help or more likely impress the girls, he stepped in with an air of calm, ready to handle the tough situation with perfect aplomb. (Actually he was terrified. It was something he'd never admit to anyone.)

He removed his shirt and handed it to one of the girls standing next to the boy Upal thought was the leader of the pack.

"Do you mind holding this until I'm done?" he said to the girl as he made meaningful eye contact with her.

Stretching out his arms and cracking his neck, he stood as big and tall as his five foot six inch body would let him and said, "Ok boys, listen up, I'm only one man. So, if you guys don't mind, I'll only take on three or four of you at a time. The rest of you will just have to wait your turn."

"Ok, who's first?" The leader took a step forward. Upal raised his right leg and landed his foot squarely on his opponent's knee, breaking it. *Snap!* The sound of the break was made worse by the cries of "Ahhhhh @!#$!" coming from the boy.

"Ok, who's next?" Upal said, bouncing up and down on his toes. Needless to say, there were no takers.

"On purpose." he mumbled to himself.

He continued to walk and sulk. He turned around to glare at the threesome sitting by the fire only to realize he could no longer see the fire or its glowing light.

"Oh no!" His heart sank.

Chapter 45 A Step Too Far

Upal's eyes darted back and forth looking for any sign of life. How far did I go? he thought to himself. Who knows how far this haunted forest has taken me? The latter thought anxiously circled through his mind. I could be halfway to who knows where. He raised himself onto his tiptoes, then squatted. He searched the blackness for something, anything that could guide him back to the camp.

He looked up, down, turned around, still nothing. The booming of his pounding heart drowned out all the other sounds of the forest. He stood silently, trying to calm himself while sweat poured down his brow. He forced himself to listen to the woods, hoping to hear the sound of Preet and Lashra talking or laughing. He was so distressed that even the sound of Crawford's annoying voice would have brought him relief.

He lowered himself close to the ground, straining, fighting, desperate to find a twinkle of firelight to guide him back to safety. He moved this way and that. Had he gone North or South? What did it matter? He didn't know where North or South were at this point.

"I can't just stay here all night." he muttered. "Which way should I go?"

Then out of nowhere something caught his eye. "Oh there it is." He saw a small sparkling light through the shrubs. His eyes darted back, he concentrated on the sparkles and glitter making their way through the woods. He could hear voices. He was safe once more.

He stopped at the edge of the camp and tried to compose himself. He could hear Lashra talking about how she feared that the joking might have gone a little too far. She reminded the two and herself of their pledge.

"All for one." she said, looking around for any sight of Upal. "Maybe we should go look for him. He's been gone for a while."

Upal was hiding at the edge of the rest area. Hearing Lashra worry about him put a smile on his face. "You can stop worrying about me, Lashra." He tried sounding ceremonious, "I have returned safe and sound. As per usual."

"I wasn't worried." she said, feeling her face go flush. "You were probably standing there the whole time." she said as she casually stoked the fire.

"It's just that it's your turn to stay up first and we're all really tired."

"I'm not that tired," said Preet.

Lashra cleared her throat as she pursed her lips, widened her eyes, tilted her head and gave Preet a vivid expression.

"Oh yeah, I was just..." he stretched out his arms and gave a big fake yawn, "Yup tired and ready for bed."

He laid down and turned away from both Lashra and Upal. He gave Crawford a passing glance. Crawford smiled understandably while nodding his head in Lashra's direction. Preet simply raised his shoulders and closed his eyes. It was an easy way out and he was taking it.

"Wait a minute." Upal said, suddenly remembering that it was actually Preet's turn to keep the first guard.

Preet was already pretending to snore.

Upal kicked him in the but. "Nice try buddy, but you get first guard tonight."

"Lashra just said I'm too tired." he responded sleepily. "And you know she's always right. Ask her yourself." Preet mumbled sleepily.

Upal wasn't tired, but he did want to get away from everyone. He laid down and closed his eyes. After a few seconds Preet opened his eyes and knew it was a losing battle.

There was no point arguing with his comrade. He got up and threw a few more branches on the fire.

The night was moving forward and even though the day had been filled with climbing, crawling, walking, shoving, deadly acid, a Spee-Eyeder and oh yeah, a witch that wasn't, they all quietly wondered what was waiting for them tomorrow.

Preet stoked the fire as the others lay on the ground hoping to find nothing more exciting than a good night's sleep.

Chapter 46 Sleep Tight

Sleep did not come easy.

Preet stoked the fire over and over again trying hard to fight the boredom of being alone. He stared up at the moon hiding behind the tree tops. "I see you." he spoke in a hushed tone. "Looks like you're full tonight."

Preet put his fire-stick down and laid on the ground to get a better look at the night sky. The moon seems larger than usual, he thought to himself. Surely it was the forest playing tricks on his mind. He tried to grasp the beauty of the night sky and all of its stars. Why does it seem more beautiful staring at it from the floor of the Rubicon? The thought made him shiver when he thought about the fact that they would most likely never leave the forest. He sat up quickly and poked at the fire and tried to forget his last thought. "Food." he exclaimed quietly, "Food fixes every problem." He silently walked to the moss tree and started to collect some of the soon to be candy. "This will fix everything. Mmmmm, candy."

Crawford closed his eyes for a few moments but he couldn't shake the thought of his father. Has he even noticed that I'm *actually* gone? Maybe he's out looking for me, he mused. "I doubt it." he said quietly to himself. What's the point of anything now? There's no way I'll ever be found here. Maybe... he fantasized, maybe someone saw me go in and word will get to my father. Then the almighty Councilor will regret his decision of choosing them over me.

He imagined his father's reaction upon hearing the tragic news. "My son, my son, I'll never see him again. How could I drive him into the Rubicon?" In his mind's eye he could see his father falling to his knees and crying out for this son whom he abandoned.

"Yes!" Crawford clenched his fists. If his father knew that he was now in the forest of death, he'd be regretting his decision to cast him out. Or… Crawford considered the alternative, maybe he's grateful. "Finally, I'm rid of the burden." he'll tell everyone.

He spoke silently to himself, "If I make it out of here, I'll do things differently. I'll be a better person, a better son. I promise." All sorts of thoughts and scenarios ran through his head, until he fell asleep.

Lashra spent the first few minutes jotting down notes and drawing out a few more sketches of things she'd discovered in the Rubicon that day. She put her things back in her bag and placed it under her head. She stared up at the star lit night and attempted to count them all. She quickly lost track and then moved on to finding star formations of the historic legends they were now looking for.

She used her finger to draw the lines in between the stars that created Paladin and his shield, "There you are." she whispered.

Patron with his helmet and Protag with her breastplate. She searched and searched the stars to find The Old Lady. "I know you're up there my teacher, my friend, my mother."

A tear drop silently found its way down her cheek and into her ear. She would swear to the others later that she heard the Old Lady's voice in that drop. Every time she tried to re-imagine the moment, it would sound like a different word, but, all of them were words of encouragement. "I will find you up there." she replied to the tear.

Upal thought about his mother. He wondered how she'd feel about the man he had become. Maybe, if she was alive he wouldn't be in his present situation? Maybe he wouldn't be this frightened and lonely little boy he knew he truly was.

Strangely, he also thought about Mrs. Nibbledent. He'd gladly take a beating from her old and wise slipper rather than being here, trying not to die. Oh, how he surprisingly missed the boredom of everyday life with his old bewitched Keeper. He smiled to himself when he realized that maybe Mrs. Nibbledent wasn't all that bad. That maybe he was partly responsible for her imbibing on such a frequent basis. "Nah." he quietly said, waving his hand in disbelief.

Preet sat alone eating the moss and listening to the sound of steady, constant breathing all around him. Everyone was asleep.

"A growing boy needs to eat more than just moss." he spoke to himself. He turned and watched Ray quietly sleeping on a log. Would it really be that bad if I ate the bird? The thought made him giggle.

At one point during the evening, one common thought ran through all their minds. How was it possible that it felt like months, even years since they'd seen their home? It had only been a couple of days, and yet so much had happened. What would transpire tomorrow and the next day? Was Demorg truly alive? If so, what was he planning and how could they stop him?

And of course Lashra, Preet and Upal wondered what had become of Saudj and what they would do if they met up with him.

In the stillness of the night Preet heard every crack, swish, rustle and scrunch in the forest. Tonight it seemed (at least to Preet), that the forest sounded more alive than the last couple of nights. It was almost like the Rubicon was also having a hard time falling asleep.

His eyes were starting to get heavy. He noticed every blink lasting a little longer. Thankfully his two hour shift was almost up. Just as he was getting up to wake Upal a frosty wave of air suddenly filled their encampment. The temperature dropped and a shiver ran through him. The iciness surrounded him. He vibrated with cold and fear. He got up and looked to the others. The chill had not escaped them. He could see they were rolling around trying to find a warmer position.

Without warning the dark forest behind him radiated. Preet turned back to glance at the woods. He saw a slow rolling misty frost moving toward the camp. The moon light bounced off of the vapors and created a distinct but intangible glow.

He tried yelling but nothing came out. He tried moving but found himself immobilized. All he could do was watch as the haze slowly rolled in.

Chapter 47 Sitting In A Tree

The ten foot wave of luminescence appeared to be fueled by the light of the moon. As it approached the camp it brought with it an eerie, frosty, calm of silence. Preet was being lulled by its beauty and rhythmic motion. The dense glowing cloud continued its slow, persistent trek toward him. He gazed around hypnotically and watched as the fog made its way around and closed in on them. All of a sudden his nose was on fire. There was a stinging, stinking smell that accompanied the fog. It was a pungent odor, much like the one found in an old rotting bottle of glumvyn.

The smell left a bitter taste in his mouth. The bitterness made its way to his throat. It became irritated and he began to hack and cough. The fog continued its haunting crawl toward the camp. A light haze covered his forearm; it was warm. No, it was hot. It quickly turned into a creeping, burning sensation.

The pain woke him from his trance. He turned away from the fog and noticed his friends were still asleep. How could they still be sleeping? He realized he hadn't said a word yet.

"Wake up!" he yelled.

Ray immediately woke up, cawed his warning and flew to higher ground.

"Wake up! It's an acid fog! It burns! He shouted as he ran around the firepit.

"Get up! Climb a tree, get off the ground, go go go!"

Preet continued screeching and bawling as he shook his friends and helped them up. He grabbed Lashra's arm and stood her in her sleep. He ran over to Crawford and kicked him, then Upal.

"Get up! Climb a tree! Get off the ground! It's an acid fog!" he repeated over and over.

He ran back to Lashra and dragged her to the nearest tree. He lifted her up as high as he could manage. "Goodness me," he grunted. "You're heavy."

"Ugh! I'm not heavy. You're weak!" she yelled back at him.

The ring of fog was drawing in closer; Preet had only seconds left. He saw that Crawford was having a hard time getting a foothold on his tree of choice and ran to help. He bent over, "Climb on my back."

Crawford obliged him and finally got off the ground.

"Oop? Where are you?" He looked around in a panic.

Upal shouted from the tree next to Preet. "I'm up here, start climbing you big oaf."

Preet reached up, took hold of a branch and tried to lift himself up. Crawford reached down and grabbed hold of the boy's arm and pulled with all his might. Preet was choking and coughing and couldn't manage to get any traction. He clumsily tried to make his way up.

"Hurry!" Upal yelled.

Crawford kept tugging, "You've got to help me Preet." grunted Crawford, as he did his best to help him.

The fog had covered most of the camp's ground. "It's burning my legs!" Preet coughed out.

His foot kept sliding off the tree, he was struggling to get off the ground. "Don't let me die! I don't want to die! Please help! Pull harder!" His cries sounded like those of a small child.

Suddenly, as if by magic, he was lifted up off the ground and was able to find a firm footing. He climbed up high enough to get above the acid mist.

Below, Preet heard the sound of someone struggling for air. It was Upal. He'd jumped down to help rescue his best friend. Gagging and wheezing, Upal made his way back to his tree and climbed until the acidic fog could not reach him.

"You saved my life Oop." Preet quietly called over to his friend.

Cough, cough, wheeze. Upal struggled to breathe. "I had no choice. If I let you die I'd never hear the end of it from your sister."

Upal's skin burned from the acid, but he didn't complain or let on of his pain.

"This must be the full moon fog," Lashra said. "I should have known." She was disappointed in herself again.

"What are you babbling about Lash?" Preet asked as he tried to make himself comfortable.

She continued. "The story goes that when this was the Forest of Eternals, the full moon fog's mist was collected by a certain fruit." She thought about it for a second. "The bromeliad fruit. Then from sunrise to sunset it would ripen. As soon as the sun went down the fruit would be harvested and eaten right away. The fruit was only edible that night. The next day it would go bad; it became unappetizing and uneatable."

"Hey, if we're lucky maybe we'll find some tomorrow." Preet's stomach was undeterred by the events of the night. "Hey Lashra? Could you maybe try remembering stuff like that, before it almost kills us?"

Crawford started reciting a childhood rhyme.

> "*The full moon brings the sour smog,*
> *That wraps a fruit that brings agog.*
> *During daylight it comes of age,*
> *Then at sunset it's all the rage.*"

"That's crazy," said Crawford. "I guess those foolish childhood nursery rhymes aren't so foolish are they? I wonder…"

"We'll have to wait for the sun to evaporate the acidic dew that's bound to be on the ground in the morning." Lashra cut Crawford off mid sentence. "Make yourselves as cozy as you can. It's going to be a long night."

They did their best to set themselves up in the trees. It wasn't going to be a night of rest after all. Preet had the hardest time. He simply sat on a thick limb stump and hugged the tree, hoping he wouldn't fall during the night.

Chapter 48 Coward

Saudj and his mother sat at the table with their heads down, quietly eating. Father on the other hand, was in the midst of a long glumvyn enduced rant.

"We are Demorgians." He slammed his fist on the table. "We are true descendants of the Sword Tribe."

He knocked his chair over as he rose from his seat, with some help from the table. He teetered from side to side, back and forth. "We!" he cried out as his hand landed on the table again and again. "Look at me!" he yelled at Saudj. The boy kept his head down.

"We are the true rulers of this gate. Umph…" He shook his head disappointedly at his son. He pointed to himself. "I… I… Me… I… I should be the true ruler of the West Gate… of all Eternal for that matter."

He did his best to stand up straight and proud. He ran his hands down his shirt to iron out the wrinkles and passed them through his dirty head of hair.

"All I see is people quaking in their shoes. Cowards with heads hung low." He took a step back to keep himself from falling down. His eyes were getting heavy. He sloshed his way forward placing his hands on the table in an effort to keep his glumvyn-soaked body from tipping over. Drool and spit flew from his mouth as he continued his diatribe.

"Why should the West feel shame? We have done nothing wrong… Nothing! Do you hear me? Nothing!"

In an eerily calm and clear tone he said, "Demorg, he tried to save our world, and this is how they repay him. How they repay us."

"You!" His paralytic hand tried to point at *one* of the Saudjs he saw. "Yes, you." His speech was getting more and more garbled.

"These fends of you... that gril... all her time at the witch's house. Ploding against me, plodden gen my people."

He attempted to restabilize himself but instead found himself laying across the table. He looked up to see Saudj still sitting at the table quietly. In a fit of rage he grabbed hold of the young boy and lifted him off his chair. He shook him like a rag doll, screaming and ranting. "Are you a spy?! Do you spy on me with that girl? Do you plot against me?!"

The acidulated smell of his father's glumvyn drenched breath was enough to make Saudj gag. He made quick contact with his father's bloodshot eyes and just as quickly regreted it.

His father mumbled. "You're worse than a spy... You're a coward."

His father threw him into the corner. Saudj's head violently slammed against the wall. The boy did not move.

The old man was back on his feet. "You," he grumbled softly in his cock-eyed-glumvyn state. He forced his eyes and yet he still couldn't focus on his son. "You, you're weak like your mother, always hiding from me. Why do I even bother?"

He stumbled over to the boy huddled on the floor. He towered over him. "Why don't you do something to make me proud of you?" He raised his large foot and kicked him. "Instead you sit there, cowering there, like... like..." He was too drunk to finish his thought. He steadied himself with the wall, raised his leg and crushed the boy with his foot. Then he spat on him for good measure.

"Coward." He managed to fumble out the word before taking a step and falling to the ground out cold.

Saudj's mother came to him and knelt down next to him. She wrapped her arms around the boy but he pushed her away. "Don't!" He shouted. "Leave me alone." he said angrily. "It's too late."

He got up and sat on the floor next to his half dead father. He patted his head and whispered gently into his ear. "We will rule again one day soon father. Then you'll be happy."

He turned to look at his mother who was sitting on the floor crying. Next to her was the Old Lady's dead carcass.

The image jolted him awake.

"I am not a coward." He crawled out of his hole. He stretched with the morning sun. "I am not a coward." he repeated to himself.

Again, he spent the day walking and going nowhere. He had no destination that he knew of. On his walk to nowhere he convinced himself that soon he would be inspired. Then he could set a plan, that inspirational plan into motion.

Maybe I'm the chosen one, the one to find the armor and reunite Eternal? We are the true leaders of Eternal. His father was no fool and neither was he.

"I am Demorgian! I am of the Sword Tribe!" he shouted at the top of his lungs. "No one will stand in our way." he encouraged himself. "If it is necessary, I'm ready to kill anyone who tries." he told the trees. *"Anyone.* After all, peace can only come after war."

The forest seemed to be instantly filled with more darkness than light. He walked a little longer and as the day was nearing its end, he longed to find a resting place and some food to fill his belly. He'd now gone almost three full days without food or drink with the exception of licking morning dew from leaves he hoped were not poisonous.

The day was giving way to the gloaming that came with the beginning of nightfall. It had been another long, lonely and deprived day. He was tired and ached for a place to rest.

He continued for a short while. There, up ahead, he could see it. Even though it was the close of day he could see a bright spot in the woods. It must be a clearing, a wonderful, welcoming savanna. He made his way to it and cast his eyes across a field. His heart sank.

His wonderful, welcoming savanna could only be described as a disturbing, tortuous landscape, and it warned its trespassers with an unambiguous message, "Visitors not welcomed." Saudj heard it with clarity.

The full moon forced its way in and pushed out the daylight. The competing shadows and highlights being cast all around the orchard made it look as though the trees were dancing. It was a painful forced dance that was both beautiful and distressing.

He wondered if he should turn back. Or maybe, should he attempt to get through now and get it over with? Perhaps, he thought, I'll make my way through in the morning.

As the moon took its rightful place in the sky, Saudj noticed a sound coming from the orchard. A soft plaintive moan floated on the breath of wind that passed him by. The longer he listened, the more he could hear the chorus of gentle whimpering wails.

Saudj felt weak and wondered if the tiredness, the nightmares, his lack of food and his desire for water were all conspiring with the breeze to drive him crazy?

He covered his ears and forced his eyes closed. He pulled his head down and shouted at the top of his lungs, "STOOOOP!"

He took in a deep breath and slowly looked up and in a solemn tone he said, "I am Saudj, ruler of the Sword Tribe and *we* are the masters of the Rubicon."

He looked across the dreaded valley of fear and lo and behold at the edge of the field a flickering of lights. Saudj was brought back to reality, "I'm not alone." he murmured.

Chapter 49 Fire Light

Sparks from a campfire, he thought to himself. What else could it be? He was sure there were people on the other side. But who could it be? He thought about whether he should cross or not. Was it safe? What if there really was someone over there? The question lingered in his mind for a few moments.

His imagination started racing. What if his friends had taken the Old Lady's words to heart? What if they had entered the Rubicon in search of the armor, in search of him?

"I could claim that I'd found the old woman lying dead." he spoke out loud, trying to figure out his plan. Yes, of course, he thought. "I came here after you." he roleplayed the encounter. "One of the kids told me you had all made your way into the Rubicon searching for the armor. Just like the Old Lady said we should. I'm so glad I finally found you." He heard his story and felt increasingly confident the more he ran the scenario through his mind.

"I should go now." Suddenly a deep dark cloud covered the moon's light and the flickering of the firelight magnified. He decided to try. He would quietly make his way through and see exactly who was on the other side. Once there, he could adjust his plan and make his next step.

The thought of being closer to another person, even an enemy, gave him a strange sense of comfort. He just didn't want to feel alone anymore.

He waited for the cloud to pass. He wasn't about to step into this gruesome… this… this, Orchard of Souls in the blackness of night. The large bank of clouds passed by and the moon's fullness had returned. He stepped into the foreboding orchard and began his trek through. A few steps in and he felt something grab at his leg. His heart exploded. His reflexive urge to jump was alarmingly and immediately halted.

Something has a hold of me. His heart pounded in his chest as he felt a wave of terror wash over him, leaving him paralyzed. *I can't move my legs.* The more he tried to pull the tighter the grip got. Frightened out of his wits, he continued to fight, but to no avail. He looked up to see if he could find something to grab on to. As he looked to the sky he suddenly realized things were about to get worse. Another large bank of clouds was moving in to cover his only source of light. An obsessive fright filled his soul.

"Harder Saudj, pull harder!" he shouted at himself. It's over he thought, darkness is coming. The clouds covered the moon. He was in total darkness but he continued hysterically fighting for his life. He was being slowly sucked into the ground. His desperation seemed to be having an effect; his attacker was loosening its grip on him. Saudj broke free.

He ran begging and pleading for the moon light to return. He focused all his energy on running and reaching the sparkles of light.

He shouted at the darkness, "Leave me!" and to the clouds he yelled, "Move out of the way!" and as if by magic, the clouds heard his pleas and the moon reappeared.

When the moon fully showed the brilliance of its light, Saudj found himself once again stuck in his tracks. His aggressor had returned, gripping him once more. He pulled and pulled in desperation. He looked down for the first time and realized it was vines that had a hold of him. He watched as they crawled up past his knees; they were climbing and wrapping themselves around his waist. Saudj screamed for help, but his screams soon turned to muffles as the vines made their way around his chest and arms, gripping, climbing, and conquering. Saudj could feel them fusing with him.

The vines were starting to wrap themselves around his neck squeezing, clutching, compressing around his entire being. His screams were barely even whispers.

"I can't breathe. I can't breathe." It became just a thought, *I can't breathe*. He tried to cry out. His final hope was that whoever was on the other side would hear him and come to his rescue.

He looked to the sky and could see the clouds coming to cover his source of light. His mind screamed "NO!" He didn't want to be trapped like this in the blackness of night. No longer able to breathe, he closed his eyes and lost consciousness.

He woke up a few minutes later in complete darkness. The Orchard had loosened its hold on him. He fought and fought and was finally able to move again. Exhausted and freed, he crawled his way to the other side.

He laid on his back a few feet away from the orchard's exit. He was distressed and drained. He let out a deep sigh of relief. He stared into the sky watching the moonlight return in full force. "Sure, now you come back." he shook his fist at the sky.

After a brief rest he got up and looked around. The sparkles seemed to have moved deeper into the forest. Something wasn't right. His gut told him to turn around and leave. He fearfully looked back at the Orchard of Souls and sensed something dreadful approaching.

The smell was somewhat familiar. It had a similar odor to the dirty glumvyn bottles he was made to clean. The same ones his father would refill with his poison. A slow moving glow moved through the orchard. The rolling mist began to burn his parched and dehydrated lungs. He turned away from the glow to suddenly see the whole forest light up as in daytime.

He started coughing and hacking and decided he'd have a better chance if he ran toward the light.

As he approached its full force he saw giant insects gathering in a swarm. Their bodies radiated a brilliant fiery light that vanquished the darkness. Saudj was stuck between this horde of giant light flies and a rolling wave of toxic fog. He looked around and thought that this was surely the end (again).

He didn't know what to do. He looked back and forth then he noticed the flying army of flies were flying high and away from the fog. Saudj was choking and wheezing, he had to do something. He decided to follow the flies. He ran and ran and ran and then *Pow!*

He ran right into a tree. He was knocked down but quickly managed to pick himself up. He realized he couldn't outrun the fog. He grabbed hold of a branch above his head and climbed his way up as high as his weakened body would take him.

Fear gripped him, he could feel his heart racing, it pounded against his chest as if trying to escape. What had he got himself into? He continued to slowly climb as close to the top of the tree as he could go. He looked down, the mist was not moving up. He'd be safe here for now. He was in no rush to come down. In fact, he had found a large bed of moss nestled between two large branches. Finally something was going his way. He stretched out and had no trouble deciding to stay there until the morning.

He stared into the night sky and as if for the first time since entering the forest, he genuinely realized he was alone. It wasn't supposed to be this way. The Rubicon was playing tricks on his mind. He was angry, bitter, sad, lonely and hated everyone but didn't want to be without anyone.

He must be going mad. Why had he killed the Old Lady? Those sparkles weren't from a fire. No one had come to find him. For all he knew the witch had survived her beating. He was sure of only one thing. "I am in the Rubicon, the place from which no one ever returns." he whispered to the moon.

Saudj closed his eyes and saw a vision of Upal, Preet and Lashra sharing the same night sky. A feeling came over him. "I'm not alone. They are here." he opened his eyes. "They've come looking for me and my armor."

"It belongs to me." he murmured to himself. Finally, he was inspired.

Chapter 50 Wake Up

Preet greeted the morning light with a *CREAK* and a *CRACK.* "*Uuuugh!*" He screeched out along with an almost unending slew of other grumbles. The sounds coming from his body added to his chorus of lamentations. "The pain!" he cried out. "In all my years…" he went on, "I have never had such a grinding, backbreaking, long-drawn-out-marathon of a night. Uuugh!" he repeated forcefully. "I need to stand up." He wiggled from side to side. "I think this branch is coming with me. It may be a permanent fixture in my caboose." he groaned.

Crawford sluggishly reported from his branch, "If I didn't hate this place before, I do now."

Preet looked at Crawford. "You didn't sleep a wink either?"

"Oh, my back." Lashra voiced wearily from the next tree.

Upal could be heard murmuring above everyone's heads. "That was the best night's sleep I've had in years." he said, still half asleep. "Keep it down a little." He rolled onto his side. "I'm gonna stay here a little longer." he said from his magical moss bed at the top of the tree.

All three looked up and watched in dismay as he casually stretched and yawned in what could only be called a soft and cozy moss bed.

"How did you manage to get all the way up there?" Preet cried up. "And why didn't you tell us about the sleeping arrangements you have up there?"

Upal mumbled, "You snooze you lose, or in my case you snooze you win." He rolled over to his other side and closed his eyes. "Just a few more minutes."

Crawford tried to move. "I'm getting down from here." He painstakingly worked his way down one branch at a time.

As soon as he reached the ground he fell to the floor and stretched out on his back. "Oh my! I never thought the ground could feel this good."

"Hold on Crawford." Lashra called out. We need to make sure the dew has evaporated before we go too far.

"I don't care. I couldn't sit or stand for another second." He hoped he wasn't being overly impetuous.

Lashra carefully landed on the ground. It seemed that some good fortune was finally on their side. "Lucky for us this morning is much warmer than the previous two mornings." She picked up some dry dirt and threw it back to the ground. "The dew vanished quickly today."

She walked around and gave Preet the thumbs up. "You can come down now brother, it's all good and safe."

Upal had decided to take his sweet time. "I'll be down in a little while. Let me know when breakfast is ready." he chuckled to himself.

They spent a fair amount of the morning stretching and trying to get back some sense of feeling into their lower extremities. Lashra went over and observed the deadly drops from the Veuve-en-Colères. After some attentive studying, she was confident in her assumption that the petals were absorbing the entirety of the lethal beads and that none of the drops were making it to the ground.

She drew a few sketches and made a few notes of her discoveries and shared them with the others. She suggested that the only way to get to the other side would be to carefully crawl underneath the golden petals.

"I had that idea yesterday, Lashra." Upal called down from his nest.

"Hey little-brain!" said Crawford to Upal. "Pushing me into the flowers, does not constitute an idea."

"I had to test my theory and uh… I volunteered you. I'd say that's an idea." Upal quipped with a dirty smile.

"Well, I guess that makes me the hero again, doesn't it?" Crawford turned and walked closer to the golden path.

"Ok!" Lashra stepped in before another word could be spoken. "So we all agree. We crawl our way through."

Preet wasn't sure it was such a good idea, after all, his size made it all but impossible for him *not* to touch the flowers.

He questioned his sister, "So you're saying we have to crawl on our hands and knees all the way?" He crouched down as he spoke.

He squinted as he eyed the path. "Hmm, I don't think it ends." he said nervously.

"Sorry to tell you Preet," Lashra answered disappointedly, "but we're all going to have to crawl through on our bellies and hope that the path is short." She shrugged her shoulders, "We have no choice."

Preet wasn't thrilled. "I have to be honest with you Lash, I'm not thrilled with the prospect of being eaten up by acid and fed to a plant."

"Plants." remarked Upal as he patted Preet on the shoulder. Preet gave him an inquisitive look. "You said *fed to a plant*, but we both know, you'd be feeding *plants, plural*." He patted him again.

Lashra's face fell and her shoulders slumped, "Shut it Upal. This is not the time for your senseless jokes."

She held her brother's hands, "We have no choice Preet."

Crawford placed a reassuring hand on his new friend's shoulder and said, "You'll be fine."

Preet started pacing the camp. "We have no choice," he said confidently. "We have no choice?" he began to panic. Of course we have a choice. Let's find another way. For example: we can go around, or…" He tried hard to think of something else. "We can go around." he finally said.

"We can swing through the trees." Upal said sarcastically.

Preet excitedly pointed at Upal. "Yes! We can swing through the trees. We can…" Preet went on a fifteen minute anxiety driven tirade and no one said another word. They all just waited patiently for it to come to an end.

When Preet had ended his diatribe he was sufficiently calm and ready to face the reality that laid before him. "Ok," he said calmly, "I've made peace with the flood of poisonous acid that will very likely overtake my body."

He looked at Upal who for some reason was smirking. "Plants Upal, I get it, plants."

He set his eyes on the path. "Bring on the curse. Bring on the affliction. Bring on the pestilence. Bring on…"

"Enough already!" Upal said exasperated, "If you don't stop you'll die of old age, before you die from the acid."

"Sure," Preet retorted, "I'd say the same if I was a little person like you and could just walk through the path, but I'm not, am I?" He shook his head.

For some unexplainable reason or maybe he was just tired of hearing Preet go on, Ray cawed a few times to get everyone's attention and then entered beneath the golden path and led the way.

"I'll take that as a good omen." Crawford said.

"Ok, here we go." Lashra breathed out a heavy sigh, laid down on the ground and started dragging herself along the floor with her elbows. "Move slow and stay safe everyone. Don't bump the leaves."

"Don't bump the leaves she says." Preet mumbled.

Chapter 51 And We're Crawling

Upal was eager to follow close behind Lashra into the golden river. His efforts were hampered by Preet who sharply pulled him back. "Do you mind going last Oop? I don't want to be left behind." he spoke quietly.

Upal pulled away, "I'm going in." He turned to make his entrance, only to see Crawford's feet vanishing under the large petals. "Ugh, foiled again. I hate that guy." he mumbled.

Upal gave Preet a sour look. Preet was confused, "What?" he said rolling his eyes. "What did I do now?"

"Hmf!" Upal laid on the ground to see how far Crawford had made it. They were a fair distance down the path. He looked up at Preet, "You're going last. I don't want you slowing me down."

Preet watched Upal disappear. He stood back and questioned the situation once again. He knew he didn't really have a choice. He got on his stomach and got on with dragging his giant torso through the latest nightmare, whispering to himself, "Forward, forward, cautiously forward." He was barely in when the thought of resting went through his mind. "I can't stop now. Bring on the virus. Bring on the outbreak. Bring on the plague…"

"Shut up!" Upal cried out.

"You shut up." he mumbled.

After an hour of painful and seemingly endless dragging and pulling, Lashra's elbows were bruised, her legs tender and her back aching. She tried to find some hope ahead, but the path truly seemed endless. She had slowed to a crawl (a slower crawl that is). She was dog-tired, worn out, done for, kaput. She had no choice but to stop and rest. She spoke quietly to Crawford. "I need to stop and rest. Pass it on."

"Thank heaven, I thought you were never going to stop." he said wearily. "Tell Preet we're going to stop for a break." he said to Upal.

Upal passed the message on to Preet, "Crowboy's too weak to go on, so we're stopping to rest." And with that, the train came to a stop.

Lashra stopped and laid her head on her arm. She closed her eyes and tried not to think about how far they'd gone and how far they might have to go. Instead she decided to focus her attention on the surrounding sounds. She listened apprehensively to the acidic drops falling onto the petals above her head. *Drip.* She counted one, two, three, four, five, six, *drip.* Another six seconds and another *drip…* and six and another and six and another and… She twinged slightly and woke from her half-sleep. "Nobody falls asleep!" she shouted. "They drip every six seconds." She wondered, "Why six seconds?" Lashra questioned everything, even the rhythm of poisonous flesh eating pariah, like the ones dripping inches above her head. "There doesn't have to be a reason for everything, Lashra." she said to herself. She shouted back, "A few more minutes and we'll have to continue!"

"Do you see Ray?" asked Crawford.

She looked up, "No, but maybe that's a good sign. Maybe he's on the other side waiting for us."

"I hope so." Crawford ached out. "I'm not sure how much more of this I can take."

Preet was squirming around. He seemed to have stopped on a small mound of rocks. He laboriously and awkwardly worked at rolling over ever so slightly so that he could get off of them. Then he suddenly realized that those weren't rocks. He reached into his pocket for the few nuts he'd secretly stashed away earlier. As luck would have it, his elbow lightly made contact with one of the petals.

His ears perked. He heard it drip. He held his breath. Frozen in fear that a drop might slip by, he waited and waited not saying a word about it to the others.

He closed his eyes tightly and laid completely still. "Lashra's gonna kill me if I die this way." His imagination took over… He could see Lashra and the others looking down on his makeshift grave.

Lashra was lamenting, "If only Preet had listened to my wise and sage advice, he should have heeded the countless warnings I gave him. Oh Preet you'd still be with us today."

He opened his eyes, "I can't give her the satisfaction. I must be in the clear by now?" He breathed out and felt a huge sense of relief. "That was too close for comfort." he thought to himself.

"What was too close for comfort?" Upal asked.

Caught by surprise and worried the others would scold him for not being cautious enough he said, "Uh, your feet and my face. *Way* too close for comfort."

Taking his time and being even more cautious, he brought the crunchy nutty fruit up to his mouth. "This will not keep me going all day." he mumbled to himself as he slowly chewed on his measly breakfast.

He quietly called to Upal, "Hey, ask Lashra how much farther?"

Upal whispered, "Hey, Crowboy, how much farth… Why am I whispering?" he asked quietly. Then he shouted to the locomotive driving the train, "Hey Lashra, how much farther?"

"I have no idea. It feels like we've been doing this for hours." she said disappointedly. "I don't know how much farther I can go."

She growled quietly and without warning she started shimmying herself forward. Crawford wiggled, Upal scooted, and Preet staying as close to the ground as possible, slinked and towed his mountain sized body forward.

The only sound they could hear was their own shimmying and grunting. As time went on Lashra's head kept filling up with more and more questions. What if they had to crawl like this through the night? What if they had to sleep under the golden flowers? What if this went on for days?

The longer they dragged on, the more she questioned herself. She felt responsible for this wearisome, drawn-out tour of the golden pathway. The deeper they went the more chances one of them had of making a false move. She thought about her brother trailing behind. *What if..?* She didn't want to finish the thought.

"Lashra?" Crawford called from behind.

She took it as an opportunity to stop and rest again. She was out of breath and any excuse to stop was welcomed. "I don't know how much farther Crawford."

"That's not it." he said. "There's something I just don't understand. If no one ever returns from here, how is it possible that our childhood nursery rhymes seem to know so much about this place? Is it just transference? I mean is it because we're in here that we're just linking the ideas together?"

Lashra welcomed the chance to answer his question. Anything to get her mind off of her troubles.

"Well," she said in a very confident but tired tone, "The Old Lady had occasional visions. One day I asked about the visions. She said the Rubicon had gone through changes over her eight hundred years and there were changes before her lifetime.

"So," Crawford interjected. "The Old Lady was able to return from here."

"In a way… Yes, I guess so." Lashra had never really thought of it that way. She continued. "All the Longevites traveled through the forest this way. For thousands of years they shared their stories about their visitations in the Rubicon. Some of the visions were written down in the Tralatitious and others were passed on verbally. Over the years parents created rhymes to remember and pass on the stories to their children. These forewarnings were meant to instill fear in children and dissuade them from approaching the Rubicon."

"Hmmm." Crawford thought about all the nursery rhymes he knew. "I guess... if you think about it, the rhymes could be used as a guide for those who do enter it. If they can decipher their meaning."

"That's a big *if*." she responded. Crawford's comment made her think about other rhymes she knew too.

The rest stops became more frequent as the hours passed. Lashra was second guessing herself at every turn and she figured the silence behind her was a sure sign that the boys were also questioning her command of the situation.

Ray, who had really been leading the way, stayed quiet as he walked and pecked at the ground. He didn't seem to worry about anything. Not one squawk or gurgle was heard from him the entire day. Suddenly the path above their heads thinned and Ray took off.

Lashra saw the bird disappear and felt a surge of energy. She hoped it was a sign that the end was near. She yelled out, "We're through. I can see the end!" She shouted it again and again.

A few minutes later they were all out of the path.

"I am never laying down again." was Preet's first comment after exiting.

Their destination appeared to be a small opening just slightly bigger than the room Upal occupied at Mrs. Nibbledent's house. The walls were made up of tightly intertwined roots, branches and vines that went up to form a deep well at least two hundred feet, straight up into the clouds.

They were completely surrounded except for one opening a few feet above the ground. Upal grabbed hold on a few vines and climbed up to take a look and see what he could see.

"What do you see?" Preet called.

Upal's voice echoed out of the tunnel, "It's just a dimly lit channel, a tunnel-like shaft made of much the same stuff as these endlessly high walls that surround us now."

"Is it a mystical portal?" Preet asked.

Upal climbed farther in and turned to face them. "Well?" he said as he waved them up. "What are you waiting for?"

Without saying a word, Lashra and Crawford knelt down directly below the entrance facing each other.

"Come on Preet." said Lashra, "We'll help you up."

Preet reached up and was only a foot short of reaching the hole. Lashra and Crawford each grabbed hold of one of Preets legs and grunted in unison as they lifted him up.

"Come on Preet, pull yourself up!" Lashra shouted.

"I'm trying." he cried out.

"Upal!" she shouted, "Can you please help?"

Upal slowly made his way back and grabbed hold of Preet's left hand. "Are you even trying to climb in?" he growled.

It took a few minutes but eventually Preet was in the tunnel. Soon after that they were all in and making their way up the long winding path.

Chapter 52 Uphill All The Way

In no time at all, they were making their way up and deeper into the shaft. Rather than being met with darkness, the lengthy straight was filled with hundreds of ambient balloon-like flowers hanging on the vines. They gave off a calm, rhythmic, hypnotic pulse of ever changing light that flowed like tongues of flames on the petals. The soft tranquil glow seemed to be gently encouraging them forward through the magical portal.

They had been climbing for what seemed like hours. All four complained of having tired and achy burning legs.

"Is the air getting thinner?" Upal asked sarcastically. "It feels like we've been climbing straight up for hours." He stopped for a moment and looked back from whence they came. "We should be in the clouds by now."

"Quit your complaining." Crawford said as he passed Upal.

"Ya, quit your complaining." Lashra smiled at him as she too passed him by.

"I wasn't complaining... I was merely asking." he mumbled.

A few more hours passed and it finally felt like the trail was flattening out.

Preet was tired and had been dragging his feet for a while now. "I'm feeling kind of dizzy. I could almost use a nap and some food. Well, food for sure, then a nap." And with no care for the others, Preet stopped and stretched out on the ground and let out a tired and well deserved sigh of relief.

Upal looked back, "That's not a bad idea." he said as he joined his buddy on the ground.

"Well if you two are stopping, I'm stopping too." Lashra was happy to see them sitting and she was in no mood to argue the point. She quickly joined in and stretched out next to them and closed her eyes. "I don't think I can do this for much longer." she said, yawning.

Upal looked over at Preet with dismay and rolled his eyes at Lashra. Preet shrugged his shoulders. The two were stunned by Lashra's indifference to them stopping.

Crawford sat with his back against the wall. "I hope the path stays flat for a while."

After a few moments of rest Crawford encouraged them to get up and continue their march. "We can't stop too long or we'll be stuck in here all night."

Preet was curled up in a fetal position, trying to get as comfortable as possible. "We don't even know how long this tunnel is. We could walk all night and still be stuck here." he complained.

Upal and Lashra both agreed with Preet, but they knew that Crawford was probably right.

They half-heartedly resumed their walk at a much slower pace. As they progressed deeper into the shaft, the balloon vines' glowing lights increased their rhythm and transformed into a bright orange stroboscopic effect. Preet's dizziness hadn't gone away and the show of lights only made things worse.

"Stop the lights." Preet said as he tried to cover his eyes. He stumbled and crashed into the side walls of the hollow shaking them. He was shocked by the unexpected showering of a liquid that cascaded from the large bucket-like flowers above his head.

The solution landed on his head, face and shoulders throwing him into a panic. "Ah! It burns! It burns!" he screamed out.

The others jumped back trying their best to avoid being splashed by the acid and being crushed by a frazzled and unhinged Preet.

"Do something Lashra!" shouted Upal.

But they could only look on as Preet uncontrollably bounced and slammed against the walls shaking the room. One side and then the other, each time activating the shower of mysterious flowing fluid. He was almost completely covered. He fell to the ground, screaming, squirming and writhing in agony. Then without warning, he stopped moving. The calm, pulsing, heartbeat paced glow of the balloon flowers returned.

Lashra, Upal and Crawford hovered over Preet's body.

Preet lay there motionless. The three just stared at Preet's peaceful body. Lashra slowly kneeled down and reached out. She was about to touch his face when suddenly one of his eyes opened ever so slowly. Then the other.

"Oh, it doesn't burn." Preet gave a dumb smile and licked his lips. "It's actually a little sweet and sticky." He ran his hand along his face and collected the syrup. He put his whole hand in his mouth and licked his fingers clean. "Ya, it's actually pretty tasty. Sorry about that."

Upal kicked him while he was down and let him have it, "What's wrong with you? We thought you were dying." He kicked him again for good measure.

They waited and watched.

"What's going on?" Preet asked.

"I think we're waiting to see if you're going to get sick or poisoned from the syrup you just ate." Crawford said nonchalantly.

"Really?" Preet said.

"No point in all of us dying." Crawford smiled sheepishly.

Preet didn't seem too worried about being poisoned; he was just happy to have found something delicious to eat, or in this case drink. He stood up onto his tiptoes, reached up and removed a bucket shaped flower from the wall. He pulled it down carefully then paused for a moment as he looked at the sticky liquid inside.

"Whatever." he said to himself as he took a few large gulps.

Their eyes were riveted on him as he drank from the flower.

"What?" he said quizzically. "I'd rather die drinking this, than starve to death." He returned to swigging the juice.

Upal agreed and jumped up to grab a flower, but alas it was too high for his littleness to reach. "Can we have some too?" he asked his bosom buddy and lifelong pal.

"Get your own." Preet laughed. "I'm kidding."

He reached up and gave each one a flower filled with the wonderful nectar. They sat for a few minutes enjoying the rest and the drink. After filling themselves they carried on and soon they were once again on an uphill journey.

A few more hours passed and their frustrations grew.

Crawford let out a sigh, "What if this thing really doesn't end? How much farther can we…"

Crawford was taken aback when Ray unexpectedly took off.

"Where's he going?" Lashra asked.

"Maybe we're getting closer." Crawford answered her.

Within a minute or two he returned with a beakful of berries.

"We must be approaching the end!" Lashra cried out.

Within minutes they were out in the fresh air again. They walked through a few hundred feet of trees and shrubs and found themselves in a somewhat open space. A few feet to their left was a lightly snow covered cliff that dropped down to an endless abyss. To their right was a narrow rock pathway covered with an impassable amount of thorn bushes filled with blue and black berries.

Directly in front of them was a large open mouth entrance to a cave. It looked like a giant monster-like creature. It had a growling furrowed brow and a mouth full of rotted and broken teeth that were ready to take a bite out of anyone who dared try to enter its jaws.

Tired and longing for rest they made a quick plan to best use the remaining sunlight. Seeing that Ray was feasting on the berries, they assumed they were safe to eat and so Crawford and Preet were put in charge of gathering food.

Lashra and Upal made their way around and gathered whatever they could find to burn. They collected wood scraps from the floor and stone walls around the area.

"Do you think we're getting close?" Upal asked Lashra.

"Retrieving in stone… I think we're almost there. I think what we're looking for is in this cave. There's nowhere else to go. We're not going to know unless we go in." she said.

They made their way back with some scraps and built a small fire by the cave's entrance. Darkness soon arrived. They sat around the fire discussing their next step.

"I wonder what's waiting for us inside that cave?" Preet asked.

Lashra's eyes were fixed on the giant teeth of the structure. "If the entrance is any indication it doesn't bode well. What I'm wondering is what are we going to do with what we find?"

"If we find anything at all." Crawford whispered.

Lashra had started feeling nauseous soon after drinking the nectar and now her back was beginning to ache. She got up and tried to walk it off. She made her way over to the pathway and started scraping and collecting moss from its walls. She didn't want to say anything about her pain to the others. She tried to distract herself. This moss is very oily, she thought. She gathered some up and figured they could use it to build torches. After all, they would need light in the cave and this moss just might do the trick.

She made her way back to the fire, dropping off the incendiary lichen. Without saying a word, she made her way to the opening of the cave and stood at its entrance. Hopefully we won't have to go too deep inside to find what we're looking for, she thought. She peered into the darkness that awaited them.

The boys were sitting around, eating everything they could get their hands on. Maybe it was the thought of finally finding something important, maybe it was tiredness, who knows, but, for the first time since coming into the Rubicon they seemed to be enjoying each other's company. Even Upal and Crawford were joking around.

Lashra could hear them laughing and for a moment it put a smile on her face, but it didn't last long. She started to well up as she thought about the pressures of leading this ragtag group of boys. She felt alone, sad and slightly depressed.

The nausea, cramps and back pain hadn't quelled. She wondered if it was all just a manifestation of the stress and anxiety she was feeling. At least that's what she hoped. I hope we didn't accidentally poison ourselves, she thought.

"Hey Lashra? You ok?" Crawford gently shouted to her.

"I'm fine." she said not turning around. "Just thinking." She wasn't ready to return.

She wasn't ready to talk to anyone about anything she was feeling. It wasn't easy always keeping everything inside, always looking like she knew what she was doing, always being in control. Sometimes she wished she could just be a girl, be herself, whatever or whoever that was. Maybe she just missed The Old Lady's companionship? Of course she did.

Crawford questioned getting up and making sure she was alright, but figured Preet and Upal would stop him and tell him that they should be the ones to check up on her.

Preet read the expression on Crawfords' face. "She'll be fine. It can't be easy hanging with us all day." he whispered.

"Speak for yourself Preet, I'm a blast to have around." Upal made a motion to get up and both Preet and Crawford put their hands on his shoulders and sat him back down. Upal understood and did not protest.

A little while later all four were sitting around the fire. Lashra had found a few sticks and they spent some of their time making and testing Lashra's torch idea. Night came in full force and no one mentioned the need to keep guard. They huddled close together by the fire and soon the exhausted brood fell asleep.

Chapter 53 Saudj And The Witch

Saudj stretched out and let out an extendedly long yawn. The stretching seemed to accentuate the pangs of hunger that caused him terrible pain. He was desperate; he had to find some food. He was ready to eat just about anything to fill the hole in his stomach. He needed something to fill the emptiness and misery.

He climbed down from his resting place and laggardly made his way through the forest. With his head down he shuffled his feet looking around for a morsel, a tidbit, a piece of anything.

Saudj's heart skipped a beat. The world around him faded away as his attention was singularly focused on the pattern in the dirt. The suddenness of the encounter caught him off guard, leaving him momentarily perplexed. He questioned what he was looking at. He bent down and purposefully ran his fingers along the ridges in the dust.

"Preet." he whispered. He stood and carefully placed his foot into the giant impression. He did the same with his other foot on and on until they stopped near a large stump. His eye caught something miraculous. Was it possible? Food.

He fell to his knees and picked up a nut, one small, wonderful nut. His eyes darted back and forth. There under the leaf, another nut and behind that one, another. He didn't care about anything else at that moment. Food, food, food. He crawled the entire camp on his hands and knees laughing like a mad man who'd just struck gold.

After about an hour of inching his way around the floor of the camp and when he was sure there was nothing left to find, he pondered where the creators of the footprints might have gone.

He sat back for a while and thought about his situation. "They have no idea where I am," he said to himself. "I have the upper hand."

He got up and carefully examined the area for signs of broken branches. Preet will have left a mess of broken branches, he thought. It didn't take long for Saudj to find indications of which way they had gone.

The brush was full and it made his travels difficult, but if he was careful he could manage to retrace their trail. He was excited to be in control, to have an advantage over the three. This thought encouraged him and motivated him to keep moving. Saudj was taken aback at the sight of someone or something just ahead of him.

He froze in place and felt a sudden sense of panic and fear. He stared long and hard. He didn't dare move a muscle. It took him a while to figure out that what he was looking at wasn't real. As he approached the statue he noticed the remnants of a once-burning fire.

"I was right." he nodded happily. He glared at the old witch sitting on her throne. "I've got them now."

He climbed onto her lap and held her face in his hands. He moved in until his nose was almost touching hers. He locked his wide eyes into hers and could see his own reflection in her emerald eyes. "I've got them now!" he cackled. "And there's nothing you can do about it." He tried to shake her as he shouted in her face, "Nothing! Nothing!"

He looked up to the sky. Darkness was falling and he was tired. He climbed down and sat by the pit and used a branch to tussle and dig into the coals. He noticed a little smoke. There were still a few small embers. He knelt down and blew on the coals. They lit up.

"Yes!" he shouted. A little fire would be great. He made his way around the camp and gathered up some more debris for his soon to be fire. "Outstanding! Excellent behavior!" he cried out as he patted himself on the shoulder. Then, from out of nowhere his eye caught a few nuts he'd missed previously.

He fed himself as he went on scouring the entire area looking for any morsels he might have missed. He was delighted when he noticed a bunch of berries on the ground under a big leaf. He lifted the leaf and found a gold mine. He soon had a fire going and was eating and filling his belly for the first time in months, or at least that's how it felt.

He sat pretending to joke around with his three friends. How nice it would be to have them there with him. Someone other than himself to keep him company. But soon the joking turned to malice and he realized they were making fun of him and questioning him about the Old Lady. They started accusing him of murder and deceit. He tried to defend himself but it was no good. Their constant attacks were infuriating him. They didn't understand, he did it for them. His mind was racing and wandering under the effects of the hypnotizing fire light.

He woke up from his day dream and realized once again that he was the one. He would show them all. "How dare they question me." he said through clenched teeth.

In the darkness of the night he got up and made his way around the camp to gather more wood. It was nice to have a fire to keep him warm and to have light throughout his solitary night.

As he made his way around he was startled by a giant glowing insect. He turned and whacked it with a stick knocking it to the ground. That was the wrong thing to do. The dazed bug lit up brightly and swirled around on the ground and on its way up stung him in the calf. Saudj jumped and howled in pain and surprise as the luciferin took off. He limped back to the fire, wailing and squealing in anguish.

The luciferin had taken a fair chunk of meat from the boy's leg. The sting's pain was piercing and biting. The abscess quickly inflamed. His calf expanded to triple its normal size. As it slowly moved up his leg he felt sure that the swelling would take over his entire body. It was undeniable, he was going to die. He sat in pain by the fire rocking and moaning, waiting for the pain to reach his heart.

The shooting sensations reminded him of his loneliness and solitude. No one was here to help care for him, to hold his hand and to tell him everything would be fine.

He thought of the time when he'd broken his leg jumping off a house during a game of chase with the others. Lashra stopped running and turned when she heard him yell. She ran to him and coddled him.

"It'll be ok, just hold on. We'll take you to the Old Lady and she'll fix you up good as new." she said reassuringly.

The pain seemed to lessen just thinking about her comforting voice. He could barely move his leg, but the pain seemed to be easing a little. Yes, he was sure it was easing. He kept his mind focused on that day, when he broke his leg. He replayed it in his mind over and over as he fell in and out of consciousness.

It was a burden-filled night, stuffed with unsettling thoughts and sleeplessness. His only comfort sat in the belief that he would survive to see another beautiful sunrise.

There it was…

Chapter 54 The Cave

The sky awakens with a soft glow as if whispering to me of the day to come. Soft wisps of clouds explode like tongues of bright red and orange flames. The morning mist in the far off mountain rolls its way down into a valley. Soon the canyon is filled with an ocean of frosty vapors. The giant trees pop up through the mist creating a magical contrast.

The sleeping forest slowly comes to life with a symphony of natural beauty. The birdsong's melodious tunes join the gentle rustling of the leaves…

"What are you writing?"

Crawford's question startled Lashra. She quickly closed her sketchbook. It was the first time she'd been able to write since entering the Rubicon.

"None of your business." she said as she tucked her book into her bag.

She got up and made her way to the edge of the cliff. She stared out and went back to her far off thoughts. Her eyes were fixed on a specific patch of land in the distance. She believed it to be the dreaded Orchard of Souls. It seemed to be never ending. She wondered if the orchard made its way all through the entirety of the Rubicon.

"We haven't seen the last of that place." she murmured.

Crawford had quietly made his way over and was standing behind her within earshot. "I hope you're wrong," he whispered in response.

She turned to see him standing close, maybe too close. Crawford read the discomfort in her eyes and stepped back a few feet.

"Sorry, I was just trying to see what had you so mesmerized. It's a nice little spot you found yourself."

Lashra smiled politely as she squeezed by. Crawford nodded, then moved closer to the edge of the cliff and proceeded to enjoy the magical view.

Lashra made her way back to the unlit fire pit. She stopped for a moment and observed Upal and Preet. They were sitting in silence just staring into the entrance of the cave.

"It's a cave. How deep can it really be?" Upal's comment came from thin air.

Preet put his arm around his pal, "Ya, you're right buddy. Ten minutes or so… I'm sure we'll be out of there in no time."

Lashra leaned in quietly and whispered in their ears. "After all, it has been pretty smooth and straightforward so far."

Preet jumped up and faced her. "You think it could get worse?" he said nervously.

Upal stretched his arms and let out a nice relaxing yawn. "We've done all the hard stuff already. We're here, let's just go in, get what's ours."

"Your brain is about as big as your size." said Crawford. He could hear Upal's big mouth blaring away. "Think about it for a second." he continued as he made his way back to the cave.

"*Lore and vision are guides for your duty.* You can check that one off your list. *Anguish will grip you with sunlight's beauty.* Check that one too. *Safely guided through the golden path, angry widows, you'll escape their wrath.* Yup, we did that too. *Retrieve from the rock what is incomplete.* I'm guessing we're about to embark on that." He took a long pause and whispered the final words (for dramatic effect). "*Altruism bestows you death's defeat.*"

"Hmm." Preet snorted. "That one doesn't sound good." He rubbed his chin. "Ya, death never sounds good."

"Death's defeat." Upal gave Preet a few friendly jabs in the ribs. "Come on… Ten minutes." He smiled at them all. "I say we fill up on breakfast, then we go."

Lashra was probably the only one to notice a slight crack in his confident demeanor.

They ate, gathered their torches and prepared to enter the cave. Upal jumped into the mouth, looked up, raised his arms for protection and screamed. The three jumped back in fear as the mouth closed in on...

"False alarm," he said calmly.

"Upal!" shouted Lashra, "You can't be doing things like that." she scolded him.

"Well, consider us even Lashra." he responded.

"Ok, so we're even." repeated Preet.

"No!" said Upal, "*We're even.*" he pointed to himself and Lashra. "I'll get you two later."

"Hey!" Crawford put his hand up. "I had nothing to do with the kissing you, thing. You can kindly leave me out. That's their weird thing."

Lashra looked sideways at Crawford. "Thing?"

Crawford looked at her straight faced. "Ya, Preet likes kissing *him*," he pointed in Upal's direction. "And you like kissing me."

Lashra pushed her way past Upal and purposefully walked into the cave without looking back or saying a word.

"Speechless?" Preet chuckled, "I don't think I've ever seen that."

They were barely a few minutes into their travels when Preet who was trailing with Upal stopped and turned around to see if the opening of the cave was still visible or maybe he wanted to see if it was still available. It wasn't. He let out a long sigh and quickly caught up with Upal.

"Hey, Oop. Just to be clear, I don't like kissing you. I mean you are nice and all, but you're you know..."

Upal stopped. Preet stopped. "Preet." he said calmly, "Please stop talking." Upal resumed walking.

"Sorry."

"*Talking.*"

236

Each one had a makeshift torch and a pocket full of moss to replenish it a few times. The other pocket was filled with whatever food they had left over. Lashra was still leading the gang down the only available route. She noticed something shiny on the side of the cave wall and moved in to have a closer look.

"It's water." She held the side of her hand against the wall and soon her cup shaped palm was filled.

The water brought with it a faint sense of hope. With nothing to drink in almost a full day, this was a surprising welcome. They got their fill and continued their journey through the large deep crevasse. Lashra's torch was reaching its end. She gestured for Crawford's torch. She lit it and continued without a word.

Hours into their trek and having used up four torches so far, they stopped for a break and questioned whether they should continue. It was a short discussion. They continued.

Preet thought he noticed a dim light in the distance. "Hey, maybe we're through? I think I see light." he said pointing deeper into the cave.

"I think you're right." said Lashra. She picked up the pace. Before long they found themselves at the edge of a cliff. Looking down they could see thousands of different sized glowing mushrooms growing all around, up and down the sides of a deep hollow. Purple, green, red, yellow, it was a plethora of luminous colors each one more magical than the other and at the very bottom they could just make out a small halo of light that seemed to be constantly changing colors.

"I wonder if they're edible?" questioned Preet.

Upal circled the thin edge around the volcano shaped shaft. Once on the other side of the hole he investigated his surroundings. There was nothing but a solid wall.

"There's no way to get through. Looks to me like we're going down." he said.

"There's a narrow path about six or seven feet down that seems to circle this giant sinkhole's walls." Upal placed his torch down and hung himself over the edge.

"Be careful. You don't know if that path is strong enough to hold…" Lashra hadn't finished her sentence and Upal had already dropped himself onto the path.

"It's not very big." he shouted back up. "We'll have to hug the wall on the way down."

It didn't take Lashra long. Soon she too was hanging over the edge. Upal scooched over, grabbed her arm and guided her down carefully. Crawford was a little more hesitant, but soon joined them.

Preet moved in closer and layed on the floor to investigate the situation a little closer. "Ya, I'm not sure that's an actual path."

He could see that the three had barely enough room for their feet on the narrow path. "Maybe I'll just wait up here?"

Preet clearly did not want to make this trip. "If you guys make it down safely I'll probably join you." he said questionably.

"Come on Preet, we're not doing this without you." Lashra said firmly. "It's not that far down." She tried to encourage him.

"Not that far down?" *down, down, down,* his voice echoed in the tube.

"Looks like danger." croaked Ray.

The bird had been traveling quietly in the comfort of Preet's hair the whole time. "Are you still here? I thought you stayed back." he said to Ray.

"Looks like danger."

"I heard you the first time." he mumbled to the bird.

Upal was already a fair distance down the path. His voice came calling, "You're just wasting time buddy." He turned and continued making his way down easily, but cautiously.

"That's easy for you to say." Preet shouted, "You have those little dwarf-like feet. You've got tons of room down there. I don't even think half of my foot will fit on the path."

Lashra looked to her right and could see Upal making his way at a steady pace. She looked up and could see Preet hadn't moved. Her patience was running low. "Come down here now!"

He begrudgingly rolled over and made his way down. "If I fall and die, I will never talk to you again." he said to his sister.

His feet touched down on the path and due to his height, his hair was still slightly over the floor of the cliff and his hands still had a tight grip on the top floor.

"You have to let go of the cliff." Crawford gently and encouragingly whispered to him. "I've got you. Let go. Just hug the wall. I won't let you fall."

Preet followed Crawford's instructions and painstakingly started making his way down the constrictive pathway. Upal on the other hand, had been making his way the whole time and was already a quarter of the way down. Lashra was not as confident as she had let on, but she still found a way to make good time.

"Oh no!" Upal shouted up the tube. "The path ends here."

There was a moment of silence, then Preet started making his way back up. "Oh well, we tried." he said happily, reversing his course.

Lashra hadn't moved yet. She was contemplating the situation trying to think up a solution.

Strangely enough, it had taken Preet very little time to climb his way back out. "Ok, come on guys, I'll help you out." he said with some joy.

"Hey Preet?" Upal shouted up. "I was just kidding. The path goes all the way down." He laughed alone.

Lashra once again was not amused with Upal's antics. "Why would you do that?"

"What?" Preet called down. "Why would you say that?"

Upal resumed making his way down. *"Now, we're even."* He nodded happily to himself.

After a short time Upal had made his way down the large corkscrewed structure. Lashra had carefully looped the long coiled cliffside path to its end too. Preet was stuck with his hands, nose and toes scraping against the wall all the way down. He took slow, small and precise side steps.

Crawford calmly encouraged Preet as they made their way down the long pathway. "Everything will be fine as long as we keep moving." he said softly.

The two of them swirled and circled the giant vertical corridor. An hour later all four had reached solid ground.

Preet, who was slightly burnt-out and unnerved, squeaked, "That was a lot easier than it looked."

Having reached the ground safely, Preet was able to admire his surroundings. He found himself under a giant mushroom. Its cap covered almost the entirety of the well, leaving only a few inches between itself and the wall. Preet jumped up but could not reach the underside of this magical mushroom.

All four stared up at the gills that gave off a radiant glow. It was constantly changing colors that moved in a rhythmic circular motion. They watched the light dancing and were hypnotized by the wave of colors going round and round.

"Wow." Preet uttered as his head began to spin.

"I know, it's so beautiful." said Lashra.

"No, I mean wow my neck is killing me." He rolled and rubbed his neck.

Upal had moved on to investigate a newly discovered fragment of their ongoing escapade through the never ending labyrinth. It was a moisture-laden path with a flat smooth surface and a low ceiling.

"Over here!" he shouted.

Lashra handed him a freshly lit torch. "I vote, we keep moving."

They were all in agreement. The sooner they found what they were looking for the sooner they could head back.

The subterranean passage was leading them down a watery path.

"The water just seems to keep getting deeper." Upal stated plainly. "Do we keep going until we can't?"

No one answered his rhetorical question; they just kept walking.

Chapter 55 The Wall

"Do you hear that?" Upal stopped and turned his ear toward the sound.

He looked back at Lashra, "Is that good or bad?"

It was the sound of gurgling water. Suddenly everyone heard it echoing throughout the cave.

"We're about to find out." said Crawford.

They continued pressing forward. The water continued to rise.

"Well, at least we know where the bubbling is coming from." Lashra said as she made her way past a large gushing jet of water.

Upal and Preet stayed back to investigate. Upal put his hand over the bubbling water. It gushed up through the cavern floor. It went up just past his waist. And being Upal, of course he couldn't resist trying to ride the powerful jet stream.

"I think this jet of water is strong enough to hold me up." he said to Preet.

He bent over and placed himself on it and was amazed that it could hold his weight.

"This is so cool, you've got to try this!" he shouted in excitement as he tried to spin himself around in circles.

"I'll pass." Preet said as he squeezed by.

"You don't know what you're missing." Upal said as he clearly enjoyed the ride.

After a few minutes Upal caught up to the group and was unamused by their unwillingness *to be* amused. "You know there's nothing wrong with a little fun once in a while people."

"Walk, walk, walk." whined Preet. "Is the ceiling getting lower? Can we drink this water? Where did Ray go?"

No one paid attention to him. They continued their walk and the water kept getting deeper. After another hour's journey, they found themselves against a wall.

"Ok, so, where do we go from here?" Crawford commented.

They stood about ten feet away from the end of the road.

Preet was quick to suggest his idea. "Let's turn back. I'm getting hungry."

They moved in closer to the wall but Upal wasn't satisfied with close, he wanted to get in even closer. He took a step and found no footing. He fell forward and almost got sucked down into the water.

"Woah!" he exclaimed as he reached back, trying not to get sucked in. Feeling himself go down, he instinctively grabbed hold of Preet's pants.

Preet looked at him straight-faced, "Who's the pant-pulling-half-wit now Upal? When I pulled your pants down, it was just a reflex. I don't know what *this* is?"

Crawford and Lashra looked at each other with confusion, shrugged their shoulders and didn't say a word.

Upal did his best to ignore Preet's comment. "Look over here. There's a dull light shining through the water, and there's a huge gap between the wall and the floor. There's something down there giving off light, I'm sure of it."

Preet walked over and put his arm against the far wall and felt the gap with his foot. "It feels like it's about a five foot wide gap, and it's pulling down pretty hard."

Upal was exasperated, "Are you serious? Why can't we just find one easy thing to do?"

Without another word he took a deep breath and went underwater to investigate. He hooked his feet onto the edge of the floor so as not to get sucked in. A few seconds later he came back up.

"Preet's right. There's a good sized gap down there and the water's pulling down pretty hard. It's going somewhere, and there is something glowing down there."

"What should we do?" said Lashra.

"We haven't come this far just to quit," said Upal. "I'm going down." No one argued.

He took a couple of deep breaths and... "No one is going to try to stop me?" he said disappointedly.

Crawford, Lashra and Preet just stared at him in silence with vacant looks on their faces.

"Of course no one is going to stop me. Why would I think anyone would try and stop me?" So, he mockingly did it himself, "Upal don't do it. You don't know what's down there. You could die." He put his hands up and shook his head, "At least one of you could fake a little concern?" he said in disbelief.

Preet put his hand on Upal's shoulder, "Oop, you don't know what's down there, don't do it."

"It's a little late for that now you nitwit." retorted Upal as he removed Preet's hand from his shoulder.

He took a couple of deep breaths and went under water to investigate one more time. As he made his way in he grabbed hold of the ledge with his toes again, so as not to be dragged down by the water's pressure. He came up a minute later.

"It feels like some kind of underwater waterfall. If that makes any sense. It's pretty deep. I couldn't touch the ground." he said disappointedly.

"So we know it's at least four feet deep then?" joked Crawford.

"Hey!" shouted Preet, "I was gonna say that."

"Really funny. Either of you malaperts want to give it a shot?" Upal remarked.

The two boys stayed silent.

"I didn't think so."

"Focus kids." Lashra tried to calm things before they got out of hand.

"Upal, do you think if we step into the current we could be pushed down to where the light is coming from?"

"Maybe…" Crawford added, "there's an air pocket or another cave of some sort?"

"I could try going down a few feet." said Upal.

"Are you sure?" they asked in unison.

"No." he replied, "But what choice do we have? I'm going in. If I'm not back in five minutes I'm either dead… or hopefully alive." he smiled awkwardly.

"Feel free to join me in a few minutes."

Upal was scared. They could see it in his eyes. Had this whole thing gone too far? Were they really going to risk their lives for this, this… what was it they were really doing? Stories, myths, legends. Lashra believed they were true. Preet and Upal wanted to believe they were true and Crawford wasn't sure what to believe.

Did any of them truly fathom the absoluteness of what they were asking of themselves at this very moment? Were they willing to lay their lives on the line for a hope, a dream, a vision? Were they going to follow through with this crazy plan?

Crawford had been apprehensive about the *whole mission* from the beginning. He reached out and grabbed Upal. "Don't do it." he said nervously.

"Too late." Upal pushed away, closed his eyes and disappeared into the unknown.

He felt himself being sucked down and all he could hear was Saudj's final warning echoing through his mind.

"Leave with me now while you still have your lives and some of your sanity. Come with me that you might be free of all this. Come with me and live."

Chapter 56 Going Down

It didn't take Upal long to start second guessing his decision. He really needed to work on thinking, *then* doing. Not the other way around.

He tried to slow his descent by bracing himself against the slimy walls of the crevasse. The space was a lot tighter than he imagined. He kept his arms and legs spread forcefully against both sides. It didn't seem to have much of an impact; he was still traveling downward at quite a hurried pace. The slithery, mucus-like coating on the walls made his efforts virtually useless. The constant downward pressure of the water both pushed and pulled on him.

The air in his lungs was getting stale. How long had he been underwater? He wasn't really sure but he knew it was long enough that he was aching for air. He tried hard to remain calm. Don't breathe out, he thought to himself. Hold on.

Pressure was building in his head. His ears began aching. The compression intensified. It hurt. He tried to focus on what he was supposed to be doing. What was he supposed to be doing? No longer able to resist, he let out a small air bubble hoping this would ease some of the pain he was feeling in his chest.

What am I doing? He had no plan. Should I let go and let the water carry me away? He stayed in control as much as possible. The walls suddenly felt coarse and less slippery. It slowed his rate of descent a little more. Where does this end? He was feeling more and more anxious as he became air hungry. His body was starving for fresh air.

Let go Upal, he heard himself say and just as he did, a light passed him by. A flash of brightness? He was sure of it.

Instinctively he spread his arms and legs out as hard as he could and reversed his course.

Grasping both sides tightly he managed to climb. Desperate for oxygen he let out a little more air. He had only one breath left in his lungs. He was feeling light-headed and foggy.

You can't be much farther, he pleaded with the light. How could he have traveled so far in such a short time? He thought about just giving up and letting go. Maybe, that's what he was supposed to do. Should he just let go and let the water take him?

Somehow he sensed the light. Yes, there it was. The soft glow; it was within reach. He extended one hand and found an edge. His fingers bonded to it in desperation. He released his final breath. He was about to pass out, his mind was cloudy and for the first time he noticed the thunderous sound of water pounding in his ears. He felt his grip loosening. It was too much, all of it, much too much.

No. Today is not my day to die. He persuaded himself to go on. He reached up with his other hand and gripped the ledge. With all his might he pulled himself toward the beacon of hope. Using the last of his energy he dragged his body upwards and was able to get his head through an opening. He heaved and gulped for air. Large amounts of water were still pouring down on and over him causing him to gag and choke.

He worked himself onto a ledge. A beautiful life saving window of hope. His body was only half way inside the newly found cavity. Dizzy, exhausted and oxygen starved, he looked up. The glowing light of the bright sun, trees, green, blue, then everything went black.

Chapter 57 Light

Upal opened his eyes. Water was still tearing down on him. He wasn't sure how much time had passed; all he knew was that his body was still gasping and in need of air. He pulled himself through the breach in the wall and crashed down on a ledge a few feet below.

"Oh my goodness!" he tried shouting through the hacking and coughing. "Woohoo! I'm alive, I'm alive!" He couldn't believe it.

He struggled to his feet and braced himself next to the large opening. He watched as an endless supply of water cascaded down with absolute power. How was it possible? Where was the water coming from? How did he manage to stay alive and make it this far? "Enough already!" he screamed at himself.

At that moment, the most important question popped up. How was he going to get word to his friends? After all, he was alive. He began to question himself.

"How long have I been gone?" He was still breathing heavily. "It couldn't be more than five minutes." He thought about it. "Come on Upal, think."

He inserted his leg through the window into the falls. He stretched and felt the other side. "They couldn't have passed me, there's not enough room." he mumbled. Then the thought occurred to him. What if they think I'm dead? Crowboy warned him not to go. What if he talked them into leaving.

"I have to go back up." He thought about it. He was completely sapped. He might be able to make it back up, but he couldn't do it without resting a while first. However long he'd been gone, it took everything out of him. It would be impossible to go back up right now.

"Hold on." Upal tried to talk things out with himself.

"They think I'm dead. Now what?" He sat on the ground keeping a close eye on the rapids passing by the window. "Will they come down if they think I'm dead? He kept talking to himself trying hard to organize his jumbled up thoughts. "One for all." He stood up and placed his hand in the waterfall. "Come on guys, I'm here." He tried hard to send them a thought transference.

He realized they might not make it. After all he was a good swimmer and he was barely able to make it. Now, he started to worry about their safety. He needed to let them know.

He shouted at the water pouring past the opening. "I made it, I made it!"

****

The trio waited and waited.

"It's been about ten minutes, what should we do?" Preet said worriedly.

"We're not leaving him alone. We know that. All for one." Lashra said quietly as she tried to evaluate the precarious situation.

Preet looked down at the water and said, "I'm going after him." and before Lashra could do anything, he'd stepped into the crevasse and was dragged down.

Preet hadn't thought about bracing himself against the wall to slow his descent. Be that as it may, his size hampered the water's efforts at dragging him down at a runaway speed. Eyes closed tightly he banged his way down from side to side.

From out of nowhere something grabbed hold of his hair. Preet tried to resist. It was Upal; he had both hands full of Preet's massive hairdo. Both of Upal's feet were braced against the wall. He pulled with every ounce of strength he had left in his tired body. At long last Preet's face made an appearance through the window. He dragged both arms into the room.

"You can let go now." Preet said calmly. Upal let go.

He shook his head to clear some of the water from his afro and made eye contact with his best friend. "Upal you're alive!" he shouted excitedly. "And I'm alive!"

Upal smiled, "Yes you are!"

Preet could see that Upal was visibly moved. Upal hugged Preet's giant head. "You risked your life for me?"

Preet reached around Upal's waist and hugged him in return.

Upal pushed himself away. "You almost broke my arms, you big lug."

Upal had thrown his arms into the waterfall and braced himself in hopes of catching the next person to come down and of all the stupid luck, it worked.

Lashra and Crawford were still in shock. "He's gone." she said.

"Ok." said Lashra "I'm not waiting any longer." She turned to Crawford, "Count to a hundred and then come join us." She paused for a moment and thought about what she had just said.

"If you want to." she said to him. She took a few deep breaths and then let herself be taken in.

"I'm doing it Ray." Crawford said to his feathered friend. "Sorry, buddy, but this is where we say goodbye."

"Looks like danger." Ray croaked out.

"This is a fine mess you've gotten me into Ray." Crawford was getting emotional. "Go, get out, go!" he shouted.

Upal had a hold of Preet's hands and was trying to pull him in. "What about the others?" he asked.

"You know how stubborn Lash… OUFFF!" he cried out. "Something's landed on me."

Lashra popped her head through the curtain of water and climbed off Preet who was eager to make his way into the cave.

"Way to put your body into that buddy." chuckled Upal. "That's one way to stop her."

"I can't believe we made it." she said.

"Come on, help me pull him out." Upal asked.

They each grabbed hold of one arm and pulled. "Careful!" cried Preet.

Then a thought popped into his head. "Actually, pull har... OUFFF!" Preet cried out. "Oh, come on already. Are you guys trying to kill me?"

"That wasn't so bad." Crawford said as soon as his head popped in the window.

"You were supposed to count to a hundred?" Lashra asked.

"I counted really fast?" Crawford said sheepishly as he finished climbing over Preet.

Preet reached out for a hand. "A little help please, before someone else lands on me."

With a little teamwork they managed to pull Preet through the window.

They all sat on the ground facing the falls watching the water power by.

"I can't believe we just did that." said Crawford.

"I just hope it was worth it." commented Upal.

A bright blast of light flashed in the cave. Their shadows burst for a fleeting moment on the wall ahead of them. Silence filled the room.

They had been so distracted with recent events that they hadn't taken notice of their surroundings. They turned to see what had caused the blast.

They were suddenly frozen, wide-eyed, open-mouthed, awestruck and speechless.

Chapter 58 Paladin

Lashra stood up and took a few steps forward. "Paladin..." her voice was filled with reverence. "the stories... they're all true." she mumbled out.

She gawked at the thirteen steps that led to a giant skeleton sitting on a throne, one that was very similar to the witch's. His left hand was firmly placed on a shield.

Lashra approached Paladin's throne with humility and respect. Her chest was tight, her hands were shaking, she hesitated for a moment and looked back.

The three boys couldn't decide whether to follow her or not. All three nodded their heads in harmony, silently encouraging her to keep going.

She swallowed hard. She forced her shaking body to move forward. Her heart was blasting, her hands were sweaty and her mind raced as she tried to process the situation.

She was mentally and physically exhausted. Step by step, she carefully moved forward until she reached the staircase that led up to Paladin's throne. She fell to her knees. The instant her hands landed on the first step, her mind was set on fire with ominous sounds and visions.

Sounds, smells, images. She was surrounded. Feelings, music, memory after memory, every moment of her life, past, present and future was being experienced at one and the same time. She bent her head down and closed her eyes trying to escape everything.

At that very instant, Paladin's sanctom was filled with thousands of dead souls, chanting and singing his praises. She recognized some of the sounds as an almost prehistoric language. She couldn't describe them, but she could feel their song. Tears of joy, of sadness, of anger and of anguish were flowing like waterfalls from her eyes. It was too much for her to take in.

She lifted her hands and covered her eyes. The immediate silence was deafening. She opened her eyes and saw Paladin. To her amazement, he was no longer a dried up thousand year old carcass.

He was a young man in his mid twenties (being Longevite he was probably about two hundred years old). He had long flowing maroon colored dreadlocks. His pale white eyes clashed with his skin. It was the color of the blackest, darkest night. His face was rugged and chiseled. He was a magnificent and flawless creature. She was mesmerized by his exquisiteness. She was fully absorbed by the man, the legend, the myth.

His eyes made contact with hers. She looked down, afraid of what she was seeing or maybe what she was imagining.

"Set your faith in the power of the shield." Paladin's deep bass voice resonated and lingered in the air. "Remember Lashra, it is not with or without but within."

She jumped when a hand touched her shoulder.

"You ok Lash?"

"What?" she asked Paladin.

She heard the familiar voice again "Are you ok?" She turned back to see Preet.

"Are you ok?" he repeated.

Lashra nodded unconvincingly. She turned back to see that Paladin had returned to a skeletal figure. Did he have more to say? The thought flashed through her mind.

Preet helped her up. "We should probably go up."

She raised her foot slowly and carefully put it on the first step. She waited. Nothing happened.

Upal clapped his hands, "Let's go, let's go, let's go!" he shouted. "Pick up the pace."

Lashra led the way up and the three boys followed a few steps behind.

She stood just inches away from the historical artifact. Paladin's hand rested on the shield, his head was slightly tilted down as if he were looking at something on the ground in front of him. She bowed her head and looked around, then noticed his right hand was clenched and his index finger seemed to be pointing to the floor. There was something etched on the floor at the base of his feet? She knelt down and brushed away the dust and dirt from the area.

Her face went flush and her blood was haunted by the presence of what she saw. Words. Mystical, prophetic words. She recited the foreboding words quietly and apprehensively.

"Altruism bestows you, death's defeat." She turned and motioned to the others to come closer so they could read the words for themselves.

The three boys came close and looked over her shoulder. Preet was confused. "How do you know that language?" he asked.

She looked up at him bewildered. "What are you talking about?" She looked back down at the script and realized she could no longer read the strange hieroglyphs.

"I could read it plain as day a moment ago." she said, a little rattled.

"It's ok," Crawford said. "This place is getting to all of us."

Lashra wasn't prepared to tell them everything she'd just seen and heard. It was all too much and so it would have to wait for another day.

"I can't believe we're this close to a piece of Pop's armor." Lashra took in a deep breath, "Aegis… safely guarded." she said as she reached out and ran her hand around the contour of the magical piece.

It was a golden color and it felt like gold should feel. It was two feet high and eighteen inches wide. There were four symbols going down the center of the shield. Lashra extended her arm and carefully traced the contour of each symbol.

The first three symbols were smaller than the fourth. Yet, all four symbols were similar in fashion. Each one was an unbroken Opal ring. In the center of each ring there was a vertical line made from the same Opal. It came up from the bottom and stopped half way up.

The first ring had one horizontal line attached at the top of the vertical one that went left. On its right, the line descended on a forty five degree angle.

The second ring had a line on its left going up at a forty five degree angle. Lashra's finger moved to the third symbol.

"She sure is taking her sweet time." Crawford cautiously mumbled.

Upal shrugged his shoulders.

Preet held the palm of his hand out. "It's getting pretty misty in here. I think it might rain."

Lashra was mesmerized and fell into a light trance. She was rounding the third symbol. Its vertical line went from top to bottom. From the center there was a forty five degree line ascending on its left.

The fourth stamp was four times the size of the others. Its ring radiated with glowing blue, green, orange, purple and red. It had one descending line on the left.

She removed her hand from the magical armor and studied her finger. In a strange way she envied it for having touched the precious armament. "I wonder what they stand for?" she uttered.

"How do you *not* know?" asked Crawford.

"I don't ever remember reading anything about symbols on the shield." she said.

"What should we do now?" Upal asked.

"I'm not sure? We need to take the shield with us but I'm not sure how we'll make it out of here." she said. "Let's investigate this hole in the ground and see if we can find another way out."

"We should split up." Crawford said.

Upal was already working on it. He figured there had to be an easier way out of this catacomb. The giant walls were filled with greenery from floor to ceiling, colorful and exotic flowers were growing everywhere. He pulled on some vines and looked behind them. He found nothing.

Lashra stood in the middle of the colossal room and looked up; she was sure she could see blue sky a mile above her head. To her left In the distance she made out a large waterfall that seemed to be coming from the sky.

"Look at that opening." she pointed up. "We must be standing in some kind of gargantuan volcano." She shouted out, "I wonder if we could somehow climb to the top?"

Upal joined her and looked up. "Even if the vines could hold our weight, it would take days to climb that high. We'd need to rest and what if we fell? The fall would kill us. I think our best chance is taking the shield and going through the window back up the falls."

"Let's keep that as our last option." she said.

Preet joined the two and looked up to see what was so interesting. There wasn't much to see. "There must be an exit somewhere," he said.

He turned and faced the Longevite's throne, "Look at how big he is." He pointed to Paladin. "There's no way he came in the same way we did."

They separated once more and continued looking. Lashra inspected the shrubs. Preet explored the greenery hanging on the walls. Upal inspected the rocks and Crawford pressed against the walls hoping to find a secret passageway, a door, a hole, anything. An hour later they were no closer to finding an exit.

Disappointedly Crawford said, "Seems like the water is our only way out."

"We should keep looking," Preet said nervously. "It might have been an easy trip for you two," he said, all bug-eyed. "After all, all you had to do was land on me. It's a pretty tight fit for me in there." He was getting a little jittery.

"I think *I* can make it back up." Upal stated.

"That's nice." Preet chirped.

"I wasn't done." Upal hissed. "We can rip some of the vines off the walls and use them as ropes. I'll take one end up with me, then when I get to the top I'll pull up the shield, then Lashra, then Crawford..."

"Wow, you called me Crawford."

"Sorry." Upal shot back. "Then *Crow Boy*, then Preet.

"Maybe we should go up in the same order we came down." Preet quickly interjected, "Oh, look that would make me number two. Well... fair is fair."

Upal shrugged his shoulders, "If you think I can pull you up all by myself I'm all for it."

Preet reached over and squeezed Upal's bicep between his index and thumb and quickly changed his mind. "I'll go last."

They went to work gathering up vines. They pulled off all the flowers and leaves and made sure they were all good and strong.

The four made their way to the opening. Lashra and Preet tied the ropes around Upal's waist.

"If I run out of breath before I make it up, I'll just let go and you guys can pull me back in and we'll figure something else out."

"I have an idea." Preet suggested. "What if we just go out the window and let the falls take us, maybe it's not that deep, maybe *that's* our escape? The water has to lead somewhere."

"What if it's miles away?" said Lashra. "I think we will try Upal's way first. If he doesn't make it back to the top, we can try your idea."

Upal put his hand in the water, "Here we go again." He climbed onto the window ledge. "Wish me luck." he said as he jumped in and started his way up.

Preet and Crawford held tight to the other end of the rope. Upal's plan of escape seemed to be working. Under the pounding pressure of the waterfall, he forced his way up. Using every ounce of strength he had he willed himself up inch by inch. Upal noticed how the walls were much less slimy since Preet and the others had gone through. It made his climb a little easier and much quicker than he'd expected. With his last breath of air escaping his lungs, he reached safety.

He was tired, his legs were burning and his arms were shaking from the stress of the climb. Even so, he wasted no time and pulled on the rope to let his friends know he had made it.

"He made it!" Preet exclaimed. "Ok, Lash, it's your turn."

She was just about to step in when she looked over at the throne. "The shield. I can't believe we almost forgot it."

Lashra ran back to Paladin's throne. She stopped at the stairs. She was actually going to do it; she was going to take hold of the shield. Her heart pounding, she ran up the stairs. She leaned in toward Paladin and picked up the shield.

As soon as the shield left his grip, water came gushing down from the top of the volcano covering all the walls on its way down. It came with such swiftness that by the time Lashra was half way down the steps, she was already standing in water.

Preet and Crawford bayed in unison, "Put it back!"

Both boys had the same instant hope, that returning the shield to its owner would halt the alluvion, this niagara that was about to take all of their lives. The water was already up to the boys' ankles and within a few seconds would be covering their only means of escape.

Lashra turned and ran back up the steps. The water was now up to Paladin's feet. She struggled to make her way through the water and back to his throne. In a panic she fell forward and threw the armament on the floor next to him, but nothing changed.

She watched as she slid back down the steps.

Preet and Crawford were terror-struck. Preet grabbed hold of Crawford and shook him frantically. "It didn't work! We're all going to drown! Do something!"

Lashra climbed and swam her way back up and in a last ditch effort placed Paladin's skeletal hand onto the shield. Instantly the inundation ceased. She waited to see if the water would recede. It did.

The large symbol on the shield began to glow. Its brightness was so great it turned the water crystal clear. The liquid became fully transparent and then as if by magic it vanished. It was all gone. Everything was dry, like it had never happened.

Lashra made her way back to the boys empty handed. "What was that?" she asked, obviously rattled by the experience. "Did that just happen?"

Preet nudged Crawford, "I told you it was going to rain."

"There is no way we can take the shield with us." said Lashra.

Crawford hemmed and hawed while rubbing his chin. "That was a crazy amount of water in a very short time." His voice was filled with trepidation.

Lashra agreed. "We'll be lucky if one of us makes it out of here alive with it."

"What if two of us go up now and one stays behind?" Preet suggested. "You said one of us could make it."

"I said we'd be lucky to make it."

Lashra felt heartsick. "Don't be crazy. The water would be ten feet over the window by the time any of us made it back with the shield. We were so close."

"We can't just leave it here!" Preet shouted in dismay.

Crawford took charge, "We'll have to come back. It's getting late, we're hungry, thirsty and tired. We know Upal survived the climb. Let's see if we can do the same. We need to get back up there and reassess the situation. There's no point in dying for nothing."

Lashra was completely discouraged. "We just can't leave without it."

Crawford put his hand on her shoulder, "We'll figure it out, Lashra. After all, you told me that the Old Lady won't let you down and that we need to trust her. Well... it's time to trust her."

Crawford's words sounded reasonable, but Lashra was having a hard time accepting them.

"Trust her now. We'll come back tomorrow." he said encouragingly.

"He's right Lash, we need to rethink our plan. We can't stay here. Let's see if we can even get out. We'll come up with something."

One by one they made their way back up the hammering waterfall and as they did they each filled Upal in with their side of the story. On the journey back to the outside world they discussed what could be done to rescue the shield. Each new idea was increasing in absurdity and zaniness. Half way through they fell into a tired silence. The four exhausted youths had only two things left on their minds, food and sleep.

"Looks like trouble." Ray's gargle echoed all around them. The bird flapped his large majestic wings with excitement. The orange light of dusk coming through the exit created a glowing halo around the beautiful bird.

They stepped out into the fresh night air.

"Look at that." Preet was the first to notice the pile of berries and nuts sitting next to the firepit. "You're quickly becoming my new best friend." He smiled at the bird as he ran to the food.

"Heyeh Hoop!" he said with a mouth full of everything available. He chewed once or twice then swallowed. "You should take notes. Ray could replace you soon."

"If I'm lucky." Upal retorted.

"You knew we'd make it back didn't you Ray?" Crawford said with a large smile.

They ate until they were full. Not long after, the four fell asleep where they sat. Preet fell asleep with his back against a large log. He was slightly curled around a stack of nuts he'd hoarded, *in case* he woke up hungry. Upal found a cozy spot just outside the entrance of the cave. Lashra had fallen asleep staring at the fire. She was half sitting and half laying. Crawford had not done much better. Somehow he'd fallen asleep leaning over a log, face first in the dirt.

The day had taken its toll on them.

Chapter 59 One More Night

"So soon?" Saudj mocked the sunrise.

"What the?" He was shocked at the size of his leg. The pain had steadied to a dull roar overnight. He hadn't noticed the swelling. "Can I even walk on this thing?" he said to himself.

He carefully worked his way to his feet and attempted to take a step. He swung his leg over and when it made contact with the ground an intense explosion of pain jetted through his body. He fell forward landing on the witch's lap.

He pushed himself up immediately and looked her square in the eyes. "This is all your doing isn't it?" He spit on the statue's face. He couldn't help but see the Old Lady's face mocking him. He bitterly turned away from her.

Not wanting to experience the shocking pain again, he literally dragged his foot around. Gently, slowly, he walked around the camp, hoping it would help reduce the blistering inflammation. "There's no way I'm going anywhere today." he said disappointedly.

He stopped next to the place where he'd found the berries the day before. He tried lowering himself to the ground carefully. His effort was futile. An excruciating, stabbing sensation brought him quickly to the ground.

"Ahh!" he screamed at the extreme and almost unendurable pain traveling through every nerve in his body. He lay motionless, jaw clenched, gripping tightly to his shirt. He groaned out in a momentary yet endless fit of agony. "I hate you!" he cried out to the Rubicon. His eyes closed. He passed out from sheer exhaustion.

Saudj slowly opened his eyes. The sun had moved up into the sky. He'd been out for a few hours. He was afraid to move. He turned his head to see an abundance of berries next to his corps. He reached over and picked at them.

After a few handfuls he worked up the courage to move. The swelling seemed to have gone down a bit. Although that could have been just wishful thinking.

"Ok." he said, working up his fortitude. "I can't stay here all day. Here goes."

He cautiously inched his way into the sitting position. He stopped for a while to revel in his accomplishment. He wasn't going to make it back onto his feet. He'd have to wait a little longer for that. Instead, he dragged himself on the ground filling up his lap with berries and collecting bits and pieces of burnables.

Hauling his way back to a stump next to his dying fire, he managed to lift himself onto a stump. He grabbed a wooden poker and nudged a few pieces of dying coal. His foot itched and he instinctively used the edge of the poker to delicately scratch his foot.

"Great," he said sarcastically. "Now I'm covered in soot."

He heard a sound coming from behind. He turned. It was just a couple of hummingbirds feeding from the witch's cap. Was he crazy or had the expression on her face changed?

"What are you smiling at?" he said with a death-stare. He turned his attention back to his blackened foot.

"Ah, what am I doing?" He attempted to clean it off but it wasn't worth the pain.

He noticed within a few minutes that areas covered in soot were itching less. He waited a little longer and noticed the swelling in those areas was also decreasing.

"What's the worst that can happen?" He said to his leg. So, he spent the rest of the day covering his leg with charcoal. By sunset the itching had subsided and the swelling was all but gone. Saudj was not ungrateful.

"I'll sleep well tonight." He turned to the witch and scowled. "Tomorrow I will discover the path they've taken and there's nothing you can do to help them."

He laid down on the ground and threw what little pieces of wood he had left on the fire. He moved in close and closed his eyes for the night.

Chapter 60 Let's Go

Lashra forced her tired eyes open and attempted to stretch out the kinks and pinches created by a night of dreadful half-sleep. "Phooey." she hushed.

She soundlessly floundered her way to the cave's entrance. She peered into the darkness and questioned whether she'd really lived through the previous day's events. She watched her long shadow disappear into the cave. She rolled her shoulders, massaged her neck and rubbed her lower back. The pain and cramps seemed to be getting worse. "What is wrong with me?" she mumbled.

She did her best to ignore the pain. "What are we going to do?" Her question bounced off the walls.

She thought about Paladin's words. "Set your faith in the power the shield provides. It is not with or without but within" Was it possible she had imagined his coming to life? Of course it was possible.

"What am I supposed to do with *Altruism bestows you, death's defeat?*" she whispered inside the cave, hoping her words would reach Paladin and that somehow he would whisper the answer in her ear.

Her mind swirled with ideas. She broke down every word from Crawford's vision. Yet, she still couldn't grasp how to unlock them. She desperately wanted to find their meaning.

Lashra stepped a few feet into the cave and stretched out her rusty body on a soft patch of hard dirt. Her lower back was aching and she found it hard to ignore. The cramps in her abdomen had returned and the nausea that followed made her question her food choices. Something wasn't right. She figured she'd question the others about their wellness when they woke up.

She had no plans to disturb their sleep. Why wake them? She thought to herself. After all there's no rush to get things started. They knew what they had to do, but had no idea how to do what they knew they should do.

She stared at the ceiling. "Altruism bestows you, death's defeat. Altruism bestows you, death's defeat." The soft sound of her voice gently echoed back in a dreamy rhythmic fashion. "Altruism bestows you, death's defeat." She kept repeating the mantra. She enjoyed the effects the cave had on her words; it was a melodious and pleasing warble.

"Hey." Preet said quietly, trying not to startle her from her zen-like state.

She jumped.

"Sorry, I was trying *not* to scare you." he said sleepily. He looked around the cave searchingly. "Where's Oop?"

"What?" Her mood shifted immediately.

"I thought I'd find Oop in here with you."

"I'm pretty sure he's still out there sleeping?" She thought about it and realized she hadn't seen him.

"No, Crawford's out there alone. Oop passed out in that shrub by the entrance." He pointed to the area.

She bolted up and out of the cave. "Upal?" she shouted. "Upal!" She looked around. There was no trace of him. "Upal!" she cried out again. "Where could he have gone?"

"Quiet down, some of us are still trying to sleep." Crawford mumbled, still half asleep and still in the same awkward position.

Preet walked over and gently kicked him. "Get up, Upal's gone."

"What? There's nowhere to go." he said, closing his eyes.

Lashra and Preet went back into the cave. She cried out his name. The sound of her voice came echoing back, but this time the reverberations sounded urgent and despondent. A light flashed behind her. She turned toward the entrance.

"Upal you had us worried." She sounded like an upset mother.

But it wasn't Upal, it was Crawford. Her heart sank as she watched him laggardly making his way into the cave. He shook his head signaling that Upal was nowhere to be found.

Lashra's eyes grew wide. "He went back for the shield alone." She hung her head and shook it perturbedly. "Why would you do that?"

"Buggeration!" Preet angrily punched his fist into his hand.

"Always trying to be a hero." Crawford uttered. "He really is about as smart as he is tall."

Neither paid attention to his remarks.

"How long do you think he's been gone?" Crawford grunted out.

"I was up a couple of hours before you two." She sounded worried. "It could be three hours or more. We need to go after him."

Chapter 61 Faster

"Grab what you can!" she shouted. "We need to get moving."

They ran out and gathered a pocket full of nuts, a couple of torches and some extra moss.

"We need to make up time. At least we know where we're going." Crawford said, trying to reassure the two.

He might not have liked Upal much, but he knew Preet and Lashra would do anything for him and that was enough for him. He took the lead and made haste.

They arrived at the mushroom shaft much sooner than they anticipated. This time, Preet didn't argue about going down. In fact, he descended first and was quick to encourage the others to pick up the pace.

From out of the blue they felt a tremor. "That's new." Preet said nervously.

The tremor was followed by a stronger shake and accompanied with a thick mist coming from below.

"*This* does not feel right." Lashra's apprehensiveness was noticeable.

The earth convulsed again. Preet lost his footing. Lashra reached over to hold on to him but it was too late.

"Ahhhhhhhhh!" Preet fell into the crevasse.

"Preeeeet!" Lashra screamed. All she could do was watch as he dropped out of view. She braced herself against the wall. Crawford moved in close and put his arm around her, holding her against the wall.

The earth trembled again. Lashra was afraid to look down.

"Wooohooo!" she heard a scream coming from the pit. "Preet?"

Yes, of course it was Preet. She was so happy.

While Preet was descending the deep tube, the giant mushroom cap was making its way up it. As good fortune would have it, the hole was filling up with water, pushing the large fungus to the top.

"Jump on before it crushes you against the wall!" he shouted up.

The ride was picking up speed. Lashra and Crawford jumped on the cap and within seconds the mushroom top came to a sudden stop. It threw the three travelers twenty feet into the air and away from the hole. All three were in for a rough landing.

"Wooo! Hooo!" exclaimed Preet in mid air. Then came the ground. "Ah! That hurt."

He laid there on the ground for a moment. "That definitely did not happen yesterday!"

Unfazed they ran back to the hole in the ground. The cap was gone. A few seconds later it reappeared.

"Here it comes again!" Lashra yelled above the sound of rushing water.

It made a sudden stop, this time a little higher up the tube. The cap was beginning to warp and bow. Crawford realized what was about to happen.

"The pressure's building," he said with a panic. "this thing is going to buckle under the pressure." His face went pale. "She's gonna blow! Run!"

Without hesitating they turned toward the exit and ran. Lashra and Crawford quickly outpaced Preet. The cave was now in a constant state of rumbling and shaking. The loudness of the reverberations was jarring and unnerving.

Lashra turned back to see Preet on the ground. She cried out above the sounds, "We have to move out! We need to leave! Get up!"

"I'm trying Lash!" he yelled at her.

Lashra hollered more warnings. "We need to get out of here, it's getting worse!"

"Yes, I know!" he shouted back at her. "Thanks for constant updates."

He got up and ran past Lashra who was waiting for him. She followed him close. A thick mist unexpectedly covered the entire area. She peeked back to see a tsunami approaching.

"Oh Buggeration!" she exclaimed.

When Preet heard her scream he knew not to look back. "This is no time to trip and fall." he said to himself.

The exit was within reach. They ran out and braced themselves against the wall outside the mouth of the cave. They watched and waited for the rush of water to end. But it didn't end. They covered their ears to block out some of the thunderous sounds escaping the cave. The giant mouth spewed its water with a vengeance, jetting and gushing with an immeasurable force. The water made its way through the long tunneled path ripping through and dragging debris down the shaft they had traveled through a couple of days before.

When it reached the small opening with the tightly intertwined root walls, it swirled and climbed up to the sky with an immense force and pressure until it exploded like a geyser.

In the distance they heard and saw a giant water volcano erupting. The water, the mist, the debris, it went up and up and up. It roared like a mythical beast with the sounds of a thousand trumpets. It was so massive that it blocked out the sun's light. They watched in awe as day turned into night.

The mouth of the entrance vomited water, until it was completely eviscerated. As quickly as it started, it stopped. A heavy and sustaining easterly wind dispersed the heavenly waters and light returned.

Carefully turning their heads in to peek, they saw to their amazement barely a drop of water on the floor.

"What should we do?" asked Preet.

He didn't wait for the others to respond. He made his way back in. There was no time to waste, they had to find him. They needed to find him and find him quickly.

After a distance, Preet was huffing and puffing. He slowed to a fast paced walk.

"He must have tried to get the shield on his own. There's no way he could have survived this." His voice was filled with sorrow. "Lashra? What if Upal was the *one* to die?" he wiped tears from his eyes.

"What?" Crawford asked.

"The Old Lady said, *one* must die to save all. What if it was Upal?" Preet choked out.

Lashra growled at him. "Don't talk like that. He's alive. If anyone is stubborn enough to withstand something like this, it's Oop."

She started running again. "Hurry!" she yelled back.

Filled with fear and sadness they accelerated their pace.

Chapter 62 Upal's In

Upal tossed and turned most of the night. He'd been stuck in a loop and kept reliving the same dream over and over. In the dream, Lashra, Crowboy and Preet were running away from him. They were yelling but he couldn't make out what they were saying. They stopped and turned around. Then he saw Preet disappear into a crack in the ground. Lashra and Crowboy followed Preet down and… Upal would wake up.

He looked up to the stars, "There's still a few hours before daylight." he said disappointedly. "I should try to get some more rest." he mumbled quietly to himself.

He closed his eyes and after a brief moment realized there was no way he could rest. There was a reason he couldn't sleep any longer. The dream, it was a sign. A couple of hours of broken up sleep would have to be enough. He knew there was no plan that could get the four of them out safely with the armor in tow. This was a one person job. Drawing to see who got the short straw? That was a bad idea. He knew he was the best person for this caper.

He grabbed a torch and made his way through the cave. "I can bring the shield back before they get up." he tried to convince himself. "With no one to slow me down, I can make my way in record time."

His mind raced as fast as he did. It felt like only minutes had passed, yet there he was soaking wet and standing at the bottom of the staircase, staring at Paladin.

"Hello my old friend." he spoke playfully to him.

He cautiously made his way up the staircase. His heart was a tight, painful beating drum. Upal stared back and forth from Paladin to the shield, the shield to Paladin. Was he really going to do this? He moved in a little closer to Paladin.

"*You* did it. You sacrificed your life so that my ancestors might live. That I might live. Your life is celebrated. As a small boy I often played the part of the great Paladin."

Upal raised his arm replaying the game. He protected himself from the fictional arrows, using his make believe shield. As he did, he recited Paladin's Parnassus.

"Paladin had a vision
Away from here to go
Left with the shield, held it tight
Arrows they did follow
Defended us
Imprisoned for me
Now I'm filled with sorrow"

"We all played the parts, we all wanted to be like the greats. But those were just games. Now look at us. Look at me." Upal was losing heart. "I need you to fill me with courage, help me get this done. How did you do it?"

He waited. Maybe, he thought, just maybe… but nothing.

"You know you could be a little more encouraging." he said to Paladin.

"Ok, what's my goal?" he asked Paladin. Upal answered himself. "Bring the shield to the surface." He tried to reach for it, but his body was frozen in place. "Come on Upal!" he shouted, trying to shake himself free of his fears. "All I have to do is make it to the surface. If worse comes to worse…" he didn't finish the thought.

"One must die to save all." The sound of the Old Lady's voice reverberated throughout the chamber.

"You're not helping!" he shouted out.

His hands were shaking as he reached out. Fear encompassed his entire being. "This is not the time to start thinking before you act." He let out a primitive "Yalp!"

True to himself, he proceeded without thinking, he grabbed the shield and ran as fast as possible, trying not to drop it; he kept his eyes glued on the hostile exit.

"Just make it to the window." he encouraged himself.

By the time he reached the bottom step, the water was waist high. He grunted, "One step at a time. One step at a time." he kept repeating as he struggled and trudged through the ever deepening waters.

He approached the raised floor that sat under the window. "Well, Lashra you were right." He shouted over the blasting sound of the falls, "I am now officially neck deep in trouble!"

By the time he reached the ledge, the water was over his head and only a few feet away from the overhang. The shield was weighing him down. He swam up toward the pocket of air hoping for a few final breaths of air. He was too late. He let the shield drag him down to the landing.

In a state of nerves he blindly hunted for the opening. One more puff of air, if only he could've gotten one more. He found the window in no time flat. He dragged himself and the armament through the hole.

He longed for air. Climb Upal, climb! his mind screamed.

A small volume of air escaped from his lungs. The downward pressure hadn't eased at all, in fact it seemed to be worse than before. The unrelenting force of the water pounded the shield. The burden was too great. The shield's size and weight made it difficult for him to move. The walls were closing in on him. He was suffocating.

Another bubble of air left his lips. Am I sinking? Panic. Terror. He clawed the walls in vain. Yes, he was sinking. Anxiety. Dread. Air, get to air, his mind could no longer hold a clear thought.

He conjured up images of dead bodies piling on top of his. His friends would also try to rescue the shield. He blew out the remainder of the oxygen he had in his body. Exhaustion overtook him, he couldn't even slow himself down anymore. He accepted that he was sinking, the downward pressure from the falls was too much to bear. He was utterly depleted, and wanted nothing more than to close his eyes and sleep.

He needed to live. He wanted to live. He attempted to stop his downward motion but he was wasted. The struggle was quick and futile. He stopped fighting. His arm was trapped in the straps of the shield and it pulled him down.

Impressions of Preet filled his mind's eye, everything they had been through, across the years. Fantasies of Lashra, her smile, her eyes, their wedding day, their children, their life together. Images of his mother, his brother, his father. Even the likeness of Mrs. Nibbledent and her slipper crossed his path. The Old Lady... her image stayed with him for the longest of moments. Then Paladin. Not the skeletal broken image he'd last seen but the young hero he'd always imagined. (The same Paladin Lashra saw the day before.)

Paladin put his hand on Upal's shoulder, looked him in the eyes and said, "Altruism will bring you death's defeat."

Upal had a moment of lucidity. He realized at that moment that he was fulfilling both prophecies: *One must die to save all, and altruism brings death's defeat. They were really the same prophecy*. His death would save them from having to die. He finally understood. No longer able to resist, his lungs and mind gasped for air. Upal inhaled only water.

The pain.

His lungs were being filled and smothered with water and it was excruciating. His body clenched and all the suffering that was being inflicted on him was gone. He smiled in that moment and let go of everything, Upal accepted his fate. Everything went white, the brightest purest white light one has ever seen or could ever imagine. It brought with it a sense of peace. He sent out a prayer for his friends. Then he was gone.

As if it wasn't enough that he was dead, the current savagely and without mercy grabbed hold of his body and dragged it downward. It slammed his limp body against the stone foundation and with all the vengeance it could muster, it whipped the boy's carcass back and forth using his lifeless corpse to sweep the base of the catacomb.

Chapter 63 Lost And Found

Upal and the shield were transported through a long dark conduit that abruptly came to a dead end. The two slammed against the wall coming to a blunt stop.

Instantly, he was sucked up by its powerful force. The two objects went straight up twenty, possibly thirty feet. With great vigor the water spewed him up from a hole in the floor. It had done it with such intense authority that, had he been alive, this alone would surely have killed him. The mighty jet of the water kept Upal's body cornered against the ceiling and a protruding wall.

Water was flowing from everywhere. It breathed out from all surfaces of the cavern. It bled from every nook and cranny; the discharge was unstoppable. Floodwaters pounded every inch of the cave. It was an overwhelming, unconquerable and irreversible deluge.

If the magical substance had been put there to protect the shield, it was fulfilling its duty with apocalyptic might.

The cataclysmic event came to a sudden stop. As if possessed, the cavern resolved to rid itself of every drop of water. Upal's ragdoll body dropped to the floor. As if in a single-minded effort to bleed the enchanted cavern of every drop of water, even from Upal's lifeless body, he began to have violent seizures. His body spewed out every last drop.

****

Hours had passed…

"There he is!" Lashra screamed as she ran toward Upal. She fell to her knees and rolled him over. His arms were still trapped within the straps of the shield. The large piece of armor covered him like a blanket. She lifted his head and gently placed it on her lap. She wept.

Overflowing with emotions she erupted in anguish and anger. She pounded his chest and berated him. "You dimwitted fool!" she cried out. "Why did you do this? It's not enough for us to lose the Old Lady?" She struck him again. "Why? Her shouting turned into a whimpering sob. "All for one Upal, all for one." She continued to beat his chest.

Preet seized her arm. "Stop it." he said, tears streaming down his face. "Stop it." He fell next to his sister. "He did this for us." As he spoke the shield let off a soft glow. "He knew we had to continue. He knew what he was doing."

She looked up at her brother and muttered, "Three arrive, three survive, three…"

Preet was confused.

"Those were her final words to me." she said as tears continued to stream down her face.

Crawford knelt down at Upal's feet. He shook his head in disbelief. He leaned over and placed his hand on the shield. "The last line," he whispered. "Altruism bestows you…" He choked up.

"Death's defeat." A hoarse murmur cut Crowboy off in mid sentence.

"You're alive!" Lashra and Preet shouted.

Upal attempted to open his eyes and speak again but his tired, battered body was fighting for air. After a few minutes of Lashra and Preet fussing over Upal, Crawford made his way to Upal's side. He smiled as he reached down and tousled his hair.

"You really are as smart as you are tall." he said, shaking his head in wonder. "But I do have to admit," he paused, as a large grin took over his face. "You're also as brave as you are short."

They all laughed.

"You did it!" Crawford said.

"We did it." Upal forced out the words with a hack. "Well, mostly me." he said. "Mostly I did it." He closed his eyes and his head fell to the side.

Lashra shook him in a panic, "Upal wake up, wake up."

"Stop it, I'm tired and sore. Let me just rest here a little bit longer." he said with a weak smile.

Even half dead, Upal could still find a way to enjoy resting his head on Lashra's lap.

As if reading his best friend's mind, "Only because you're too weak to try anything." Preet interjected.

Lashra smiled. She was happy to be holding him, happy that he was alive. She couldn't imagine life without both Preet and Upal. Holding him like this, stroking his hair, she felt something. She wasn't sure what it was. So, she passed it off as cramps and indigestion. The thought made her laugh on the inside and her smile grew wider.

"What's so funny?" Preet caught his sister's smile.

"Just another crazy day in the Rubicon." she said.

"You were dead Upal. Did you know that?" Preet nudged him gently with his foot.

"Dead?" He looked up and met Lashra's eyes. "But I'm alive."

All of a sudden, looking into his eyes made her feel self-conscious. She quickly got up and Upal's head hit the ground. "Ahhh!" he grunted.

"Come on Preet help me get him up." she said, slightly flustered.

They reached down and took him by the arms, gently lifting him up. His legs were weak and unstable. Crawford walked over and placed himself between Lashra and Upal. Lashra lifted Upal's arm and tenderly placed his hand on Crawford's shoulder.

"I'll help you until you get your feet under you." Crawford said.

He placed his arm around Upal's waist and held him to keep him on his feet.

"I'll be fine." Upal said as he attempted to remove his arm from Crawford's shoulder but he found the task to be quite challenging. "Well, maybe the first few feet."

Preet picked up the shield and placed his arms through the leather straps. *Clang,* the armor hit the wall.

"Be careful with that Preet, I had to die to get that thing."

"But not really though, because you are alive." Crawford was more than happy to point out that fact.

Miraculously Upal had no broken bones, although he was severely battered and bruised. The long trek back to the outside world took a considerable amount of time.

Preet, Lashra and Crawford all took turns assisting Upal on his journey. They stopped multiple times along the way to allow him to rest and recover.

"Light," Upal nodded toward the exit. "Finally. I can make it out on my own."

"Two and half steps away and *now* he can do it on his own." Crawford laughed rhetorically.

Thankfully Preet caught Upal just outside the exit. Two and a half steps was almost unbearable. He delicately helped his friend to the ground and made him as comfortable as he could.

Crawford stretched out and kicked back near the edge of the cliff. He saw a beautiful canopy of green; the morning fog had long lifted. They were so high up that the tops of the trees below looked like rolling grass.

He turned toward the gang and quipped, "I have to say, after everything we've gone through in the last few days, salvaging Paladin's shield was rather anticlimactic."

"What? Need I remind you I died for that shield?" Upal uttered out in dismay. "Tell him Preet."

Crawford had a faint smile as he continued with his erroneous comments, "I'm just saying, if that's the best that the Rubicon can throw at us, I think we'll be fine."

"Preet?" Upal wanted a little help from his best friend. "Can you remind this guy" he said as he exhaustedly nodded his head in Crawford's direction, "of my tragic death?"

"But Oop, you're still alive." He chuckled and gently shoved Upal, who was too weak to hold himself up and just fell over.

"I guess *dying* is just another thing you're not good at Upal." Crawford said as he turned away laughing.

"Leave him alone guys. He's been through enough today." Lashra said in a disapproving tone. "Here you go. Eat up. These berries will help with the bruising and your recovery."

Upal moaned out, "A couple of momes, that's what they are. Just a couple of momes." He ate a few berries then closed his eyes and fell asleep.

Preet was about to shake him awake when Lashra stopped him. "Leave him alone. He needs to rest. He's going to need all day and night to have any chance of making it back tomorrow."

"Back to where?" asked Preet.

"Back to the witch, I guess?" she responded. "Upal's in no shape to climb down a cliff and that's about the only other choice we have. Now that we have the shield..." she stopped in mid sentence.

She wasn't sure what to do and neither Crawford nor Preet were offering up suggestions.

"Maybe we wait for another vision?" Preet suggested.

Lashra was weary and sore and starting to feel grumpy. "I'm getting a little sick and tired of this whole situation. What was the Old Lady thinking of, sending us into the Rubicon?"

Preet could hear her exasperation. "You're right." He opened his arms wide and embraced her in a giant hug.

"There's no point going farther. He needs his rest and we can all use a few hours without excitement."

They took their turns admiring the shield. The shape, the metal, the colors, the symbols. It was all so surreal.

Nightfall was approaching and they decided to take no chances, someone had to stay awake just in case. Crawford drew the short straw and therefore he would keep first guard. Upal, who had spent the entire day sleeping, would continue his well deserved rest and get the night off.

"My eyes are starting to burn, I need to shut them for a while." said Preet. "Three hours comes quickly."

Within seconds they were asleep. Crawford sat with Ray warming his back by the fire. "Thanks for always being there little buddy. You truly are my best friend." He smiled and petted the raven. "Well, at least now you're not my only friend."

Crack, the sudden sound was unnerving in the silence of the night.

Crawford held his breath and turned his ear toward the sound. He carefully and quietly got up to light a torch. Waving it high above his head he lit up as much of the area as possible.

"Did you hear that? he whispered loudly to Ray. He looked over at the bird. Ray's back was hunched over, his beak pointing at the ground; he too was fast asleep. "Great. Forget everything I said about being my best friend."

With trepidation he made his way silently and slowly toward the sound he thought he heard. I hope nothing jumps out at me, he thought to himself. A sense of horror began to fill him, a chill ran through his body and he could feel every hair standing on end. He moved the flame around to see if he could see anything or hopefully scare away anything that could possibly be out there.

He stopped and listened for a minute. He breathed a sigh of relief. It must have been my imagination. He peered to his left and his right and could see nothing out of sorts, although his heart and stomach said something completely different.

Content with the fact that he found nothing out there, he retraced his steps backwards when suddenly something grabbed his foot and dragged him to the ground. A sense of horror filled him, terror stabbed his heart. He looked around in a panic and realized he'd tripped over the log he'd been sitting on. His body felt numb.

He put his hand over his heart and massaged the aching muscle. "Buggeration this place is driving me to madness." he hissed to himself.

He wondered if all the commotion was enough to have woken the others. It wasn't.

"I won't have to worry about falling asleep tonight." he spoke quietly but also loudly enough to be heard by whoever or whatever was out there listening. He did whatever he could to comfort himself.

He held his breath and turned his ear once again to a soft sound coming from the tunnel's direction. What was murmuring out there? Was it the wind or a large flying insect that glows? Or, or, or, he was too frightened to continue his thought. No, it was just his overworked and tired imagination. That's all it was, he tried to convince himself. He thought about waking up the others but he could already hear Upal's voice lamenting.

"I died and you woke us up because you heard a noise?"

That was enough incentive to let them sleep.

He sat for a short time in silence, thinking of the most horrible things that might happen to him if he didn't stay alert. Then he tried hard to think of comforting thoughts. He would have taken *any* comforting thought.

"Ahh yes," he spoke out loud to himself, trying hard to forget the self-perceived horror of his situation. "What was Lashra saying earlier about the Scrolls of Tralatitious? What was it she said? They were never seen again?" The thought discouraged him.

"She could've ended that lesson on a more positive note. Maybe I should wake her up and ask her what happened next?"

Chapter 64 Saudj's End

"Where am I?" Saudj's voice echoed. He was in the unknown, surrounded by the purest blackness he'd ever experienced. A strange yet delicate buzzing sound surrounded him. He carefully stretched out his arms and spun slowly in place trying to feel for something, anything that might help him figure out where he'd landed. "Where am I?" he repeated.

He took a small step to one side and his hand felt a monstrous slimy something. He quickly removed his hand and wiped it on his shirt. "That was creepy." he muttered softly.

Carefully waving his arms in front of himself he took a step. Suddenly a light went off in his face. He instinctively flailed his arms and struck an object. The light started blinking on and off a few times then the glow remained permanent and steady. It was a Luciferin.

"Not this again?!"

He waited for a moment preparing himself for the imminent attack. But it never came. Why was it here? Why was he here? The insect regained flight and moved forward on some kind of path. Saudj squinted, trying to see where it was going. The creature's light was only able to illuminate a small area at a time.

"Where are you leading me?" he questioned the Luciferin.

It stopped in mid flight and turned around. Saudj jumped back in terror. He tripped over his own feet and fell to the ground. He looked up at its sinister face as it approached him. He couldn't fully make it out in the darkness. The glow became so intense it lit up the entire area. It couldn't be?

"I must be dreaming. This has to be a dream!" he cried out. "No, not you!?"

He tried to convince himself it was all a dream. Saudj closed his eyes but the image bore down on him. He could feel it, the Luciferin had stopped and hovered only inches from his face. He could feel the breath of air created by the flying nightmare. He uncovered his eyes and came face to face with him.

It was Upal. He was forcefully staring into his eyes. Saudj was dumbfounded. He could see the shield in the glint of Upal's eyes. Like a shot, Upal the Luciferin repeatedly stung his nemesis. Saudj was defenseless and screamed in agony.

"Ahh! Uhh?!" Saudj was jolted from his nightmare. He sat up, batting his arms, trying to rid himself of the monster. He looked around in a state of shock, slowly coming to the realization that it had been a nightmare.

"He did it, he found the shield." Saudj was still stunned by the trauma.

He looked to the sky. The sun would be up in a matter of an hour or so. He wasn't going back to sleep. He got up and was grateful for the lack of pain. He hobbled around the camp in search of fuel for his fire. He made his way back and threw a few pieces onto the coals. He bent down and blew. After a few puffs the fire was going. He got up and fell back from the dizziness.

He sat and stoked the fire a little. The flames had disappeared. Just as he was about to bend down and resume blowing, a gentle westerly breeze made its way through the camp and reignited the flames.

"Your shield." the wind whispered. It was scarcely perceptible and Saudj was sure he had imagined it.

The clear sky brought with it a rather warm start to his day. He sat staring into the fire; he couldn't seem to shake the image of Luciferin Upal from his mind's eye.

"Something strange is going on, I can feel it in my bones."

He rose and walked around the camp again. He gathered whatever goodies he could find to fill the hole in his belly. The sun beamed its light into the camp, hitting the scrolls that lay by the fire. He'd had them all this time and didn't bother to read them.

He struggled to remember why he'd even grabbed them. There were thousands of pages in the Old Lady's library. Why was she holding these that fateful night? He held them up and was about to throw them in the fire. He stopped himself. He unrolled them and grabbed a page and read a random passage.

"They vanished into the Rubicon and the remaining Longevites called out to everyone. "Today we start a new chapter in the history of Eternal. Let us never forget all the tragedies that we have withstood in the recent past. Our brothers, sisters, mothers, fathers and children, yes, even our own selves have been damaged and destroyed, because of our lawlessness.

Our transgressions have doomed three blameless souls to the Rubicon. This day in our history should never be disregarded. Every year at this time, we shall celebrate for three days the lives of those who died for us. Today and for the next two, we shall unite in peace and friendship in the Celebration of Liberation."

Saudj was convinced that some things in the scrolls had to be true. After all, there were days ordained to commemorate the historical events. But the magic and myths of Demorg and his blasphemies? Those stories were added to keep his people down, to enslave their minds and their souls. That he was sure of.

"I should've burned the whole place down." he said as he threw the scrolls on the ground; at that moment the earth shook. Saudj braced himself. The rumbling only lasted a few seconds. He immediately grabbed the scrolls and tucked them away.

Unharmed, he toured the camp once more. He looked high and low, trying to figure out where those darn kids could've gone. "There's got to be a trace of them somewhere."

He stopped in mid step, the same soft buzzing sound from his dream had returned. No, it wasn't a buzz, it was more of a *purr, a hiss*. He forced himself to focus and to listen attentively. It was an indistinct continuous whispering sound.

"What is that?" He turned his ear to the sound and closed his eyes to help reduce the distractions. Whatever was causing the sound, he was sure that it wasn't good.

Saudj got up and walked towards the sound. He was standing directly in front of the Angry Widows. The earth beneath his feet shook and rumbled again. The sound returned and it seemed to be coming from somewhere in the flowers direction. He looked down and noticed a bit of a rut under the flowers.

"Hmmf. I knew I'd find you."

He bent down to take a look under the Golden Flowers and sure enough, there was the trail he was looking for.

"Trying to sneak out of here are you?"

He started to question why they would choose to crawl out. Did they know they were being followed? It didn't make any sense. He peered deep into the underbrush and then noticed the hissing sound had turned into a rushing sound. A wave of water appeared and it was close-at-hand. He turned and ran with a painful limp.

He fell to the ground a short distance away. He watched in awe as the wave destroyed the path. It crashed up against the witch's throne, shattering it to bits and pieces. Saudj was completely covered with debris yet he felt he was out of danger. He thought it remarkable that the wave magically stopped where the throne once sat. In that same instant the sky grew dark and the day had turned to night. Then out of the blue the light returned, bringing with it a heavy mist.

And just like that the water was gone and a clear path lay ahead of him.

"If I had to guess... I'd say they went this way."

He made his way through and soon found himself climbing up and up and up. About half way through the tunnel he was exhausted and decided to rest. He closed his eyes and soon he was asleep.

He woke up and wasn't sure how long he'd been asleep. The tunnel seemed much darker than before. He needed to get a move on. A few hours later he found himself walking out of the tunnel in the dead of night.

He looked up and could just make out the moon through the canopy. He decided to move forward with hopes of finding a good resting place for the night. A few feet into his journey he spotted twinkling lights. Was it more of those futile glowing bugs? He quietly moved in for a closer look.

Saudj heard an unfamiliar sound by the twinkling lights. He was too close. He stepped back and...

Crack... Saudj stopped and took a deep breath. The sound of the snapping branch under his foot echoed throughout the Rubicon and it paralyzed him with fear. Oh no, I've been exposed; his thoughts were barely audible over the blasts of his pounding heart, a fresh sense of terror reared up within him.

He saw a light in the not too far distance, it was high and it was moving back and forth. Then he saw a large dark shadowy figure that seemed to grow and shrink with every move. It held light and it was coming for him, he didn't dare move.

What have I done? His panic increased with every step the shadow took. Why did I get so close? The thoughts were screaming in his head. His eyes widened with alarm.

Somehow he had been lulled into a false sense of security brought on by the flickering firelight and the faint crackling and snapping sounds of the fire. His aloneness had gotten to him, and now it had drawn him in close, much too close, dangerously close. If only he could get out of this situation, he swore he would not be this careless again.

"Did you hear that?" A strange sense of relief fell over Saudj, as he heard the voice.

It's human, he thought to himself, at least I have a chance. He realized it wasn't Preet or Upal's voice that he'd heard. Could there be survivors like himself roaming the forest? Did this stranger know that his friends were in here? Was he working with them, plotting against him?

Saudj heard the footsteps moving away from him. The man hadn't traveled far and Saudj realized how close he was to their camp. I need to see it. I need to see who's there. "Be careful Saudj, move slowly, thoughtfully. Don't make a sound." he unknowingly mumbled to himself.

He moved deliberately and without a sound. He approached the clearing and could see the stranger warming his hands by the fire. He took another step needing to get a closer look. *Crack...* not again. He stopped.

Saudj could see them. Preet and Upal, one on each side of the fire. Where was Lashra? She must be on the backside, he thought. Then, as if by magic he laid his eyes on the shield.

"They did it. They found the shield, they really did it." he mumbled quietly.

Then he heard the stranger's voice again.

"What was Lashra saying earlier about the Scrolls of Tralatitious? What was it she said? They were never seen again? She could've ended that lesson on a more positive note. Maybe I should wake her up and ask her what happened next?"

Saudj did everything he could not to move. He was stuck. Now he had to figure out how much time he would have to stand there before he could make his move and leave.

It was going to be a long night.

Chapter 65 Upal's Window

Mrs. Nibbledent sat on the large trunk darning the mattress cover. It was hard to imagine that the children had been with her less than a week. The thought brought a smile to her face. She could not recall a time she'd felt more fulfilled or satisfied.

She paused from her task at hand for a moment and peacefully listened to the voices coming from the street below. She listened as the children sang and skipped rope in time with their rhymes.

"Paladin had a vision
Away from here to go
Left with the shield, held it tight
Arrows they did follow
Defended us
Imprisoned for me
Now I'm filled with sorrow"

The song brought back memories of another Longevite. It was so surreal that the Old Lady was dead. She'd been murdered; it was so strange, otherworldly.

Mrs. Nibbledent was unexpectedly shaken off the trunk by a powerful tremor. Luckily she'd fallen on the mattress next to the trunk. She rolled off as quickly as her old body would let her. She scrambled to her feet and she stumbled her way to Upal's window (as the children had come to know it).

She looked down and was relieved to see that the children were safe and sound.

"What's going on?" the oldest child (her name was Culy) cried up from the street below.

Mrs. Nibbledent's eyes were gaping and unblinking, her mouth wide open and her arm was stretched out pointing westward. Terror seemed to thunder down on her.

Something must be happening near the Rubicon, thought Culy.

The woman tried to utter a sound that would convey what she was seeing but nothing came out. A monstrous waterspout was jetting out of the Rubicon. It flowed endlessly up, filling the sky with all types of debris. As it reached its pinnacle it spread out like a giant mushroom. Day turned to night.

Everyone in Eternal who witnessed the event fell to their knees. The daylight slowly returned with the help of a breeze coming from the Rubicon. Soon the entire city was covered with a thick murky mist. Everyone recognized the moment as a fulfillment of some kind of prophecy. Most likely one that involved the murder of the last known Longevite.

Without a second of delay people began explicating the sign of the times.

The North Gate untangled the event and told its people that it was the Old Lady sending a message to the world. She had found her murderer and had passed judgment on him. The release of water was a sign. She was free and not even the Rubicon could hold her back. The dark mist that fell over the city was a remnant of the transgressor's burial.

The South Gate instructed its people that they should see it as a sign that the return of Demorg was imminent. The Old Lady was the only thing stopping his return. With her murder (obviously planned by Demorg), he was now able to return and finish what he'd started thousands of years ago. The earthquake and the explosion of water was a warning to them that Demorg had retrieved the armor and murdered all Longevites. The thick mist that covered the city was symbolic of the Longevites' blood.

The East Gate counseled their people in this way. "There will be more signs to come." their mentors preached. "It is the fulfillment of the *One*'s prophecy. The Old Lady's murder was the turning point. The unfettered display of water was a celebration of life, freedom and joy. The opaque mist that traveled from the Rubicon and covered the city was a sign that everything will be ours again."

The West Gate leaders with their long history of being outcasts, soon spread stories of a soon coming war. One that would bring redemption to its long enslaved people. The Old Lady was displeased with the descendants of Demorg. Not only had they murdered her, but they let her murderer go unpunished.

Saudj's father preached to his neighbors. "The Old Lady has joined forces with Paladin, Protag and Patron. She seeks to punish us for our supposed betrayal."

People were quick to gather around and listen. "The battle for the Rubicon and all of Eternal has begun. You cannot deny the signs. Demorg is *The One* and he will soon return to avenge our years of torment. We will no longer be oppressed." The gathered mob nodded and cheered him on.

"The dark muddy mist that has fallen on us, is a sign to us that these walls will be destroyed and washed away. Rejoice! We will soon be free. Go and share the good news with your neighbors and let the Romas know we will all be one again."

He released the pack and they swarmed the West Gate spreading their message.

"Mrs. Nibbledent!" Culy cried up from the street below. "Mrs. Nibbledent?"

She couldn't take her eyes off the vision. What does this mean? she thought to herself. At that moment she traveled back to the last time she saw Upal. He had been staring out this very window, *his* arm extending out to the Rubicon, shouting impulsively.

293

Oh my precious Upal, she thought. You said one word and it was a prophecy.

Culy shouted and waved her arms, trying everything to shake the woman from her trance. "Mrs. Nibbledent!"

Culy read her lips and seemed to understand when Mrs. Nibbledent whispered in the wind "Murder."